Herring in the Smoke

By L. C. Tyler

Herring in the Smoke

L. C. TYLER

Allison & Busby Limited
12 Fitzroy Mews
London W1T 6DW
allisonandbusby.com

First published in Great Britain by Allison & Busby in 2017.
This paperback edition published by Allison & Busby in 2018.

A CIP catalogue record for this book is available from
the British Library.

10 9 8 7 6 5 4 3 2 1

ISBN 978-0-7490-2174-0

Typeset in 10.5/15.5 pt Sabon by
Allison & Busby Ltd.

The paper used for this Allison & Busby publication
has been produced from trees that have been legally sourced
from well-managed and credibly certified forests.

Printed and bound by
CPI Group (UK) Ltd, Croydon, CR0 4YY

In memory of Uncle Len

CHAPTER ONE

It was at his own memorial service that I first spoke to Roger Norton Vane.

I had arrived slightly late, being less used than I once was to London's Byzantine one-way systems and parking regulations. By the time I had found a more or less legal place to leave my car within walking distance of the church, I was uncomfortably aware that I might not get a seat. Vane had been well known and (at least with the general public) popular. I ended up being ushered into a pew at the very back, along with an amiable old gentleman dressed incongruously in beige cotton trousers, open sandals and a heavy, navy-blue overcoat, who was equally late but either unaware of the fact or not much bothered.

At first he ignored me, craning his neck one way and another to see who occupied the seats in the many rows in front of us. Occasionally he nodded, as if approving of what he saw. Now and then he pulled a face. Once he rather theatrically held his nose. Then finally he turned in my direction.

'Just flew in this morning,' he said, at a volume that suggested the whole church deserved to know. He jabbed with his thumb at his thick woollen lapels. 'I'd forgotten how cold it was back here. Isn't March supposed to be spring or something? Daffodils? Easter bonnets? Fluffy little lambs, waiting to be turned into chops? Flew over with not so much as a sweater in my suitcase. Certainly nothing for this weather. So, I asked the taxi driver to stop off at' – he named an outfitter who had gone out of business some fifteen years before – 'and the damned fool said he'd never heard of it. Took me to Marks and Spencer. Said they had loads of overcoats there. Actually they'd already switched to their summer stock. Still, they had this little number in pure English wool on the Reduced rail. Quite natty. Made in Vietnam, oddly enough. Funny, when you think about it. Vietnam. Right next door to us.'

'Ah . . .' I said. I glanced nervously towards the distant lectern in case things were about to begin. I wasn't sure we had time for a long explanation about how he got his new coat, or why Vietnam was just next door to Islington, and I didn't want to find myself in lone mid-conversation as an otherwise respectful silence descended.

My companion, however, was clearly not worried that he was in danger of interrupting anything important. He looked knowingly at me and then uttered something in a language I didn't understand – lilting, musical but at the same time slightly harsh.

8

'Sorry?' I said.

He repeated it with a grin. 'I live in Laos, you see,' he added. He pronounced it 'Lao', without the final 's', which I've always regarded as a bit of an affectation; but maybe not if you actually live there and speak the language, as he apparently did. 'Decent little country, all things considered. Still twenty years behind Vietnam and at least forty behind Singapore. But comfortable enough these days. And well run. No hint of democracy, thank goodness. No human rights to speak of. Absolutely top place. Do you know it at all?'

I smiled apologetically and looked again towards the far end of the church, but there was no indication that anyone had plans to begin on time. A very famous writer, who was due to speak at the service, was leaning against a pew, checking his notes in an unhurried way. Vane's niece, whom I had got to know well over the past month or so, was standing and chatting to guests. It was all remarkably relaxed; but this was, I kept having to remind myself, not a funeral but a joyous celebration of the life and work of Roger Norton Vane. There was no need for solemnity. It seemed impolite not to introduce myself to my talkative neighbour.

'I'm Ethelred Tressider,' I said, holding out my hand.

The gentleman in the glossy new overcoat responded with a remarkably firm handshake.

'But I usually write my novels as Peter Fielding,' I added. 'I'm a writer, you see . . .'

He shook his head. He hadn't heard of me. I felt I was losing his attention.

'And sometimes I write as J. R. Elliott,' I added anyway. 'Historical crime set in the fourteenth century. Maybe you might have . . . ?'

He shook his head again. Sometimes people make an initial pretence, purely out of politeness, of trying to remember whether they've read one of my books; but his look made it crystal clear that he couldn't be even remotely arsed. I decided not to enquire if he'd come across any of the lightweight romances I write as Amanda Collins. I had just turned back to my service sheet when he said something that I was sure I must have misheard.

'Sorry,' I replied, looking up, 'I thought just for a moment that you said you were Roger Norton Vane.' I smiled at my error.

'No, that's what I said,' he replied.

'You mean you're some relative of the writer . . .'

'No, I mean I am the person in whose honour today's festivities are being organised. I am Roger Vane. The writer. Recently deceased.'

I looked at the photo on the order of service that I had been handed as I came in, and then at the gentleman next to me. I knew the photo well. I had actually supplied it to the organisers myself. If this was Roger Norton Vane beside me, he had aged considerably since the picture was taken. But twenty years is a long time.

'You don't believe me, do you?' he asked.

'I don't know what to believe,' I said. 'It's just that . . .'

'You thought I was dead?'

'Everyone thought that,' I said. 'That's why we're all here. In this church. It's your memorial service. What I was going to say was: it's just that I'm your biographer.'

'Are you? You'll probably be wondering what I've been doing for the past twenty years, then.'

'Yes,' I said. 'When writing the final chapters I did wonder a bit.'

'Bet you did. So, I have a biographer now, do I? I've clearly gone up in the world since I died. Who did you say you were?'

I told him again. Just the Tressider bit this time.

'Well, maybe not that far up,' he said. 'Were you the best they could manage?'

'I'm not sure I was the publisher's first choice,' I said apologetically.

'I certainly hope you weren't,' he said. 'Still, we are where we are. We'll need to have a chat. Properly. Now I'm back in the Smoke. I'll have plenty of stories to tell you, and not just about my time in the East. Let the literary world tremble in its kitten heels. I could spin you a yarn or two about him . . . and her.' His thumb indicated a prominent television presenter and the CEO of a big publishing house. Neither was actually trembling at that moment, but I appreciated that they might be soon. Like the rest of the congregation, they were tied up in their own conversations, exchanging platitudes, swapping lies about sales figures. Nobody had felt it worthwhile to listen to us – the loud-mouthed man in a blue overcoat and his tall but slightly nervous companion.

'So you mean you've been in Laos for the past twenty years?' I asked.

Roger Norton Vane gave me a broad smile. 'There

and other places. And unfortunately not quite as dead as everyone thought,' he said. 'They're all going to look a bit silly, don't you think? Everyone except you and me, Ethelred.'

He gave me a conspiratorial wink. Then, finally, the organ finally began playing and the human voices around us were stilled, one by one, as if by a vast wave rolling inexorably from the front to the back of the packed church. At the same moment the sun suddenly burst through the great stained glass window above the altar, sending a bright technicolour dawn into the chancel. We both turned towards the renascent glow, each curious, in our own way, to see what would happen next.

CHAPTER TWO

It had been twenty years before the memorial service that
Roger Norton Vane had vanished without trace. Twenty
years to the day.

Vane had, when I first came across his work, been
a moderately successful writer of crime novels set in the
nineteen fifties – which at that time just about qualified
as historical fiction. Later the books were turned into
a television series and his face became as familiar to the
public as his well-illustrated covers. One of my reasons
for believing that he had indeed now returned from the
dead was that I recognised the voice – I'd heard it often on
television and radio and, as guest of honour, at crime writing
conferences. I told you that I'd never spoken to him, which
is true, but I'd listened to him more times than I could recall.
I started to read his books because everyone else was doing
so and continued because they were genuinely very good –
not pastiche fifties, but quirky modern novels that evoked

13

the period wonderfully well. His rise seemed unstoppable. Then, quite suddenly and at the height of his fame, he had disappeared without trace.

He had gone on holiday to Thailand, with his then partner, Tim Macdonald. One afternoon they had set off from their hotel on a walk through the jungle. Adventurous though this may sound, the mountain forest path was in fact much used and well signposted. An averagely fit person could complete the circular route, as described invitingly in the hotel brochure, in just over two and a half hours. The path was surprisingly flat, for the most part an old logging road, hugging the contours of the adjacent slopes. Many walked it in trainers in the dry season. Both men were fit and more than capable of a gentle stroll of this sort. They had, according to the hotel, been advised to stick strictly to the trail, though Macdonald later denied that any such warning had been given. It was subsequently agreed by all that they had left at two o'clock and had a very adequate four hours of daylight to complete their circuit. Macdonald returned alone at quarter to five, saying that his friend had decided to continue a bit further alone, but should be back shortly. That was his entire explanation. Macdonald went to their room to take a shower. At five-thirty he came to reception to return the walking stick he had borrowed and to enquire whether his partner had shown up and perhaps gone straight to the bar. He hadn't. The receptionist noted that Tim had a scratch on his face, which he claimed was from a thorn. Since there were in fact thorns in the jungle, the receptionist did not think to probe any further. With hindsight, he subsequently admitted, perhaps he should have done.

Later – very much later – the official enquiry into the matter established that a proper search did not begin until well after dark, for which Macdonald and the hotel blamed each other with equal enthusiasm. Hotel staff had retraced Vane's journey, their small handheld torches casting a feeble light on the trunks of the huge, vaulting forest trees and none at all into the vast black expanses beyond. They were not helped by the fact that Macdonald was unclear at exactly which point the two had parted company, especially since the torch batteries were by that stage nearly exhausted and one liana-clad tree looked much like another.

A second attempt was made at first light, with every spare staff member – for the most part city-bred and unfamiliar with the scary green waste around them – now urgently scouring the jungle. The police were finally called in towards midday, over twenty hours after Vane and Macdonald had set out. The local chief superintendent would eventually tell the investigating committee that by then it was far too late – Vane had already perished or wandered well beyond the area they were searching. There were, he hinted, one or two scrawny tigers still in the area who might arguably have been looking for breakfast at a time when the police had yet to be alerted. The hotel manager counterclaimed that if helicopters had been deployed straight away, as he had frantically demanded over the phone, they could have covered the larger search area that the chief superintendent rightly referred to. In seven years at the hotel he had never seen a tiger. He said that poachers had hopefully shot the last of them years before. The one pictured in the brochure lived in Bangkok Zoo and was for illustrative purposes only. Both implied, as much as they dared, that Macdonald had been negligent of his friend's welfare – that he should not have left him in the first place and that he should subsequently have been less amenable to the suggestion that nothing untoward had happened in the possibly-tiger-haunted jungle. He should not have gone to the bar and ordered a Singapore gin sling with fried cashew nuts on the side. Had bitter recriminations alone taken the investigation forward, Vane would have been located at once. But he wasn't.

When three days of searching had come to a fruitless conclusion, Macdonald was briefly and very publicly arrested for murder and flown to Bangkok for questioning, the almost-healed scratch on his face now being regarded as incriminating in the extreme. His explanation that his friend had decided to continue alone was minutely dissected – to where would Vane have continued on a circular path, other than back to the hotel? Did Macdonald mean that he had turned back and Vane carried on round the path? Or did he mean that he had carried on and Vane retraced his steps? Or something else entirely? Macdonald seemed unsure which he meant, raising further doubts in the mind of the police. Why had he taken the walking stick to his room rather than return it immediately to the hotel desk? Macdonald conceded that he had cleaned it before returning it but said his intentions had been helpful rather than otherwise. Had he used it as a murder weapon, he argued, he would have thrown it into the jungle and risked being charged twenty Baht for its non-return.

These false and hurtful accusations, Macdonald later argued, caused the scaling down of the search at a critical time. He was eventually released without charges being laid and left for England early the following morning, a precipitous departure for which he was criticised by anyone looking to shift the blame from themselves. As it turned out, he could have stayed for another twenty years without being able to play any meaningful part in the investigation.

Of course, in the months that followed, there were countless sightings. A German couple, staying at the same hotel a few weeks later, reported seeing a man in the jungle, who had smiled and waved at them. A hat, not entirely unlike the one Vane had been wearing but possibly of a different colour, was found shortly after by somebody who had themselves accidentally strayed off the path, and vouched for the ease with which it could be done.

A girl in a bar in Bangkok said she had definitely served Vane a double Mekhong and Coke with ice and lemon, but she wasn't sure when. He was seen getting into a taxi in Kuala Lumpur and getting out of one in Penang. He was seen crossing the road very, very carefully in Hanoi. He bought a newspaper in Hong Kong and told the vendor to keep the change, which was admittedly not a great deal. He won a large sum of money at a casino in Macao. He was most certainly seen, a year or so later, begging by the side of the road in Calcutta, wearing a blue T-shirt and green shorts with the logo of the Brazilian football team.

He had a long conversation with a British pensioner on the beach in Galle, and definitely said that his name was 'Vane' or 'Vine' or 'Lane' or 'Villiers' or something very much like it – it had proved difficult to buy hearing-aid batteries of the right type in Sri Lanka. He bought a ticket at Wimbledon Tube Station and said quite specifically that he did not need a return, in spite of the saving he might have made.

The local Thai police treated each sighting with mild interest. They were aware that nobody survived more than a few days alone in the jungle and, if he was alive anywhere, it wasn't on their patch. After six months, a team from Scotland Yard had the good fortune to be sent to Thailand to help the police with their investigations. They stayed as long as they could and were interviewed several times on local and international television. One of the policemen got sunburn and one contracted a sexually transmitted disease.

Then, finally, there was a genuine piece of evidence – the only one that would surface in twenty years. A fisherman at a beach resort was caught trying to sell a very expensive watch. It was inscribed: 'To Roger, with all my love, Tim'. The fisherman was arrested and was triumphantly presented to the press, in handcuffs. He claimed, however, to have bought the watch from an Englishman who said that he didn't need it any more. He was no thief, he said. He'd paid a lot of money for it – several thousand Baht – which he'd borrowed from a friend. A friend quickly emerged to confirm that he had indeed lent the fisherman money, so that he could purchase the watch at the bargain price the Englishman had named. The fisherman also found or purchased several impeccable witnesses to confirm he had been fishing, far out at sea, when Vane had vanished. After a while the suspect was quietly released, without handcuffs, to explain to his friend why he could not repay the loan in the foreseeable future. The watch remained in an evidence bag in a police station on the Thai coast, pending future investigations.

As the years passed, the sightings became fewer. The television series continued with new plots devised by various scriptwriters, as they would have done anyway. The old episodes were repeated. Sales of the books remained steady, especially with the new television-tie-in covers. Royalties piled up in a bank account. Vane's reputation, in fact, remained high, fuelled in part by his thrilling absence. On the fifth and tenth anniversaries of his vanishing there were long pieces in the Sunday papers, speculating on what had happened, but coming up with nothing that was both credible and new. Tim Macdonald refused to be interviewed or even to appear on reality television shows. The fifteenth anniversary passed largely unnoticed. As we neared the twentieth, it was proposed that there should finally be a memorial service. And I was asked to write a biography, somewhat late in the day, to cash in on what the publisher hoped would be at least a brief renewal of interest in his books.

When I received my invitation to the service I almost declined it. It seemed strange to mourn for somebody I had never had a conversation with. But being his biographer (even though the book was far from complete) tipped the balance. I had to be there – not to lament his passing but, as the fashion now is, to celebrate his life and work. Especially when I had supplied the photograph for the order of service.

Thus it was that I was able to send the first tweet when it all kicked off. As Elsie later pointed out – one day it could be the only thing that I am still remembered for.

CHAPTER THREE

So, that is what I knew – no more, no less – as I sat beside a dead man in a church in north London, wondering if things would go well or badly.

On this last point, Vane himself seemed willing to keep an open mind. Hands in his pockets, he slouched in the pew and listened to the various tributes being paid to him. Occasionally he half-turned to me and nodded his approval, or he muttered 'that's complete crap' or 'I hope you've got the correct version of that story in your book' or, more succinctly, 'arsehole'.

Though his posture was that of a sulky teenager, I think on the whole he was enjoying himself. Few of us get to hear what our friends will say of us after our deaths and for the most part they spoke quite well of him.

It was not until Tim MacDonald took to the stage that I noticed he tensed a little. Vane frowned and leant forwards. Tim, now I had a chance to study him, was an undoubtedly good-looking man, who appeared to both possess and use a gym membership. He was slightly younger than Vane, but his hair was showing the very first signs of grey at the sides. He was, I knew, an illustrator of children's books – successful enough in his own right and still occupying Vane's old flat in Canonbury. I had never seen the flat because Tim had refused to cooperate in any way with the biography – it was one of the many reasons why the book was still not finished. He paused before addressing us, apparently half amused, half contemptuous of the packed church before him. Slowly he took out a single sheet of thick cream paper, which he laid carefully on the lectern. He took from another pocket a pair of bright-green reading glasses and put them on. He knew we'd have to wait until he was good and ready. What others had said was merely a build-up to this, the definitive verdict on Roger Norton Vane.

'I hope you've got your phone handy,' said Vane without looking at me. He was staring fixedly at Tim.

'It's switched off,' I whispered. 'They told us to . . .'

'And you actually did?'

'Yes.'

'Switch it back on, then, because in about thirty seconds you're going to need it,' said Vane.

An elaborate cough from behind us hinted that somebody would rather listen to Tim than to us. I suspected that, whatever Vane had in mind, it might not go entirely well. But it was, and for once quite literally, his funeral.

I fumbled in my pocket and so missed the first few words that Tim Macdonald spoke. But I did catch what he said next. 'Some might say that Roger Norton Vane was loved and loathed in equal measure . . .' It was at that point that Vane finally broke cover. One moment he was there beside me. The next it was just an empty space.

I heard a sharp intake of breath from all sides. Then somebody said: 'Good grief! Surely not? It's actually him.'

When I looked up, phone at the ready, Vane was already striding rapidly down the aisle, blue overcoat billowing out behind him, bearing down on the man who had once been accused of murdering him. My tweet carried a picture of his back, about halfway to his intended target. Based on this rear view alone, it was just somebody walking quickly down the aisle – but the evident consternation on people's faces made it clear that this was a novel and unplanned feature of the service. The picture was retweeted several thousand times before the day was out. (Seventeen retweets was my previous best.) Even today, if you google 'blue M&S overcoat' it's one of the first images to come up.

Thus it was that the world first heard of Roger Norton Vane's resurrection, and thus it was that the congregation were informed firmly but politely that they could all piss off back to where they came from. Tim Macdonald included.

'Of course, it has implications,' said Elsie. 'You realise that, I hope?'

I had arranged to see my agent after the service because, as I've said, I am rarely in London these days and she had suggested a catch-up coffee, which we were now having. I noted that her inviting me had not prevented my paying. But Elsie had not suggested we went anywhere expensive, in case she accidentally stumbled into footing the bill herself. It had, it seemed, happened at least once before.

'It's very exciting,' I said, passing Elsie the sugar. 'I mean . . . a writer reappearing after a twenty-year absence. After years of speculating, we'll all finally know what happened to him.'

'It will certainly increase the sales of the biography,' she said.

'I hadn't thought of that,' I said.

'No, you wouldn't have. That's why you have me as your agent. To think of that.'

'Well, it's a good thing, however you look at it. I can ask Roger all sorts of questions that had been puzzling me.'

Elsie nodded thoughtfully. 'Of course, we can't now do the hatchet job we'd planned.'

'Hatchet job?'

'Oh, don't look so innocent, Ethelred. You knew that's what Lucinda wanted. I told her – Ethelred has read all of Vane's books, and loves them, but he will be quite happy to write the biography exactly as you wish. He'll make Vane look a total prick, if that's what you'd like. No extra charge.'

'Is that why Bill Stanstead was stood down?'

Another writer had originally been commissioned to write the biography but had quit or been sacked, according to which version you wanted to believe. I was a last-minute replacement for him – Lucinda's sixth or seventh choice, according to Elsie, and lucky to get the work on any terms. That was another reason why the project was running so late and I was chasing round trying to finish the research as quickly as I could.

'There were reasons,' said Elsie vaguely.

'Why does Lucinda want a hatchet job, anyway?'

'Don't you listen to any of the literary gossip?'

'Not really.'

'Then you have some catching up to do. Are you sitting comfortably? Then I'll begin. And please don't interrupt until I've finished.'

'I won't,' I said.

'You just did,' she said. 'So, a long time ago, in a galaxy far, far away, Vane got Lucinda fired from her job as assistant editor at the big publisher she was then with. Vane wanted to move elsewhere and cited Lucinda's failure to do something or other – missing a rogue semicolon during proofreading, or something equally serious – as his reason for quitting. He moved. She got the boot. Same day.'

'That was a little unfair.'

'I never said it wasn't.'

'But anyway she's now a commissioning editor . . .'

'Elsewhere. Yes, I know. But only for crap books like the one you're writing. So, it's not surprising she still hates his guts. She wanted the plain unvarnished truth – or plain unvarnished lies, if we could get away with it. Being dead he wouldn't have been able to sue you or her or me or anyone else.'

'Whereas now . . .'

'Whereas now you've messed it up. According to your tweet, he's alive and well.'

'You never told me that,' I said. 'I mean that Lucinda wanted me to portray him as being in any way unpleasant.

I thought I'd got the commission because Lucinda liked my work.'

'Why would you think that?'

I sighed. 'Well, I've always admired him – I mean his books – I'd never met him before today.'

'I'm sure I did tell you, Ethelred.'

'When?'

'In an email.'

'I don't remember that.'

'You remember all your emails?'

'Yes.'

'Then it must have gone astray. That's probably why you didn't get it. It happens. They go astray. Like dogs chasing rabbits. Anyway, the point is, Ethelred, that now he can sue us, so Lucinda's not going to be pleased with you.'

'He's not alive just because I tweeted it.'

'A lot of people won't see it that way, Ethelred. Your presence on social media is pretty much a definition of whether you are alive or not. You have brought him back to life, a bit like that Frankenstein.'

There are plenty of times when it isn't worth arguing with Elsie, not unless you are a great fan of logic being tested to destruction.

'Fine. I'm to blame, then,' I said, taking up my default position with Elsie. 'At least I can just write the book I was always planning to write.'

'Sadly, that is what you'll have to do, unless the lawyers can find a way round it. Of course he was a shit. Always charming when he appeared on television or whatever, but not a nice man. If he didn't like you, he'd make it clear he didn't like you. If he hadn't heard of you, he'd make it very clear he hadn't heard of you.' She looked at me and raised an eyebrow.

'Possibly,' I said.

'And poor Tim won't be pleased to see him back.'

'No?'

'Don't you listen to any gossip at all?'

'No, not even to the nice gossip.'

'Ethelred, there's no such thing as nice gossip. Not in publishing. What you may already know is that, pre-vanishing, Roger Vane and Tim were about to split up.'

'Yes, I do know that,' I said. 'It was reported by some papers at the time. That's why they thought Tim might have killed him. That and a rather confused account of what had happened on the day of Vane's disappearance. Plus a scratch on his face. Plus getting out of Thailand before he could be questioned further.'

'Indeed. All of those things. Circumstantial but damning nonetheless. The trip to Thailand was one last attempt to put it all right. But they quarrelled every evening. Loudly. In public. Other diners complained to the management. The hotel faced bankruptcy, having to refund people their restaurant bills. Travel agents noted an inexplicable drop in bookings to Thailand . . .'

'Can you stick to something like the facts?' I asked.

'What? The real facts? OK, if that's what you prefer. They had a very public falling out. Fact. Roger Vane disappeared. Fact. Tim returned to the hotel and ordered a gin sling. Fact. That, as you say, is why the Thai police thought Roger Norton Vane had been done in by Tim.

Lovers' tiff. Plenty of people here thought that too. But, and this is what you may not know, they also thought he'd been quite justified in doing so. If you'd asked anyone within ten miles of Fitzroy Square what they reckoned, they'd have replied: "The kid done 'im in right enough, but nobody round this manor's going to grass 'im up to the Old Bill."'

'Are you imitating Vane's substandard cockney dialogue by any chance?'

'I thought I was imitating your substandard cockney dialogue, but I stand corrected as always. Anyway, most people did sympathise with Tim. I certainly did. I've told him so.'

'He's a friend, then?'

'As it happens, I represent him. I signed him up a few weeks ago. He knows I'm always there for him if he needs me. He has merely to call.'

Elsie's phone beeped. She held her hand up, as a polite instruction that I was not to interrupt whatever important thing was about to happen, and then checked the screen.

'It's Tim Macdonald,' she said. 'He wants a bed for the night. Roger Vane has thrown him out of the flat. That was quick work, even for him. Respect.'

CHAPTER FOUR

I had an appointment to see Cynthia Vane the following day. There seemed no reason not to keep it, just because the subject of my book was now more alive than we had suspected.

'I looked out the photos you wanted,' she said. 'That's Uncle Roger with my father, just before he vanished. That's both brothers while they were still at school. Looks as if they're on holiday somewhere. Norfolk maybe? Flat and sandy, anyway. I've also got one or two reviews of the earlier books that you may not have seen – my father must have cut them out and kept them. He was always very proud of Uncle Roger – even before they made the television series.'

'It must have been a shock for you, yesterday. A very pleasant one, I assume, but a shock all the same.'

'Pleasant? You think so? I'm not sure Uncle Roger was aiming for pleasant. But it was certainly a surprise for a lot of people. As you know, we'd already started the process of having him declared dead – legally, I mean. We'd accepted he was actually dead long ago. Except it turns out he was alive and living in Laos. Nice of him to keep us informed. It would have served him right if he'd shown up a couple months late and we'd given all his books to Oxfam. Some might call that harsh, but if you don't contact your family for twenty years, it's the sort of risk you take.'

'So, what would have happened exactly, if he'd been declared dead – legally?'

'Apart from Oxfam lucking out? His will would have been dusted off. Probate would have been obtained. Inheritance tax would have been paid. Distant and largely forgotten members of the family would have fought to the death over the ormolu clock. His gardening coat would finally have gone to a tip with facilities for dealing with hazardous waste. The flat would have been put on the market and been sold to some venture capitalist from Novgorod. His material existence would have been shattered into a thousand tiny fragments. I've no idea how you undo something like that.'

'And who would have inherited the bulk of the estate once he was legally dead, if that isn't an indelicate question? Tim, I suppose?'

'Oh, no. Tim may have got something, but most of it came to me. That was one of the reasons why my father wanted to have Uncle Roger declared dead years ago – he'd long since given up any hope his brother was coming home and thought it was better the money and the flat were mine. But I've never felt inclined to push for it myself.'

'The flat will have increased a bit in value in the meantime.'

'I would imagine so. It's all a bit theoretical now that he's back. I've never done the sums anyway, so I'm honestly not sure how much money I've lost. Not that I wouldn't always have preferred to have had Uncle Roger alive and well. If you're planning to quote me in the biography, then just say his impoverished niece was delighted to see the rich, devious bastard back. As indeed I am.'

'Tim couldn't have been too keen on having Roger declared dead, though. He'd have lost his home. He's lived there for twenty years.'

'Well over twenty years. They'd been together for a while, in spite of frequent fallings out.'

'He couldn't have claimed anything as a right . . . if Roger hadn't returned?'

'I don't think so. There was never anything formal – no civil partnership, for example. I'm not sure they had them then. The discovery that Uncle Roger was alive should have meant Tim could stay on – except Uncle Roger has thrown him out anyway. When you think about it, it's not surprising he did – they were apparently about to split up when he disappeared. Tim's had rent-free accommodation for twenty years longer than he might. And he's got money. He can afford to buy somewhere of his own at long last. He can't complain.'

There was a discernible note of contempt in her voice. But I had to agree – however things turned out, Tim couldn't complain. As for her own financial loss, Cynthia seemed to be taking it well. She'd lost a flat but gained an uncle.

'So,' I said. 'It's all as if Roger had never gone away.'

Cynthia paused and looked at me. 'Not quite. In some ways Uncle Roger is the same . . .'

'But he's altered in others? I have to say the years don't seem to have softened him much.'

'He's lost none of his old venom, I'll give him that. But he's much greyer. And somehow smaller. I scarcely recognised him at first. It was only when the rest of the congregation started to exclaim it was him . . . Then you sort of saw it. The face. The posture. The way of walking. But sometimes you don't immediately recognise somebody you've not seen for a few months if they've dyed their hair or lost a lot of weight. You can change a hell of a lot in twenty years.'

'He probably had the same problem with the rest of you.'

'That's the odd thing – he didn't. He recognised me straight away. Not even a hesitant "well, you must be little Cynthia". I mean, I was in my early teens when he vanished. But he came right up to me and kissed me on the cheek. Not a moment's doubt.'

'There are photos of most of us on the Internet these days – Facebook, Twitter and all the new ones I've no plans to sign up to. It wouldn't have been hard to find out what you looked like now.'

'That's true. There were other things, though, that he seemed to have inexplicably forgotten.'

Cynthia looked at me as if inviting the question. I obliged.

'Such as?' I asked.

'Oh, he and my father had a terrier called Bramble when they were younger, but when I mentioned Bramble he just looked completely blank. Then, claiming to recall the animal after all, he referred to Bramble as "he", when he would have known she was a bitch. You don't forget things like that. It would be like thinking you had a son when you had a daughter.'

'A slip of the tongue.'

'I suppose it could be. It's easily done. You think of dogs as "he" don't you? And cats as "she". But even then . . .'

'Do you mean you think it isn't him?'

'It looks pretty much like him, and certainly sounds like him . . . I'd like it to be him. Really I would. Uncle Roger is the only close member of family I have left, apart from my mother. But even so . . . What do you think, Ethelred?'

'I never really knew him before,' I said. 'Certainly not like you did. But I saw him plenty of times on television and once or twice on the stage. There's nothing to make me think he's an imposter.'

It was, I had to admit, not the most ringing of endorsements. But surely nobody would attempt to impersonate a figure as famous as Vane – especially when there were two close members of his family still around?

'He knew who cousin Wilbert was,' said Cynthia thoughtfully.

'There you are, then. I haven't come across Wilbert. Distant relation?'

'Non-existent relation. Possibly on my father's side. I made him up on the spur of the moment. "Cousin Wilbert will be pleased to see you again," I said. "I've always liked Wilbert," he replied.'

'So he failed the Wilbert test?'

'I'd say so, wouldn't you?'

'Maybe he misheard?'

'That's charitable of you, Ethelred. Your good nature shines through in a generally shitty world. But no, I don't think there's anything wrong with his hearing. It's more to do with the fact that . . . how can I put this? . . . I think there's just a chance he's a total fake.'

'Really?'

'Don't look at me like that. The money has nothing to do with it at all. Except that I wouldn't want Uncle Roger's money going to a gold-plated shyster. Whatever's going on, I'm going to get to the bottom of it. Then quite possibly I'm going to kick some ass.'

'Good for you.'

'Yes, that was what I thought too. I have a plan, Ethelred. There are still plenty of people around who will remember him well. I won't be the only one with doubts.'

'Probably not. I'll need to write a slightly different book, of course, if he is an imposter.'

'Not really. Just a different postscript. Don't worry, I'll keep you informed. He may still prove to be a genuine uncle with a poor recollection of dogs. What can I do for you in the meantime?'

'Just one or two queries about his time at university,' I said. 'Then I'd like you to run over the last time you saw him – before the memorial service, that is.'

'OK, try me,' she said.

It was an hour or so later that she suggested a break for coffee. She switched on the television because Roger

Norton Vane's reappearance was still news. The previous evening, crime writers had queued up to say how delighted they were that he was still alive. Bookshop owners were interviewed, saying that their shelves had been stripped of anything by Vane or by anyone remotely resembling him. It was likely there would be more of the same this afternoon, though perhaps only as a brief final item. In fact he was second on, after something on the US presidential election.

The announcer switched from the bemused smile appropriate to the previous item to a disapproving frown and said: 'And now over to our arts editor for some surprising developments in the Roger Norton Vane affair.'

Cynthia placed a mug of coffee in front of me, but her eyes were glued to the television. She sat down beside me without a glance in my direction. On the screen we could see a great deal of the arts editor's back. The face we saw beyond it was Tim Macdonald's. The camera slowly panned in on him.

'You've known Roger Norton Vane for some time, I think?'

'For almost thirty years,' said Tim, with some feeling.

'And you are very close to him?'

'To Roger, yes. Of course, I was. But not to this imposter who has suddenly emerged from nowhere.'

'So, you don't think that the man who claims to be Roger Vane is in fact him?'

'Isn't that what I said?'

'I'm just clarifying. For the viewers.'

'Why? Are they slow on the uptake?'

The interviewer paused slightly too long before replying: 'Of course not. I just meant, why do you think that?'

'The Roger I knew was caring, loving . . . The man who burst into my flat yesterday and ejected me into the street does not resemble him in the slightest.'

'You say your flat . . .'

'Oh, Roger's flat, if you insist. My home for almost thirty years. That's the point.'

'But most other people do seem to have accepted that this is Roger Norton Vane.'

'Do you think I don't know my own partner?'

'It has been twenty years.'

Tim drew himself to his full height. 'Did Penelope not know Odysseus after twenty years?' he demanded.

'I thought it was Argos the dog who recognised Odysseus? Penelope demanded improbable feats of strength. But perhaps we are straying from—'

'I was hardly given time to demand anything. This strange man charged in and told me to pack and be gone. As for feats of strength, he didn't even help me carry my bags.'

'So, if he is an imposter as you say, why do you think that so many people believe him?'

Tim looked straight into the camera lens. 'It's a conspiracy. The forces of evil are gathering around us. But I shall fight them with the sword of Truth and the shield of . . . something else . . . Cunning, possibly. Whatever. Right will triumph!'

There was a stunned silence and then the arts editor said: 'Thank you, Mr Macdonald. That was very . . . And so, it's back to the studio. Er . . . Sophie.'

* * *

It was at least half a minute before either of us picked up our coffee and took a thoughtful sip.

'I'm not sure any of that proves Roger really is an imposter,' I said. 'Quite the reverse when you think about it. All he's done so far is to show up in a blue overcoat and evict Tim from Canonbury Square. If Tim did try to kill him, all those years ago, then of course Roger would want him out of the flat. I mean, you wouldn't want to spend a night with your assailant sleeping in the next room, or indeed the same bed.'

'Equally, if Tim Macdonald knew he had killed Uncle Roger that would explain why he is so convinced it couldn't be him. I mean, Tim would be the one person who'd know for sure if it could be Uncle Roger. And he did seem very certain it couldn't . . .' Cynthia looked at me significantly.

'He was never charged,' I said.

'A lot of people thought he did do it, though,' said Cynthia.

'I know,' I said. 'Everyone within a ten-mile radius of Fitzroy Square, apparently.'

'There you are, then,' said Cynthia.

The television now showed a famous athlete who was trying to explain why she had been on a particular prescription drug for most of her career. It was not, she said, for any purported performance-enhancing reasons, a little-known side effect of which she had been made aware only within the last few days. It had all been a terrible mistake and she hoped this apology would draw a line under things. That seemed unlikely.

'Twenty years is a long time,' I said, finally turning to Cynthia. 'People change. People forget things.'

'Maybe. I still wouldn't forget the name of my dog, though.'

'No,' I said. 'You wouldn't forget the name of your dog.'

CHAPTER FIVE

'So, that's a flat white for me and a chocolate with marshmallows and whipped cream for you,' I said.

For the second time in two days I was having coffee with my agent.

'Was mine the chocolate, though?' asked Elsie. 'I thought I'd said a small skinny something . . . But you've got it now, so I suppose I'll have to drink it. Shame to waste good chocolate. My turn to buy next time. Shouldn't there be at least four marshmallows, by the way? They've only given me three.'

'I thought you said yesterday it was your turn to get the coffees next time,' I said, taking my seat.

'And so it is,' said Elsie. 'Next time. What?'

'Nothing. It's fine,' I said. 'I was only joking.'

'Look,' said Elsie, 'I can hardly hand in a receipt to Tuesday listing a hot chocolate with whipped cream and a contractual minimum of four marshmallows.'

'You could tell her that I had the chocolate and you had the small flat white.'

Elsie considered this and then shook her head. 'No, she'd know,' she said darkly. 'She always does.'

'Are you afraid of your own assistant?' I asked. 'You don't have to diet if you don't want to. You could just say you fancied a hot chocolate. Or you could simply not reclaim the money from the agency budget.'

She shook her head. 'That would be so wrong on so many levels,' she said vaguely. 'How did the meeting with Cynthia go?'

'She seems to have very real doubts that Roger Vane is the genuine article,' I said. 'A bit like Tim in that respect, but without resorting to the Shield of Cunning.'

'Yes, good wasn't it, that interview? That will help sell a few books. Just needed to get onto one of my contacts at the BBC and, bingo, there we were. Doubts sown in the minds of the public.'

I looked at her across my coffee. 'Elsie, you didn't put him up to it?'

'Not especially,' she said. 'He might have done it anyway. And I quite specifically said the Shield of Justice. What on earth would a Shield of Cunning look like?'

'Well, I'm not sure if people will believe him. I mean, since he's been thrown out of the flat, he's hardly impartial.'

'He'd have known better than anyone,' said Elsie.

'So – let's say you're right, just to save ten minutes of my day – why did Tim let this imposter throw him out?'

'He said to avoid an unseemly row. It's Tim's greatest fear for some reason – unseemly rows. In which case,

God knows what he ever saw in Roger Norton Vane. Also the Pseudo-Vane threatened him with lawyers and the police if he didn't get his sorry arse and his colouring set out of there.'

'But Tim must have had some reason to think it really was Vane at the time or he would have called the police.'

'Well, he's sure enough about it all now. After talking to his agent, who explained things.'

'If Roger Vane is not genuine, there are a lot of people who will spot it. His own agent, for example.'

'Ah yes, George, his own agent. There's another interesting development.'

'In the sense that . . .'

'In the sense that Roger Vane has just accused him of fraud, duplicity and false accounting. George just phoned me up. He's very upset. He's been paying all of the royalties, less perfectly reasonable agency deductions, into an account he'd set up in Vane's absence. It amounts to a tidy sum, I can tell you, after twenty years. More than you'll ever see.'

'Are the deductions excessive?'

'They're less than I'm charging you.'

'Why not pay directly into Vane's own account?'

'Initially George was advised not to. Vane's wallet and credit cards were missing. There was a chance that somebody could move in and clean out his entire bank balance. It was a wise precaution. He carried on because it was simpler to do so. All the money was in one place, earning good interest – easy to account for to Vane or to his executors.'

'But Vane thinks there's not enough there?'

'A slander against a highly respected agent.'

'I'm seeing Roger Vane tomorrow,' I said.

'The person claiming to be Roger Vane.'

'The person claiming to be Roger Vane, if you insist. He's promised me some interesting stories.'

'I bet. If it proves to be Roger – and I'm not saying it will – he won't hold anything back just to save anyone's hurt feelings. The list of people regretting his return must be growing by the hour.'

'I'll tell you if he has anything to say about you,' I joked.

Elsie considered then shook her head. 'No,' she said. 'He'd have had no way of finding out. I'm safe enough. If it's him. Which it isn't.'

'That'll wake you up,' said Roger Norton Vane, as I took a tentative sip of the thick brown liquid. 'Very strong coffee and condensed milk. Plonk it in the cup. Give it a quick stir. That's all there is to it. Usually drink it iced in Laos, of course. They serve it everywhere. By the cup in restaurants. In plastic bags with a straw sticking out of them at the roadside stalls. That way you can drink it while you drive your moped with the other hand, so long as you're not too worried about braking.'

I placed the small cup back on the table. 'Very nice,' I said politely.

'Of course, you can't have it after about six in the evening, or you'll never sleep. Fine if you want to write all night.'

'Have you done much writing while you were . . . away?'

Vane looked me in the eye and gave me a crooked smile.

'Now and then. Plenty of books left to write. Plenty of stories left to tell. I've done the research, unlike a lot of my colleagues. I'm one of the few crime writers who was actually a practising criminal.'

I nodded. It was a story he'd told many times, on television chat shows and newspaper interviews and panels at conferences. 'Hot-wiring a car,' I said. 'Theft of an automobile. Driving at seventy miles an hour in a thirty mile an hour zone. Attempting to pervert the course of justice.'

He nodded. 'Me and a mate at school. Not Eton, like most of the Cabinet – just an inner-city joint with a bit of a drug problem. Learnt how to hot-wire from the metalwork teacher – he'd been a getaway driver for the Kray brothers. Schooldays – happiest days of my life. So, how far have you got with this book of yours? The one about me. Not the science fiction, or whatever it is you normally do.'

'I took over from another writer called Bill Stanstead . . .'

'Really?' Vane nodded, impressed. He had clearly heard of him. 'I always thought Bill had a lot of integrity. Good man. You can't push him around. Wouldn't have been able to get him to turn out whatever crap the editor wanted.'

'You can't entirely ignore what your publisher wants,' I said.

'Depends if you're capable of standing up for yourself,' said Vane.

'Anyway,' I continued, 'Bill couldn't do it in the end and we're not as far advanced as we should be. I think Lucinda wanted the book out by now, but I'm still finishing the research. There are plenty of gaps that I hope you can fill in. Such as exactly what happened in Thailand. And why.'

'Ah yes, that. I thought you might ask. You've spoken to Tim Macdonald, I take it?'

'He has declined to be interviewed. He wouldn't speak to Bill, either.'

'Bet he wouldn't. You know Tim claims I'm an imposter?'

'Yes,' I said. 'He said so on the BBC News.'

'Wouldn't know the Sword of Truth if it came up and slapped him on the face. As for the Shield of Cunning . . . But I'm not certain dear little Cynthia's entirely convinced of my bona fides, either. Bless her.'

'Really?'

'Don't try to sound surprised, Ethelred. I'm sure she's said something of the sort to you.'

'She said something about your not knowing the name of some dog you and your brother had.'

'That's Bramble?'

'Yes.'

'No such animal. She's getting things mixed up. Long before her time, of course. No reason why she should remember. My brother had a bitch named Briar Rose – always called her Briar. Lakeland terrier. He doted on her, but I would have been about three or four when Briar died. Scarcely remember her myself. Then we had a dog called Bracken, who was pretty much a joint enterprise. Cynthia's adding two and two and coming up with Bramble. Took me a while to work out what she was on about. Then she started on about Wilbert for some reason.'

'The distant cousin?'

'So she mentioned that too? Thought she might. Thanks for confirming what she's up to.'

'Well, I mean, she did, sort of . . . .'

'Your blushes do you credit, but I'm not stupid, Ethelred. I could see what she meant all along. Another little test for Uncle Roger, eh?' He paused and then smiled. 'Actually I'm amazed she knew. That really was A-level family history. You see, Wilbert was just a nickname he had for a couple of years at school. Dropped that forty years ago, at least. No idea how Cynthia even found out. She'd have known him as Graham. All credit to her, though. Bit of a card, Graham – which is another word for a pain in the arse. Good to know he's still alive, anyway – must be almost ninety now. Didn't get many Christmas cards in Laos, you see? Especially when they all hope you're pushing up daisies. You don't get the latest news on births, marriages and deaths. Half the family could be six feet under for all I know or care. I'll find out when this year's cards turn up. How's your coffee?'

'Fine. Very . . . sweet. And milky. And strong. So, what did happen on the afternoon you went missing?'

Vane looked out the window. Out in the square, the daffodils were making a fine display. Forsythia was about to bloom. The early afternoon traffic rumbled untroubled, ever onwards towards newly gentrified Hackney and Hoxton. It was all a long way from the primeval green wilderness into which he had disappeared.

'Maybe we could leave that for a subsequent meeting?' he asked. 'Seeing Tim again, here in my own flat . . . it's all still a bit raw. You see what I mean? He hurt me – and I don't just mean physically . . .'

'Yes, of course,' I said. 'But afterwards . . . after whatever happened . . . you somehow made it over the border into Laos?'

Vane turned away from the view over England and blinked a couple of times.

'Yes, I didn't go there directly. Took a bit of a roundabout route. I went south at first, down to the coast. There are plenty of ways you can get across the border down there. For a couple of quid I hitched a ride on a fishing boat that had business at a secluded cove in Cambodia. I had my passport and some cash with me. You can live cheaply over there – or you could in those days. You could buy a whole cooked chicken for ten pence and they pretty much paid you to take the rice and vegetables away. Biggest expense was bottled water – couldn't risk dysentery and having to see a doctor. Worked my way upcountry by easy stages and into Laos – not a difficult border crossing if you do it at night in a small boat. Got work in the first town I came to, as an English teacher then as a translator then as a copywriter. Moved around. Changed my name more than once. Became a Lao citizen. Did all right. More sex than you could believe. Bloody fantastic. How's your coffee?'

'You asked me that. It's fine. I'm just taking it slowly. So which town did you live in?'

'Here and there. Vientiane mainly – right on the Thai border and almost back to where I'd started. And other places you wouldn't have heard of. Look, Ethelred, could you do me a favour?'

'Certainly.'

'You see, my bank's being a bit sticky about my identity.'

'They don't believe you either?'

46

'Just bureaucracy. I don't have all of the paperwork they'd like. Actually, I don't have any of it.'

'You must have your passport? You said you had it with you.'

'Twenty years ago I did. And, as I say, I later changed my name and destroyed everything that might have connected me with Roger Norton Vane. It seemed wise at the time. Wasn't planning to come back. So I don't have anything with today's date on it saying who I really am.'

'Well, it must be possible to produce something . . . a driving licence?'

'Lost in the jungle, old boy.'

'What else do you have?'

'Nothing at all. And don't suggest dental records could settle it. My old dentist retired even before I went to Thailand. I was always planning to sign up with a new one . . . Don't know where you'd even start to look for my old X-rays after twenty years. But if you were willing to swear that it was me – I mean, you are my biographer and all that. They'd trust you.'

He smiled engagingly with his undocumented teeth. Jaundiced though his view was of the rest of humanity, I was his friend and he wanted me to know it. Somehow this did not make me as comfortable as was intended. I felt I was being pushed into a mess I ought to stay out of.

'Wouldn't Cynthia be better?' I asked.

'Well, there's a thing. You see, Cynthia's a fine girl, but she's not been quite as open with you as she might.'

'No?'

'She's been pressing for a while for me to be declared

dead so that she could inherit the pittance I possess and make poor Tim homeless.'

Vane seemed to have done a quite good job of making poor Tim homeless himself. Perhaps his point was that in her case it was out of character.

'Really?' I said. 'She doesn't seem the sort . . .'

'Don't be fooled, Ethelred. One of the first things she said to me was that she wouldn't be inheriting now. She made it sound like a joke, of course, but I happen to know she needs the money. So does her mother – and pretty urgently too. She's a nice enough girl, Cynthia, but her mum's putting pressure on her. It would suit Cynthia if everyone thought I was a fake and she could inherit the cash after all. And I've got no way of proving who I am – or at least not to the satisfaction of officialdom. So she may just succeed.'

'Hang on – what about a DNA test? Cynthia's a close relative. It would be conclusive.'

'She's scarcely going to cooperate with that, is she? Not in her interest.'

'Other family?'

'Blood relations? My brother's dead. I'm not counting on Wilbert.'

'What about your agent? He must have known you for years. He could vouch for you.'

'I think I've rather burnt my boats with George. Inadvisable with hindsight. Always be nice to your agent, Ethelred. That's my advice. Never know when you'll need one. Well, there it is; what's done is done. But you, Ethelred . . . when we first met, you said straight away that you believed me. A man of discernment, I thought.

The sort of chap you can trust. And as my biographer, you are the world expert on me.'

'Well, yes . . .' I said a little doubtfully. I couldn't remember quite what I'd said. My tweet saying he was alive probably wasn't legally binding. 'I suppose . . .'

'Excellent,' he said, rubbing his hands together. 'I may have some forms for you to sign shortly. If you'll excuse me, though, I have to go and see my lawyer now. One or two things to discuss. Let's meet up again in a day or two.'

'I'm afraid I'm based down in Sussex,' I said.

'Good. Not too far for you to come then. I'll send you a text to say when we need you. Can you find your own way out?'

'Thanks for the coffee,' I said.

'Not at all, my dear chap. Plenty more condensed milk where that came from.'

The train rattled southwards, with rain streaming down the windows in diagonal lines. March had turned suddenly, as it so often does, from spring back into winter. I hoped that Roger Norton Vane had purchased an umbrella as well as an overcoat.

I read through the notes that I had taken. There were undeniably still gaps in the narrative – especially concerning the day of his disappearance. But, when listening to Vane, I felt instinctively that he was the man I had heard speak at conferences twenty years before. His hair was greyer, his face more lined, he'd lost weight. But he was Vane, for all that – arrogant, alternately ingratiating and bullying, and always ready to pick a fight with anyone. And the voice was absolutely right. If he had forgotten the name of his dog it was because he didn't really care for dogs any more than he cared for humans. Through the miasma, I could just see the distant outline of Arundel Castle, sitting in cold comfort on its hill above the flat, misty, willow-studded plain of the Arun. In a few minutes the train would stop at Barnham, then I would need to begin to get my things together. I closed my notebook and placed in it my bag. I got my coat down from the rack and carefully unfolded it.

Ten minutes later I was getting off the train in Chichester, no clearer on the Roger Vane matter than I had been before. A few days ago, nobody knew that Roger Norton Vane might still be alive. Now, all over London, opinions were hardening one way or the other. Was it really him? I was amongst those who saw no good reason to disbelieve him. Those who had the greatest doubts were those who had personal reasons for doubting. Cynthia had lost an inheritance, or at least had an indefinite delay placed upon receipt. Tim Macdonald had lost his home prematurely. Vane's agent, George, had suddenly been jolted out of a pleasant state of watching royalties pile up with little effort, and had been brusquely and perhaps unfairly called to account.

It was all getting very complicated. It would have been interesting to know what Elsie really thought of it all.

CHAPTER SIX

Elsie

So, what I really think is this: flat chocolate is much easier to smuggle into the office than lumpy chocolate. You can slip it into your briefcase between two files. Which points to investing in a bar of Lindt hazelnut, for example, or maybe Montezuma's salty Sea Dog or the nice Co-Op one with orange oil, which you should definitely try if you don't know it. But, conversely, there's nothing more embarrassing than being caught with a herbal tea (no sugar) in one hand and a solid slab of high-calorie indulgence, with an awkwardly large bite taken out of it, in the other. So that indicates a need for smaller, scientifically targeted dosages that can, if necessary, be crammed into my mouth the moment I hear footsteps outside my door. The chocolate should preferably be unwrapped too, to avoid the danger of having to swallow a wrapping in an emergency, which is always unpleasant. M&M's might fit the bill here. Or a large box of Maltesers. But then we're back to how you get them in under the radar.

As with climate change, there's no simple solution.

Like most people, I've toyed with the idea of hiding balls of chocolate inside grape skins. But then Tuesday might be tempted to help herself to one. And who has the time to stuff grapes with chocolate these days?

Yes, yes – obviously it's my agency and I can eat chocolate in it if I want to, but it's the look more of sorrow than in anger on Tuesday's face that causes me to employ, not subterfuge in any way, shape or form, but . . . let's say . . . tact, whenever I reward myself with a small, thoroughly deserved snack.

There was a knock on the door. I flicked the half-eaten Mars Bar into an open drawer with a well-practised movement, rammed it shut with my knee, swallowed hard and called out: 'Come in!'

Tuesday's face appeared. 'Are you free to see Lucinda?'

'Absolutely.'

Tuesday gave me a strange look. 'You weren't having lunch or anything?'

I passed my tongue over my top lip. Mmmm . . . chocolate . . . good in one way but maybe not so good in another way.

'No, it won't be lunchtime for a while yet.'

Tuesday said nothing, as befits her status as a mere lackey in the Elsie Thirkettle Agency, doubtless silenced by my icy stare. Or maybe she just felt she'd made her point. Whatever.

'I'll show her in, then,' she said primly. 'She wants to talk to you about the Vane biography. You'll need to lick your chin, too, if you want to get rid of all the chocolate.'

I looked towards the drawer and wondered if I had time for

another bite before having to face Lucinda, but she must have been hovering at Tuesday's shoulder because she shot into the office the moment Tuesday stepped back. As publishers go, she certainly fell into the small and nippy category.

'So, when will it be ready?' she demanded.

'Ethelred's only been working on it for a couple of months,' I said.

'What does he need to find out, for goodness' sake? He's read all Vane's books, or so you told me. The rest is probably on Wikipedia or somewhere.'

'He's talking to people who knew him. And to the formerly dead Roger Norton Vane. Vane turning up was a stroke of luck, when you think about it. A real plus. Look, Lucinda, Ethelred can still be rude about him – just enough to really upset him – but without giving Vane any cause to sue you.'

'Is that possible?'

'Absolutely,' I said.

Lucinda considered this. 'OK. But Ethelred's not going to make himself too popular.'

'He's not that popular, anyway. He really isn't at risk of losing a lot of friends. And frankly, one more person who thinks he's a tosser won't make a lot of difference to anything.'

'No, I suppose not. The main thing is speed. Quality isn't important or we'd have got somebody else to do it. We'll just do one paperback print run. Interestingly, though, I've heard there's a rival biography on its way – from Tim Macdonald.'

She raised an eyebrow.

'Is there?' I enquired with genuine interest.

'You bloody represent him, Elsie. You represent both of

them. You've sold the same book to two publishers. What the shit's going on?'

It was a good point and deserved due consideration.

'Hmmmm . . . let me think . . . Tim . . . is he writing a biography? . . . of Roger Norton Vane? For somebody else? I suppose he might be. Just a bit.'

'How much of a bit?'

'The whole of a bit,' I conceded.

'Well, we're going to get Ethelred's out first. Aren't we, Elsie?'

That could be tricky since I'd promised Tim's publisher the same thing and for much the same reason. Still, one of the books was bound to come out first. I couldn't be wrong in both cases. 'Yes, of course, Lucinda,' I said. 'We shall absolutely get your book finished before the other one.'

She breathed in, possibly for the first time since she had entered the office, and suddenly sat back in the chair. 'So what do you make of this guy claiming to actually be Vane? Fake? Or the real deal?'

'Ethelred says real, but then he still believes in Father Christmas. Tim says fake, but he doesn't believe in anything much.'

'Tim only saw him for a couple of minutes while he was having his speech thrown in his face, and then later when he was being shown the door of his flat. And on the latter occasion he was weeping many bitter tears, according to at least one version of the story. So, how could he tell?'

'Well, what do you think? You knew him. You were his editor for a while, though not for very long, of course.' I smiled at her sympathetically.

'He's Roger Norton Vane as I remember him. Smug. Abrasive. Unconcerned about anyone's interests except his own. The big question is why he chose to come back now.'

'And,' I said, 'why he disappeared in the first place. That's also the big question.'

'His last couple of books were crap,' said Lucinda, with relish. 'After he switched publishers he was complete rubbish. Maybe he knew he'd done all he could . . .'

I shook my head. 'Writers never know that,' I said. 'Sit them at a desk with a laptop in front of them and they can't help themselves. Tap, tap, tap. It's an addiction . . .' Which reminded me. I opened the chocolate drawer and took out one I'd begun earlier. I peeled back the wrapper. Chocolate, nougat and caramel caressed my tastebuds. 'Sorry – would you like one of these? I've got another somewhere – a fresh one, obviously.'

Lucinda shook her head. She was size minus six or something and could have fitted in any number of Mars Bars without noticing it. Maybe her attention was elsewhere. Her loss, not mine. I checked the drawer to see if the other one was indeed within easy reach. It might seem rude if I had to rummage through every single hiding place while Lucinda was talking. Nope, there was one visible. I wouldn't need to.

'Do you know what I think?' said Lucinda, leaning forward confidentially. 'I think he realised his career was on the slide and decided to vanish, like Agatha Christie did, for the publicity. But, unlike Christie, there was no banjo player around to recognise him and tip off the press, so he was stuck with what he'd done. He had to stay put in the jungle or look like a complete idiot. Which he was, anyway.'

'Christie had certainly had a row with her other half prior to vanishing,' I said. 'Just like Vane and Tim Macdonald. People can do strange things when they're really pissed off. Christie only got as far as Harrogate, though. Vientiane is a bit extreme. So's twenty years. It's too long to be believable in any context except real life. Anyway, why does he come back now? Has he finally written a masterpiece?'

'As if. Plenty of writers go from genius to shite in three books, but nobody goes from shite to genius. Can't be done. No, he'd just had enough of sweet iced coffee. I tried it in Vietnam. Fun to begin with – a bit like Facebook. Then the nausea sets in. He also might have heard that it was his last chance to come back before he was declared dead and his accumulated royalties were divvied up amongst the undeserving. That must focus your mind a bit.'

'True,' I said.

'It's absolutely true,' she said.

'Totally true.'

'One hundred per cent true.'

There didn't seem to be too much I could add to that. A hundred per cent always seems conclusive. A hundred and one per cent, theoretically better, just seems like the first small step on the long road to infinity and one per cent, a quotient usually recognised only by ten-year-olds.

Then Lucinda looked straight at me and gave the only good reason to date for wanting Vane to be the real deal. 'It would have been fun screwing him over when he was dead. But, now I think about it, if we play our cards right, we can have even more fun if he's actually alive.'

* * *

'How long?' asked Ethelred, with totally unjustified annoyance. I couldn't see his face, because he was phoning, but it would have been much like Tuesday's if she'd caught me in the pick-and-mix section when I said I'd popped out to buy stationery.

'Two months,' I said. 'I told her you'd have it all tied up by then. Five thousand words a day – you'll finish with a week or so to spare. You weren't planning to go anywhere, were you?'

'I might have all sorts of other things to do.'

'Except you don't,' I said.

'And what about the quality of what I'm writing?'

'Oh, she's not worried about that,' I said. 'She'd have got Barry Forshaw or Martin Edwards or somebody to do it if she'd wanted it well written.'

'That's very comforting,' he said.

'That's what I'm here for, Ethelred,' I said. 'To support you and give you that extra little bit of confidence that all second-rate writers need.'

He told me how grateful he was. Or at least he used those words. He may have meant something else.

'Lucinda wants you to say that the person claiming to be Vane really is him,' I said. 'I agreed there would be more money in it that way.'

'More money for whom?' asked Ethelred.

'Mainly for her but, don't worry, there's a bit more for me as well.'

'Well, that's what I think, anyway. It's him.'

'So you said, but why?' I asked.

'There are too many people around who remember Vane,'

he said. 'He might be able to keep it up for a day or two, but the fact that he's lasted even this long suggests to me that it must be him. Or somebody who was very, very close to him – and I can't think who that would be. His brother's dead. No first cousins, just one very distant one. But if I'm wrong, then we'll know pretty soon. Is it true that Tim Macdonald's writing his own version of the biography, by the way?'

'That's what I'm told.'

'But you represent him, so you'd know what contracts he had signed. There's no point in pretending, Elsie – it will probably be up on Amazon soon.'

That was a good point. Actually it was up on Amazon already.

'All right. But this is in strict confidence. Tim is doing a Vane book too. A very different one. Not in any way like yours. More . . . literary.'

'Thank you.'

'More of a bestseller.'

'Thank you.'

'More aimed at selling the US and translation rights. And maybe television or a film.'

'Thank you.'

'My pleasure. You only had to ask.'

'But mine will at least be out first?'

'Absolutely,' I said. 'I'd scarcely let you waste your time otherwise, would I?'

CHAPTER SEVEN

The cottage was not far from where I live in Sussex – just over on the far side of Chichester, in fact. It was small, quaint and had lavender growing on both sides of the path – now severely pruned but promising lush swathes of pale purple once summer arrived. Both the roof and the small porch were thatched, though many loose strands of wispy reed were blowing freely in the breeze.

I knocked on the door. It was opened by a small, trim woman with grey hair. I could see the resemblance to Cynthia at once.

'Margery Vane?' I asked unnecessarily.

'Absolutely. And you must be Ethelred,' she said. 'Come in and I'll put the kettle on.'

Cynthia's mother was somebody else whom I had arranged to see as part of my attempt to get inside the enigma that was Roger Norton Vane. Twenty years ago she would have known him well – better in most ways than

Cynthia would. I'd hoped, in the days when I had no hope of speaking to Vane himself, that she would be a valuable source of information. As with Cynthia, I had seen no reason not to keep the appointment just because Vane was now available in person. I suspected that Margery might have a slightly different perspective on Vane from the one he had on himself.

'I'd so hoped he was dead,' she said, as she poured the tea. 'Better for everyone, really. I was quite upset when Cynthia told me he hadn't been murdered. I didn't go to that service thing they held – I couldn't see much to celebrate in his life and work. I was just looking forward to Cynthia finally inheriting what was rightfully hers. There's nothing to come from me . . . oh, she won't get the cottage, I'm afraid. What you have to understand is that Cynthia's father made almost no money until he was fifty-two and then died when he was fifty-three. Inconsiderate and irritating to the very end. We sold the house in London and bought this. It was fine for a while, then the crash came and interest rates dropped to nothing. So I signed up for an equity release scheme. The cottage is mine for life but it will be the bank's when I die. Cynthia had always said that, once she inherited Roger's money, she'd pass some of it onto me – which was sweet of her but it won't be happening now.'

'So, you could have bought the freehold back?'

'Oh no, not enough for that. But the thatch needs repairing and the damp needs fixing – both rising and descending – and the gardener frankly hasn't been paid for months. "Genteel poverty" doesn't do justice to the position I'll be in by this time next year. I don't mind the bank inheriting a ruin, but I'm not sure I actually want to live in one. Still, unless you happen to do a bit of thatching or parge work on the side, I doubt that's of much interest to you. What can I tell you about my brother-in-law?'

'Anything you like. It's all grist to the biographical mill. I suppose you saw a lot of him?'

'No more than I had to. He would descend on us from time to time to ruin Christmas or Easter. There was something about him that was almost childlike, in the sense that children get a really big kick out of sadism. It's what makes Roald Dahl so popular. It's a basic instinct to laugh at somebody else's extreme discomfort. Only as you grow older do you learn to empathise with an incompetent headmistress out of her depth or a gamekeeper just trying to do his job and feed his family. There but for the grace of God . . . Turning the gamekeeper into a rabbit who gets caught in one of his own traps doesn't seem so funny after you're thirty-five or so. Roger, bless him, never grew up. So, it always seemed funny to him.'

'You sound as if you hated him.'

Margery paused in her rearrangement of a much-stained tea cosy.

'No, I didn't. Not most of the time, anyway. He was very good-looking in those days. It's always easier to forgive people you lust after. And I could empathise with his inability to empathise with others. It's just the way he was. My husband was a bit like that too. But I loved them both in different ways.'

'Loved?'

'Yes, I think so. Roger, anyway.'

'Family trait? The insensitivity, I mean.'

'Oh no. Nothing to do with the family. My parents-in-law were nice enough. If I blame anyone I blame that school.'

'I'm not even sure which school it was – Wikipedia is silent on the subject – just says he was educated in London and at Oxford. Roger said it was some inner-city comprehensive.'

'He actually told you that?'

'Well, he said it was some inner-city place with a drug problem.'

'The Cordwainers School? An inner-city comprehensive? I think not.'

'Is that where he was? He's kept quiet about that.'

'Didn't fit the image, I would imagine. One of the country's most expensive private schools, albeit based in central London. I was occasionally taken, as a spouse, to alumni events – I suppose that's what you'd call them – but I always felt an outsider, because that is what I was and nobody ever saw fit to invite me inside. Cordwainers isn't the sort of place that cares about anywhere else. It's often said that Cordwainers boys aren't snobbish, but that's because they are so confident of their own superiority that they can't be bothered to look down on anyone. Too much effort. To despise somebody you have to acknowledge their existence.'

'Who were his contemporaries at Cordwainers?'

'Roger's? No idea. I could tell you one or two very famous names from my husband's year, but Roger was three years younger. He'd have mixed with a different crowd.'

Then something occurred to me.

'Does the name Cousin Wilbert mean anything to you?'
I asked.

She shook her head. 'Should it?'

'Roger mentioned him.'

'Then one must conclude he is a cousin on that side
of the family. But I can't ever remember the name being
mentioned. Wilbert? Not a name you would forget.'

'You might have known him as Graham?'

'Oh Graham . . . why didn't you say so? Yes, he died
last year . . . or the year before? One funeral merges into
another after a while. But I never heard him referred to as
Wilbert. Why would anyone want to do that to him?'

'Roger said it was a nickname he'd had.'

She shook her head again. 'Sorry – can't help you at all
there. My husband would have known, of course, but there
we are. What I can do is to show you some photographs.
You might be able to use some of them.'

An hour later I left the cottage with an envelope full
of pictures of Roger Norton Vane, sitting or standing with
various combinations of the Vane family as it had been
twenty years before. I also took away growing doubts that
I had been misled by Roger Vane in some way that I could
not yet put my finger on.

But I had further interviews in London. Hopefully they
would clear things up.

CHAPTER EIGHT

'Biscuit?'

'Thank you.' I took one and then wondered what to do
with it. My notebook was perched on the side of William
Ogilvie's cluttered desk, with a dainty bone china cup and
saucer beside it. I could see no space for a biscuit anywhere.
I eventually placed it precariously on the edge of the small,
gold-rimmed saucer. The lawyer said nothing, but helped
himself from the pile of brightly coloured iced circles that
could have graced any nursery tea. He bit into it with relish,
spraying crumbs in my direction. If he normally ate with
such gusto, he looked well on it. He was tall, thin and, to
judge by the speed with which he had led me from the lift
to his office, very fit.

'You've always represented Mr Vane?' I enquired.

'Ever since I qualified. Ever since he needed to defend
himself in defamation cases. That means we go back a
long way.'

'A colourful character?'

Ogilvie laughed. 'To the extent that I ought to comment on my clients to a third party, yes, a colourful character. With a colourful tongue. Still, it's a matter of public record that he has been sued for libel several times. And sued somebody else once. He lost, of course. It's difficult finding something to say about him that's completely untrue.'

'He doesn't seem too concerned about his own reputation. I mean, he's very open about his criminal past . . .'

I stopped, aware of a sudden tension in the air. The lawyer's eyes now had a steely tone that I had not noticed before. 'I wouldn't believe everything he tells you, especially that.'

'Really? You mean it's not true?'

'Along with many other things he says, it's not completely untrue. I mean, when he was at school he did learn how to start a car without using a key and did remove one from the school grounds – the deputy head's, as it happens. He was stopped fairly quickly by a policeman who thought he looked a bit young to be driving. The deputy head generously didn't press charges. The police were content to leave it to the school to sort out and ignore the small matters of the lack of a driving licence or insurance and of any danger to the public resultant from underage toffs hot-wiring cars. They probably wouldn't do that now, but they did then. The past is a foreign country, as they say. But who wants to go to a foreign country? I always think you're much safer holidaying in Britain. Much better all round on a nice English beach. Deckchair. Bucket and spade. Nothing nasty lurking in the water.'

There seemed to be a message hiding not far below the surface – one that had nothing to do with travel bookings.

'I can't see why I shouldn't quote it,' I said. 'It's a story he told me himself, after all.'

'In writing?'

'No.'

'In front of witnesses?'

'No.'

'There you are, then. Best to stay in Bognor Regis, don't you think?'

'I thought it was one of the more interesting anecdotes about him.'

'It is. Of course it is. That's why he tells it. But it doesn't mean that it's true or that nobody will take offence if you repeat it. The school acted with a certain amount of generosity. They might not take kindly to your implying that they'd prosecuted one of their pupils – which they emphatically did not. And there were others involved, who might not want their names mentioned – especially if your version, obtained from Roger, differed from the truth in even the most trivial way. I'm not offering you legal advice, but I would suggest you'd be much safer leaving it out of any account you are writing. Roger has always had a difficult relationship with the truth. Sometimes he's been on speaking terms with it, sometimes not. Hence the work he's kindly put my way over the years. Help yourself to biscuits, by the way.'

Mentally I deleted an entire chapter of my book. There was plenty of other stuff, of course. I wondered whether I could put the story in while at the same time denying its veracity. It would be tricky. Maybe I shouldn't.

'And I'm told the school was Cordwainers?'

'That's right. One of London's leading schools – along with St Paul's and Westminster. Of course, it's still on its original site, unlike St Paul's. Right in the middle of Holborn. A bit cramped, but they bought up some houses nearby back in the thirties, evicted the tenants and built a new gymnasium and science block. It was all fine . . . fine as a school, not fine for the tenants. They never seemed to feed you enough, and what they did give you was never terribly good, but none of us had any real complaints.'

'He always tried to make it sound tough.'

'It was in its way. If he'd really gone to prison, as he has occasionally tried to suggest he did, he'd have got a more comfortable bed and much better grub. And time off for good behaviour. It was what you'd describe as character building.'

'He said the metalwork master had been a getaway driver for the Krays.'

'Ah . . . that may have been true. No DBS checks in those days. I doubt he was the only one with a dodgy past. But it was a top school, then and now. That was why the police stayed out of it when he took the car. They wouldn't have interfered in the internal affairs of a national institution.'

'Who would have been at school with him? I guess with a place like that some of them would be in quite prominent positions now?'

Ogilvie nodded thoughtfully. 'Pretty well all of them would be in prominent positions. That's what their parents paid for. You could check in Who's Who, I suppose, to see who was around in Roger's time. Let me think . . . You might want to talk to Lord Davies. He would have been there.'

Ogilvie smiled, as if he had just given me unusually helpful advice. I could, however, see an immediate impediment.

'The fund manager?' I said.

'That's right. People normally add the qualifier "billionaire" when mentioning him these days, but fund manager will do.'

'He never gives interviews,' I said.

'He might. This time.'

'Really? I'll try to book an appointment with his secretary, then.'

'She'll say no. Because he never gives interviews. But I can let you have you his private email. Known just to his friends. Say you met me and I suggested it.' He scribbled something on a torn-off slip of paper and passed it across the desk. I looked at it doubtfully, then pocketed it.

'I'll try it,' I said. 'Thank you.'

'My pleasure. I always like to be helpful when I can.'

'And you have no doubts that the person claiming to be Vane really is him?' I asked.

Ogilvie frowned and leant back in his chair, clutching his cup in both hands. He pursed his lips. 'When he first came through that door, I genuinely didn't recognise him. Right sort of height, right sort of bearing, but somehow . . .' Ogilvie pulled a face indicative of extreme and justified legal doubt. 'But then he spoke and I'd have known the voice anywhere. We chatted. He'd forgotten a few things I'd have expected him to remember, but then I suppose he might have said the same for me. I ended up completely convinced. I know young Cynthia's still got her doubts, though.'

'She's been to see you?'

'Yes, earlier today. I told her what I told you. In my humble opinion, it's Roger returned from the dead. We had quite a long chat about this and that in the end – bit of a catch-up. Hopefully I managed to reassure her, in some ways at least. Sadly not in others.'

'Well, now he's back, there'll be more work for you,' I joked.

'Maybe. I'll be doing slightly less legal work from now on. I'm standing for Parliament in the next election. Safe-ish seat in Hampshire. The current incumbent is retiring, if the old buffer lasts long enough. Unless he cuts down a bit on his drinking, there could be a by-election in the very near future. They don't mind moribund MPs in our party, but we draw the line at dead. The call may come any day or any hour.' Ogilvie smiled. 'Not that his constituency will be sorry to see the back of him. He's gone a bit liberal in his old age. I'm reassuring the voters that I at least will be properly representing their views on inheritance tax, policing and immigration. I'm starting to spend more time down there, getting my face known. Ensuring they understand I'm one of them – not some city lawyer on the make at their expense. I don't want them to listen to the siren calls of UKIP. I may drop hints I'd bring back hanging, for sheep stealing if not for murder. What you have to understand, Ethelred, is that if there are too few police, then the illegal migrants nick all your sheep, leaving you with nothing but shit-covered grassland to pass on to the kids. It's a point I can't make to the local press too often. Even a six thousand majority can evaporate if you're not careful.'

In spite of my doubts, Lord Davies replied to my email within a few minutes of my sending it. He could see me for half an hour tomorrow, if I wished. At his office in Cheapside.

I phoned Elsie.

'I'm making better progress than I expected,' I said. 'Ogilvie, the lawyer, was helpful and he's put me onto Lord Davies, who was at school with Vane. Did you know he was at Cordwainers?'

'Roger Vane?' said Elsie. 'Yes, I think so.'

'Did you? He kept that quiet. It's not in any of the main sources – nothing on the Internet, nothing in the standard reference books. Told me it was an inner-city place with a drugs problem.'

'Question of image,' said Elsie. 'Not edgy enough. Oxford was fine. Anyone can get into Oxford – you, for example. But you need wads of cash for a place like Cordwainers. And it has to be old cash – new money isn't accepted. Or it wasn't then. It's probably all oligarchs' kids now, ferried backwards and forwards in gold-plated Rolls Royces. But it did have a drugs problem in those days. I reckon a lot went on that you couldn't get away with now. There will be plenty of respectable Old Cordwainers out there wondering what stories Vane is going to tell you. Drugs. Drink. And the rest. I'm not surprised Ogilvie tipped Davies off that he ought to see you.'

'You think so?' I asked. 'I thought Ogilvie was just being helpful.'

'As if.'

'Davies was certainly very keen to meet me,' I said.

'Bet he was,' said Elsie. 'Who wouldn't be if they were shitting their pants?'

CHAPTER NINE

'Biscuit?'

I nodded and took another. I wondered from which obscure but expensive artisanal supplier they came – small, unevenly shaped, not too sweet but richly buttery and melting in the mouth. Elsie would have appreciated them more than I did.

Davies' office was large and shiny. The wood was pale and highly polished. The chrome was slightly too immaculate to be the genuine 1930s article. Its spectacular sweeps and curves glistened. The few books and artworks on display were carefully chosen, carefully placed by people who charged for both services. The largest single object in the room was undoubtedly a Henry Moore. The whole succeeded in conveying multiple messages – it was fashionable, expensive and no aspect of it was unintended or left to chance. You knew that you had entered Lord Davies' world, in which everything was exactly as he intended it to be. For a few minutes, you too had your place here. As part of his world.

'So, is it him or not?' he asked.

'Opinions are divided,' I said.

Davies snorted. He didn't have time for divided opinions.

'And your own?' he demanded. 'What might those be, Mr Tressider?'

I paused in mid-bite. It was as if, on a clear summer's day, I'd heard the distant but unmistakeable rumble of thunder. I'd been warned to expect this: the sudden switch from affable host to implacable inquisitor. They said it was deliberate. He never wanted the person on the far side of the desk, and it was a very large desk, to feel entirely at ease.

What surprised me, though, was how old Davies looked. His grey hair was thinning and there were deeply etched lines across his forehead. The pictures supplied to newspapers by his PR people always showed a smiling, smooth-faced man with a square jaw and wavy hair – there was something vaguely nautical about the image that he wished to project. Easy-going, liked by his crew but efficient and nobody's fool. The captain of an aircraft carrier perhaps, though a submarine might have suited him better: Davies liked to operate beneath the surface, unobserved and creating as few ripples as possible. The kinder articles on him, and he had the influence to ensure there were just the right number, said that he valued his privacy. Others called him secretive – they might have gone further but even 'very secretive' might have ended up in court. Anything approaching the truth would have been instantly stopped in its tracks by an injunction.

'To the extent that I can judge,' I said carefully, 'I can see no reason why it should not be Mr Vane. He resembles him physically. The voice is very much his voice.'

'I can tell that myself,' he observed. 'I thought you were supposed to be his biographer? That you actually knew something about him?'

We looked at each other across the windswept acres of mahogany.

'You've known him for much longer than I have,' I said. 'You were at school with him.'

'Is that what he says?'

'Isn't it in the public domain?'

'It depends what you define as the public domain. Vane was always free with opinions on anything, but he has tended to be rather vague about that part of his education. I think he'd have liked to have gone to a comprehensive – the Cordwainers School wasn't quite "street" enough – I believe that's what they say now – my children say it, anyway. Interesting term, though it ignores the fact that Park Lane is a street too, and a perfectly functional one. I was always very happy to be at Cordwainers – proud to be there. I rather hoped he'd disowned us.'

'Hoped?'

'Sorry, slip of the tongue – I meant I thought he'd disowned us. I have no hopes for him one way or the other. The school has plenty of famous old boys – Old Cordwainers as we say – it won't worry about whether Roger Norton Vane still wishes to associate himself with the rest of us.'

'You don't seem to have liked him?'

'I felt he was a bit of a clown, to be honest. Not just

always in trouble but always in trouble so unnecessarily. He pretty much had a reserved place outside the Head Man's study. Always standing there awaiting whatever punishment he was due next – lines, detention, cane. Not somebody you wanted to associate with if you wished to stay out of trouble yourself. I'm assuming he doesn't claim me as a friend?'

'He's said very little so far. I'm hoping to get more out of him about his early life when he's finally willing to talk to me. My first interview with him was not as helpful as I'd hoped. There was an incident at school – he stole somebody's car?'

'More coffee, Ethelred?' asked Davies, indicating the pot.

'I'm fine, thanks.'

'Well, just say when you do.'

'Thank you. So, did he steal a car?' I asked.

'You've already asked me that.' Davies' tone was very much that of a parent to an overdemanding child.

'But you didn't reply.'

'Possibly not. Why would you want to know?'

'I was merely curious,' I said.

'Really? Just curious? You aren't planning to include it in your book, for example?'

'William Ogilvie advised against it.'

'Sounds good lawyerly advice to me. You could end up in all sorts of trouble publishing unsubstantiated gossip. If you check your contract you'll probably find you indemnify your publisher for all legal costs if it is found that anything you have written is libellous. That could be expensive – lawyers' bills and so on. For you and your publisher. Another biscuit,

Ethelred? There are three sorts there, I believe – plain, vanilla and ginger – though the difference is fairly subtle. Subtlety's expensive too. If you want to know what you're actually eating you need to pay a lot less. But I can afford to indulge myself in any way I wish. Any way at all.'

'I thought I could taste ginger in the last one,' I said. 'It was rather good.'

'A man of discernment,' he said approvingly. 'A man who knows what's what. A man who doesn't blunder into things. At least, I hope you don't.' He took a biscuit himself and chewed thoughtfully. 'Ginger,' he said. 'My favourite too. We clearly have similar tastes, Ethelred. That's good.'

I looked at my notebook. The page was headed 'Lord Davies' but was still otherwise empty. I took my pen and added 'Vane had reserved place outside the Head Man's study'. I doubted I'd actually quote that, but the blank page was an accusation of idleness.

'You knew him fairly well?' I asked. 'He would have been in your year?'

'It was a big school. You knew the boys in your own house of course. Friendships in other houses were not encouraged. Not discouraged exactly, but not encouraged either. I don't know why. That's how it was then.'

He glanced at the half-eaten biscuit in his hand and placed it on his saucer. Maybe he wasn't that keen on ginger, after all.

'And Vane wasn't in your house?' I asked.

Davies considered this carefully. 'Let me see: there was Philips and Mac and Dusty and Viscount Fitzstephen and whatisname . . . oh, dear, what was he called? . . . he became Sultan of somewhere in later life. Every year he had to present his subjects with his weight in cloves. Or was it nutmeg? I could probably find out which, if you were really interested to know. He grew rather fat in later life and had to be declared bankrupt. I'm sure I'd have a photograph of us all somewhere . . . Did Vane tell you any other little anecdotes from his schooldays?'

'No, not so far. Just the car one.' I said. 'Do you have anything I could use?'

Davies proceeded to tell me a long and convoluted tale about a bucket of water placed on top of a door, which emptied on the French master as he entered the room. The master was saved only by a particularly firm mortarboard. He had uttered some French words that the boys had not previously encountered. The story was, at best, no more than mildly amusing and could have been taken directly from a 1950s school novel.

'And that was Vane?'

'It was never proven.'

'But you witnessed it yourself?'

'I may have simply been told about it. You should definitely include it. After all, you probably won't have a lot to say about his schooldays, will you?'

I opened my notebook and wrote: 'Bucket story – unusually firm mortarboard – not proven. Jolly jape. Frank Richards???'

'Thank you,' I said.

'My pleasure,' he said. 'I'm keen to assist you as much as I can. I'll see if I can find out a bit more about that sultan chap, who so interested you.'

Davies looked at his watch. It was not large or showy, but, like everything else, it was clearly expensive. He opened a leather-bound diary, the only object other than his coffee cup and a half-eaten biscuit on his desk, slid his finger quickly down the page and then looked at me. My time was apparently up.

'If Vane does tell you any other little stories – about his time at Cordwainers – you might like to run them past me for accuracy,' said Davies, shaking my hand. 'I'd be happy to help. I could get my lawyer's opinion too. He could tell you what was safe to print. Safe for your publisher. Safe for you. No charge for that, of course. It would be my pleasure.'

'That's very kind,' I said. 'If I need advice of that sort, I'll certainly do as you suggest.'

'You are very wise,' he said. 'My secretary will show you to the lift.'

'How did things go with Davies?'

'No better than average,' I told Elsie. 'He was friendly enough and fed me expensive biscuits. But I didn't get much out of him on Vane's schooldays. Told me some story about putting a bucket of water on top of a door to drench the French teacher.'

'Sounds like Greyfriars.'

I shifted my phone to the other ear to allow me to consult my notebook.

'Precisely. Even the words he used made it sound like Frank Richards. Everyone involved was described as "a fellow" or "a chap" – and he actually used the word "jape". And "jolly". Except nobody owned up and took their punishment like a man, as they would have done at Greyfriars. Otherwise straight cliché from beginning to end.'

'Maybe it really was like that at Cordwainers: daily floggings from prefects and secretly roasting a whole ox on Big Side by moonlight. I mean, I didn't go to that sort of school. Wrong sex, wrong accent, wrong bank balance. How would I know what they all did to each other?'

I didn't go to that sort of school either, and my father taught at the one I did go to. I wouldn't have risked trying anything with a bucket of water, then or now. I wouldn't have had the money even for half an ox.

'I won't be including it,' I said. 'He also kindly suggested I ran any other stories I heard past him.'

'Him or his lawyers?'

'Both. I think the real purpose of the interview was to warn me how easily it would be to sue the shit out of me. But it was the same with Ogilvie. Nobody wants to tell me anything about Vane's early years. Nobody wants me to write anything, either. I may as well give up on it if Lucinda wants the book as quickly as you say. Unless I can find somebody who will spill the beans.'

'Slide,' said Elsie.

'Sorry?'

'Don't mention it. Slide. You're not telling me the name means nothing to you?'

'Titus Slide . . .' I said. 'Where have I come across that name?'

'In the same place you found Eustace Slide and Hieronymus Slide.'

'Hieronymus Slide was Inspector Gascoyne's low-life

informant in Vane's first book – really slimy character. He gets shot in the last chapter. In the groin at close range.'

'Spot on. And Eustace Slide? I'll give you a clue – his mother's portrait is tattooed on his arse.'

'Oh yes, the drug dealer in Vane's second book – another minor character – he turns out to be a paedophile and is found hanged in a warehouse. They never catch the killer.'

'Hanged upside down. Like Mussolini. Dies very slowly. Titus Slide is the rapist in The Follower. You only discover who the narrator is at the very end. It's him. You think he's got away with it but he falls down a ladder into the cellar and breaks both legs. He can't get out again. The rats eat his eyes. A week later he dies of thirst.'

'Yes . . . don't remind me. I wonder why he used the same surname in all three cases?'

'There's a Slide in every book, though I couldn't name them all offhand. Often only one of the supporting cast, but always obnoxious – usually killed in a painful way. You can miss them if you aren't looking out for them, but spotting them is fun if you are in on the joke. The production company didn't risk following suit with the TV series.'

'So, why did he choose that name?'

'Dr Jonathan Slide was his housemaster at school.'

'You know him?'

'He once sent me a novel about a school. Nothing you could publish legally. Once it had circulated round the office for us all to read, it got a standard rejection slip. But the story of Vane's Revenge is well known in publishing circles.'

'So that's why he chose the name? It feels a bit like

a Roald-Dahl-style punishment of a tyrannical teacher.'

'I suppose it might have been a gracious compliment – a sort of thank you for fifteen terms of top-class education. What do you think?'

'However bad a housemaster he was, I think that it was a bit unkind.'

'That's Vane for you. Once the school caught on – round about book two – it disowned him. The head wrote and informed Vane it wasn't the sort of thing a chap was supposed to do. Not to a chap's housemaster.'

I thought of Davies' 'hope' that Vane had forgotten them. Not a slip of the tongue, then.

'I wonder how Dr Slide felt about that? Did anyone ever ask him?' I said.

'No, but you can,' said Elsie.

'He's still alive?'

'Just about. Alive enough to dish the dirt on Vane if he wishes to.'

'He'd probably be hard to find.'

'He lives in Putney. Tuesday has his contact details. It took her a while to get them – hours of trawling through our records of rejected manuscripts, poor thing – but I find it helps to keep her fully occupied and at her desk. I'll email them to you, if you like. I'm sure he'd welcome a visit. He doesn't get out much. Not any more.'

CHAPTER TEN

'Biscuit?'

'No thanks,' I said. 'I've just had lunch.'

'Late lunch, then?'

'Yes,' I said.

The four digestives on the plate seemed to have been at the back of the cupboard for some time. They had an odd grey tinge to them and a slightly furry surface. Jonathan Slide wisely made no effort to select one for himself. Perhaps he'd had a late lunch too.

He was wearing an old tweed jacket with leather patches on the elbows, a checked shirt and a crumpled, brown woollen tie, almost as if trying to caricature a retired schoolteacher. He had not noticed, or did not care about, the numerous stains of various colours on his khaki trousers. From the window of his small flat we had a fine view over the river and Putney Bridge.

'Always something going on down there,' he said,

hobbling a couple of steps towards the window. 'You can never be bored with a view like that. Never bored or dwelling on the past. Doesn't pay to dwell on the past, however wronged you've been. That's the London Rowing Club first eight – the one with blue and white stripes on their blades. Thames have red, white and black. Westminster School have pink. The Cordwainers' boathouse is up in Hammersmith – but they row past sometimes – blue blades with a gold rose. Can't miss them. For a year or two they had blue blades with two gold stripes, but we made the boat club go back to the rose. They'd had the gold rose for a hundred years – you can't change a tradition just because it's cheaper to paint a stripe than a flower or somebody thinks it looks "better". Most change is for the worse, I find. In Victorian times the young men often used to row naked from the waist up. Did you know that? In 1869, when Harvard raced Oxford on this stretch of the water, the Harvard crew were all bare-chested, though they did wear crimson handkerchiefs on their heads.'

'Including the cox?' I asked. I took a sip of tea. It was very weak and milky. I'd noticed Side had carefully retained the used tea bag after he'd extracted it from my cup. It was now drying by the sink.

'No idea about the cox,' he said. 'I wouldn't have thought so, would you? Now they all wear these lycra suits. I suppose it must be warmer. But still . . .'

We watched London Rowing Club make a practice start. For about twenty seconds water flew everywhere. The coach was unhappy and it was repeated with slightly less spray. They halted again and the coach berated them for a while via a crackly loudhailer. Both eight and coaching launch drifted slowly upstream with the incoming tide until they were lost to view.

'You're from Chichester, then?' asked Slide, breaking the silence.

'West Wittering,' I said. 'Do you know it?'

'A bit. I've always taken holidays in Selsey, just down the coast from you. Not as smart as the Witterings – more scope to do as you wish. Not as much scope as Brighton, but more than enough for my purposes. I'd go there every summer when I was teaching. I'm off down there again next week. Same B&B I always use. We should meet up.'

'I don't get to Selsey much,' I said.

'I'm often in Chichester,' said Slide. 'That's no distance from you. And free with your pensioner's bus pass.'

'I'm not quite old enough to qualify . . .' I said.

'Aren't you? You look as if you are. Well, you can afford the bus fare, I dare say. Just because you dress like that doesn't mean you're a complete pauper. Plenty of places to meet and chat. There are one or two bars I know, though they might not be to your taste. Still, we could have tea at the cathedral. That's nice, though it tends to be full of Christians, I find. Or anywhere in the centre of town – I get around quite well with my stick.'

'That would be very pleasant,' I said. The invitation seemed sufficiently insincere that I could accept it without risk. 'My mobile number is on my card.'

'Did you give me a card?'

'Yes.'

'Really? Well, I'm sure I'll find it. I do have a portable

phone myself. Don't use it a lot, but one day it may come in handy. You have to keep charging them up or they go flat or something. Did you know that?'

'Yes,' I said. I handed him another card. He looked at it suspiciously, then stuffed it in his top pocket, joining the one I'd already given him. Hopefully he wouldn't demand a third.

'More tea?' he asked.

I shook my head and reached for a biscuit, then thought better of it.

'So, you were Roger Norton Vane's housemaster?' I asked.

'I thought that's why you wanted to see me. If it isn't, I can't think why you're here. I didn't know him in any other capacity and you don't seem to know a great deal about rowing.'

'Yes, of course. I'm just . . . just checking I've got that right. He never mentioned Cordwainers himself. In some ways it's been quite difficult to get any real facts about his early life.'

'Has it? I would have thought you would just have to ask him – now he's back.'

'He is not always as forthcoming as a biographer would like. Perhaps he's forgotten some things.'

'Really? Well, I remember him, anyway. Nasty little boy. Some boys get into trouble through high spirits – do well enough afterwards. A few – not many – are just plain nasty. Born nasty. Are nasty. Stay nasty. They often do quite well too, of course. Cordwainers opened all sorts of doors for everyone. We could take the son of some utterly

86

undistinguished father – a writer, say, like yourself – and turn him into a gentleman. Fit for the Foreign Office or the Navy or Shell or the Bar or any firm in the City. Once a recruiter knew a fellow was from Cordwainers, there was no need to interview the rest. I remember a professor at Guy's Hospital saying to me: "We've never regretted taking a Cordwainers boy. Some of them weren't too bright, but they were all gentlemen through and through. I'd rather lose the occasional patient and have the port passed to me from the right direction." That was how it was then – at Guy's, anyway. A sense of proportion. Now it's all targets for this and targets for that . . . Are you sure you won't have a biscuit? Sometimes they're all right if you heat them up in the oven. They go hard again. The first time, anyway. Would you like me to do that for you? It would be no trouble.'

'I'm good,' I said.

'Are you?' he said, looking at me. He took off his spectacles and polished them on his tie. 'Well, unlike you, Vane was out and out bad. Came from a perfectly decent family, I believe. Professional people. But that's no guarantee of anything. Not any more.'

'You think it really is Vane?'

'I saw him on television. Still being snide and unpleasant. Never liked him. Never will. I'd love to throttle him with my bare hands. That's between you and me, of course. Not for publication.'

'He clearly didn't like you . . .'

'Why do you say that?'

'I mean – the characters in his books with your name.'

'So I'm told. It was only my surname. I don't read that

sort of trash anyway – crime novels. You are at least a biographer. Decent trade. Almost respectable. You haven't fallen quite that low yourself.'

'No,' I said. 'Did you resent it? The use of your name?'

'It didn't surprise me, if that's what you mean. If he hadn't done that he'd have done something else. Nasty child.'

'Lord Davies said he didn't know Vane well – that he was in another house . . .'

'No, they were both very much in my house. Can't understand why Davies would have said that. You must have misunderstood. Same house, same year, same dorm. So was that boy who became a lawyer. Liked those circular biscuits with lurid icing on them. He was still eating one when I last saw him – went there to get my will changed. Not that I've got a lot to leave anyone, but I don't want it going to the government and being used to help refugees or feminists or something awful like that. What was he called? Oh dear, my memory isn't what it was . . .'

'Ogilvie?'

'That's him. Ogilvie. How on earth did you know that? Yes, Vane, Davies and Ogilvie were quite thick with each other. I was afraid that Vane would lead the other two astray, but they turned out all right. Davies has made a lot of money, I'm told. Thousands.'

'Ogilvie's planning to stand for Parliament,' I said.

'Conservative?'

'I think so. He's in favour of money and hanging, anyway.'

Slide nodded, slightly reassured. 'I believe I took Ogilvie to Selsey once. I did that sometimes – take a few of the boys down to Sussex with me. Fun and games on the beach. Nothing illegal. Very jolly.'

'Is it true that Vane stole a car?' I asked.

'At school or later? I haven't followed his subsequent career very much, as you will have gathered.'

'At school. The deputy head's.'

'Oh, that . . . Borrowed, rather than stole, I'd have said. It was the Head Man's – no, you're right, the deputy head's. I think he had a bit of a thing for Vane, because he could have got him expelled. Vane wasn't at all bad-looking then. Not that I fancied him myself. Not really my type.'

'So there were no actual criminal charges?'

'No. Not for Vane or his companion in crime.'

'Who was . . . ?'

'Let me think . . . let me think . . . I'm sure it will come back to me. Possibly the same boy who was his editor and salesman when he published that poem of his.'

'I didn't know he wrote much poetry.'

'He didn't. He wrote only one when he was at Cordwainers – five pages stapled together and sold for a shilling.'

'That's more than most poetry makes.'

'It was gay porn, really, with a few rhymes thrown in.'

'Good grief. What did the school make of that?'

'I think it sold out quite quickly. I've probably still got my copy somewhere.'

CHAPTER ELEVEN

Elsie

'Biscuit?'

'Correct,' I said, swallowing the last of it. 'What I eat while I'm on the phone to you, Ethelred, is my own affair. How did you get on with the Hieronymus Slide?'

'He's called Jonathan Slide. I got on fine. I spent the whole meeting wondering who he reminded me of.'

'And it was . . .'

'Roger Vane. In some ways they're very different people, but the same capacity for sweeping generalisations. The same underlying arrogance. The same unpleasantness.'

'He hadn't heard of you either, then?'

'That isn't relevant. My point is that Roger Vane seems to have been far more influenced by his housemaster than either would care to admit. Or maybe it's just a Cordwainers thing. Maybe that's how they turn them out. They seem to have a very high opinion of themselves.'

'Of course they do. And, having been starved for five

years, a lifelong obsession with food. So did you discover anything new?'

'Davies, Ogilvie and Vane were apparently all good friends at school, which neither Ogilvie nor Davies were anxious to own up to. Slide also gave me an interesting account of an erotic poem that Vane produced at school and that one of his chums marketed for him.'

'Nothing worse than that? I'd been hoping for much more. Slide must hate Vane's guts for making him a character in his books. If he didn't know anything bad about Vane, you'd have thought he might have been arsed to make something up.'

'I don't think Slide likes Vane but he bears him no ill will over the character names business. He says that he's never read the books and doesn't much care.'

'He really said that?'

'Yes, that's what I've just said to you. He said that. That was what I meant.'

'Ethelred, I happen to know, because Tim told me, that Slide famously went out and bought each of the books the moment they hit the shops. Day of publication. Hardback. Full price. No Amazon Prime in those days. The one thing you can't afford to be as a teacher is a laughing stock. But that's what Slide became. He would spend the weeks preceding each publication date sweating over what Vane was going to do to him this time. The moment he got the book he would leaf through it until he came to the relevant text, then he would read with growing horror what his namesake had done. At or around book four he had a complete nervous breakdown. He was off work for a year. He had to give up being housemaster.

He largely gave up teaching. The school found him some admin role – careers advice, I think. Not too difficult in that most of the boys had jobs lined up for them from birth. But his own career as a teacher was a total write-off.'

'He didn't tell me that.'

'Which is interesting in itself. Did he think the man claiming to be Vane is genuine?'

'Yes,' he said. 'I rather think he did – on balance.'

'Tim still doesn't,' I said.

'Well, I do,' said Ethelred. 'There are one or two things that he's clearly misremembered, but he has been away a long time. And in the last resort a DNA test should prove it. Roger thought Cynthia wouldn't play ball – the inheritance and all that – and that there was no point in asking her to do it. But there must be some way of persuading her. In the end she must want to know too.'

'He said that? She wouldn't play ball?'

'I don't remember the exact words, but that was more or less what he told me.'

'That's why there'd be no point in even asking?'

'Yes. I'm not sure why you're labouring this point,' said Ethelred in his most patronising voice. 'She wouldn't cooperate and there would therefore be no point in raising the matter. As I say, I think that he may be wrong. But he was very clear about his reason.'

'He didn't mention in passing that Cynthia was no blood relation of his?' I asked.

'She's his niece.'

'Cynthia's adopted. His brother and his wife couldn't have children of their own.'

'Maybe he doesn't know . . .'

'How likely is that? Your brother adopts a child and you don't know about it? A baby miraculously appears in the household without the necessity for pregnancy?'

'Well, he certainly didn't tell me that and it would, as you say, have been an obvious objection. Perhaps he was just being funny at my expense?'

'Well, that's happened before. But in this case, maybe, because he's an imposter, he has no way of knowing she's adopted? It's exactly the sort of thing that might trip somebody up, no matter how well they've researched their target. Look, Ethelred, first he doesn't know his dog's name . . .'

'The dog's sex.'

'Name. Sex. Whatever. Then he falls for an invented cousin.'

'Wilbert. A genuine cousin whose nickname Cynthia was unaware of, but who was really called Graham.'

'Cynthia's mother was also unaware of the nickname.'

'True. But she said there really was a cousin called Graham. A distant cousin of her husband's, it would seem. It's not surprising she didn't know.'

'And, when coming up with a fake cousin, Cynthia just happened to hit accidentally on that one name, out of the thousands of other nicknames he might have had? Wilbert's not the most common name, except possibly in the part of the country you and Thomas Hardy come from.'

'Maybe she'd heard his nickname mentioned years ago and so, when she was thinking of what to call this invented cousin, she came up with something she dimly remembered . . .'

'Though her mother had never heard the name?'

'Or had also forgotten it.'

'Again, let me enquire: how likely is that?'

'Actually it's perfectly possible,' said Ethelred. There are times when you might as well try to reason with a traffic warden. Still, it was worth one more go.

'Look, Ethelred, here's how it is: Cynthia, Vane's closest living relation, and Tim his (admittedly very ex) partner both think he's a fake. You, who never spoke to him before this week, have decided, however, that he's the genuine article. Which of you would a rational being decide to believe? Count to ten before you reply.'

'I'd want to see the evidence,' said Ethelred huffily, after a count of eight.

'Then, my sweet, I shall get it for you,' I said.

Because I had already set the wheels in motion – wheels that I knew would grind on and crush the so-called Roger Vane into the dirt, in much the same way that financier Sir Jasper Slide was ground into the dirt by a combine harvester in *The Killing on Two Tree Farm*.

'When's Cynthia arriving?' Tim asked, as I terminated my call to Ethelred.

'In a few minutes,' I said. 'You put the coffee on. What else will we need? . . . Yes, of course, biscuits.'

CHAPTER TWELVE

Elsie

'Coffee?'

'Black. No sugar,' said Cynthia, settling back into the armchair.

Tim was in the other armchair, because my modestly sized flat possesses precisely two of them. Shortly, I would sit on the dining chair that I had pulled up facing them, but for the moment I was being the epitome of a domestic goddess, pouring actual genuine coffee from a proper coffee pot. It was a while since I'd made the real thing, and I could no longer remember the correct ratios of coffee and water. Ten parts one to one part of the other one? But ten parts of which? What I was pouring might be hot water carrying the distant memory of coffee or (after they'd chewed their way through it) might keep them on the ceiling for the next three days. We'd soon see.

'Mmmm . . . coffee,' said Cynthia, taking a sip.

I waited for her to tell me what sort of coffee, but she didn't.

'I've probably got some biscuits somewhere,' I said.

'No thanks, I'm on a diet,' said Cynthia.

'My assistant's always trying to get me to cut down on biscuits,' I said. 'And chocolate. And crisps. And whipped cream. And mayonnaise. And chips. Not all together, of course. And absolutely not mayonnaise with chocolate – you'd think it would work but it really doesn't. Anyway, you certainly don't need to diet, Cynthia.'

I waited for her to say 'well, nor do you, Elsie' but she didn't. I decided I liked her slightly less. And frankly she did need to diet. Losing four or five pounds would have done her no harm at all.

'So, why are we here?' she asked.

'To discuss the man calling himself Roger Norton Vane,' I said. 'Between us we have the knowledge, skill and cunning to bring him down.'

'You seem very sure of that.'

'You've caught him out twice already – Bramble and Wilbert,' I reminded her.

'Uncle Graham was apparently called Wilbert,' she said. 'At least according to the man claiming to be Uncle Roger. Graham died a couple of years ago so I've no way of checking. I did wonder if maybe I had some distant memory of that. It might even have been mentioned at the funeral . . .'

'Your mother didn't remember Graham having a nickname.'

'You've spoken to my mother?'

'Ethelred did. In the line of biographical research.'

'Oh yes, I think she mentioned he was going to call

round. I'm afraid her memory isn't what it was. That she doesn't remember somebody called Wilbert honestly doesn't prove anything.'

'This isn't the time to start changing your mind,' I said.

'I'm not really. It was just a brief and uncharacteristic moment of self-doubt. It has passed. My normal arrogance is restored. The man's a charlatan. Everything points to it. What is your plan, Elsie? Torture? Blackmail? Seduction?'

'Not seduction, unless you fancy it yourself – and it would have to feel slightly weird seducing a man claiming to be your uncle. No, I was thinking more in terms of my natural cleverness – augmented of course by your own. It's very simple. Between us we come up with ten questions, say, that only the real Roger Vane could answer.'

'And then one of us gets to go and ask him?' said Cynthia.

'No,' I said. 'He knows we all have doubts about him – especially you. He'll be cautious and evasive. We'll give the questions to Ethelred, whom he trusts, and then get Ethelred to report back.'

'Will Ethelred be happy doing that?' asked Cynthia.

'He doesn't need to be happy,' I said. 'He just needs to ask the questions.'

'So, where do we begin?' asked Tim.

'With you. Tell us what actually happened the day Roger Vane vanished. And it will have to be the truth for this to work. No evasions. No holding back merely to save your own feelings.'

'Hang on a minute . . .' he said.

'Is there any problem with telling us the truth?' I

enquired. 'I mean, you have nothing you would wish to hide behind your Shield of Cunning, do you?'

We both looked at him. If Tim was about to confess he killed Vane and buried him in a hole in the ground, then that in itself would be conclusive. It was very, very unlikely Vane would have been able to show up at a memorial service. We could probably shelve the whole question-setting thing.

'It's just I'm not sure about this,' said Tim. 'I mean, I don't come out of it well.'

'I honestly never thought you would,' I said.

'Nor me,' said Cynthia. 'Our expectations of you are not high. You're good to go.'

'Thanks,' said Tim.

'The truth – however embarrassing or illegal – need never go beyond the three of us,' I added reassuringly. 'And beyond Ethelred. And the man claiming to be Vane, or there would be no point in any of it. And maybe Roger Vane's lawyer. But what the hell . . . even if you did kill him, there must be some sort of statute of limitations after twenty years. Just trust us and we'll work out how to get you off the murder charge as and when.'

'You won't need to get me off any charge, because I didn't kill him. As I say, I'm not proud of what I did, but it wasn't murder.'

'OK,' I said. 'We've had the prologue. Very nice. Now cut to the chase. I'd like to hear the story while I'm still young enough to enjoy it.'

Tim sighed. 'All right. It begins much as you've already been told. We argued from the moment we got on board the plane. That afternoon the cause of the argument was a member of the hotel staff that Roger had been blatantly chatting up. If it sounds silly and trivial now it's because it was silly and trivial then. But that didn't stop us. Eventually, I said to Roger I'd had enough of it and I was going back to the hotel. Roger laughed. That was when I took a swing at him with my walking stick. I didn't mean to hit him, let alone hurt him.'

'But . . .'

'But the stick had a pointed metal tip. It . . . it sort of cut him a bit . . . right by his shoulder blade. Not life-threatening, exactly, though a bit of antiseptic would not have gone amiss. I suppose it was painful. For a moment we both looked at the blood seeping onto his T-shirt, then he took a couple of steps back and slipped – he fell and started rolling down the slope, away from the path. I thought it was very theatrical. After a bit of rolling, he hit a tree and just lay there. I could tell he wasn't hurt – not really – I actually saw him open an eye and look at me and then close it again. It was just a stupid game to make me feel guilty – or maybe he wanted me to run down the slope after him and then he'd try to attack me or something. So, I stayed put. I'm not saying he didn't have the right to attack me; but I wasn't going all the way down there just so he could do it. I called to him to get up, but he didn't, so I thought the best thing was just to leave him there to come to his senses and make his way back to the hotel when he felt inclined to. But before I did, I hid close by and watched him. I peered through some thorn bushes – that was how I managed to cut my own face. After a bit I saw him get up, examine the minor scratch I'd given him and then sit down again with his back to the tree as if wondering what to do. He was fine, though the T-shirt possibly needed soaking to get the blood out. It's always much better to work on stains straight away. Cold water is often fine if you're quick enough.'

'That is so true,' I said. 'Soak overnight, then wash with biological powder.'

'Best to soak in biological powder too,' said Cynthia. 'If it's blood.'

'True,' I said. 'Comes up like new.'

'Anyway,' Tim continued, 'having confirmed I hadn't killed him, I walked back slowly, expecting him to overtake me. When he didn't, I went and had a shower and then checked the bar around five-thirty. The rest you know.'

'And you didn't tell the police any of that?' I asked.

'I told them as much as I needed to. I hadn't killed Roger, but I had no wish to give them evidence that suggested I might have done. Had I told them the whole story they would have realised that I would have been absolutely justified in killing him.'

'So that was all you did?'

'I also took the stick to my room and washed it clean.'

'Why?'

'I don't know. It just seemed the right thing to do. A stick covered in blood would also have been . . . misleading.'

'Was it in fact covered in blood?'

'Just the very tip.'

'Have you told anyone else since?'

'Of course not.'

'Then only you and the real Roger Vane know all this,' I said.

'Unless Uncle Roger – the real Uncle Roger – told

anyone subsequently,' said Cynthia. 'He could have run into somebody in Laos or wherever he went and told them in a bar . . . or something.'

'True. That's why we need several tests,' I said. 'There must be things that he simply wouldn't have gossiped about to casual acquaintances. What have you got for us, Cynthia?'

'Well, he won't have forgotten Christmas when I was about three. He told me on Christmas morning that there was no such thing as Father Christmas. Mum and Dad were furious. Uncle Roger critiqued their parenting skills in some detail, then stormed off into the snow and missed Christmas lunch. We smoothed things over, of course, and I don't think any of us decided to go public with the full details. I'd have sold the story to the *News of the World* if I'd known how to work a phone, but I was three and didn't. So it's only me and Mum and Uncle Roger left who would know about it. You could also try him on what I used to call myself at that age.'

'Which was?'

'Pobble.'

'And you've told nobody about that lately?'

'Pobble? What do you think?'

'Good. Unless your mother has been leaking information to the false Roger Vane, we're in the clear. How about you, Tim? Did you have a nickname? Perhaps dog-related in view of Roger Vane's liking for terriers?'

'It was,' he said, 'in no way dog-related, nor is it something you need to know. But I can offer you something useful. We first met at a party given by a friend of Roger's – Jeremy something or other. The real Roger would remember that.'

'Noted,' I said. 'Jeremy something or other. Very memorable.'

'There's no need to sound so sarcastic.'

'That's your opinion,' I said.

'When I was little,' said Cynthia, frowning, 'Uncle Roger drove an MG Midget for a while – chrome bumpers. But he had problems with the roof and traded it in for something more conventional.'

'MG? That's good,' I said. I scribbled a note on a pad.

'What about the television programmes?' said Tim. 'There was that actor in the first series, who they replaced. He got dropped and didn't appear in very much after that. I can't remember his name, because nobody does any more, but the real Roger Vane would. They were quite good buddies. Actually a bit more than that. Roy Johnston? Do any of you remember him?'

Cynthia shook her head quickly. 'Before my time,' she said.

I also shook my head. 'Can't really picture him.'

'Then that would be a very good question,' said Tim. 'Roger would hardly have forgotten him, even if everyone else has.'

'On the contrary,' said Cynthia with a sigh. 'It would be much too easy for the false Roger Vane to find out. He'll have researched everything that's publicly available.'

'Cynthia's right,' I said. 'All of that stuff will be in Wikipedia or somewhere. There's an official website for the programme. You can get an episode-by-episode guide – even

104

the most minor parts are listed. There are blogs too – and some Twitter accounts – more or less devoted to it. Anyone could look them up and discover all sorts of odd facts about the series. We need to stick to the stuff that's not out there on the Internet and that only Roger Vane could know.'

'Agreed,' Tim said reluctantly.

Eventually we put together a dozen questions that Ethelred could test Vane with, ranging over his working and personal life. I was quite impressed. We were, frankly, on fire. Now we just needed to get Ethelred to ask them.

'I'm not sure about this,' said Ethelred.

'Because it will prove me right?'

'Because I'm writing his biography. He tells me things in the sincere belief I will behave responsibly. And that is what I shall do. I do have some duty of care towards him.'

'No you don't,' I said. 'You are the biographer of the real Roger Vane – not this fake one. The real one – the one you've always admired – would be pleased you've exposed him. He'd say: "Well done, Ethelred. You have exposed the man who was impersonating me. I'm very, very grateful." Anyway, you'll look a total dick if you claim he's the real Vane and he turns out to be a fake. Your reputation depends on this. You owe it to the literally several fans of your work.'

There was a silence at the other end of the phone as Ethelred's professional vanity wrestled with his conscience. The result seemed to be a points victory for his vanity. 'It will have to be on Saturday,' he said. 'I'm visiting Cordwainers School tomorrow.'

'Your horoscope said that Saturday will be an excellent day for betraying those close to you,' I said.

There was another silence. I saw the mistake I'd just made by mentioning 'betrayal' – it was as if I'd taken Ethelred's conscience into its corner, slapped its face a bit and told it to get back out there and fight like a man. It struggled to its feet.

'It's not going to work,' said Ethelred's conscience. 'Most of the questions aren't relevant to the biography, anyway. He'll smell a rat. I think—'

'No you don't,' I said. 'You don't need to think at all. You simply have to say the words on the paper. They are good questions, they are. Not rubbish that you can pick up on the Internet like who was the first actor to play Inspector Gascoyne in the TV series.'

'You mean Roy Johnston?'

'You know that? I was forgetting you were a fan.'

'I agree there'd be no point in asking him that question to test his bona fides. Actually, loads of people would know it was Johnston. Now, there's somebody else who would cheerfully murder Roger Vane.'

'Why would he do that?'

'Don't you listen to any of the gossip?'

'Stop sounding smug, Tressider. It doesn't suit you. I listen to relevant gossip, which up to this moment that was not. What did Roger Vane do to him?'

'Johnston was once Vane's boyfriend as well as being the lead actor in the series – but they fell out. When Roy was dumped from one role he was dumped from the other too. Word on the street is that it was no coincidence. They say Johnston was lucky to get the part in the first place. He had a track record of playing endearing and slightly eccentric characters but wasn't exactly a matinee idol. He never worked much afterwards – not as an actor, at least.'

'So, what does he do now?' I asked.

'I've no idea. I think he went off to Australia. His last film or TV credit listed on the Internet is some Australian soap about ten years ago. He had a bit of a drink problem too. Probably happily working in a bar or something now.'

'So, he's not likely in practice to come back and murder Roger Vane?'

'No need,' said Ethelred. 'At the rate Roger is making enemies, somebody else will do it for him. His ex-partner. His agent. His former publisher. His niece. His housemaster. One of his contemporaries at school.'

'You'd better get a move on with your questions, then. I'd hate to have him die again before I know the answers.'

'I'll do it on Saturday. After I've been to Cordwainers. I'm talking to the headmaster.'

'Whatever,' I said. 'Just don't mess up.'

CHAPTER THIRTEEN

'Cocaine?'

The headmaster shook his head at my suggestion. 'Cannabis mainly,' he said. 'Things have changed a lot since Roger Vane's time here, of course. We have a zero-tolerance policy these days. Any boy caught with drugs of any sort can expect to be expelled immediately. But even when Vane was here, there wasn't a problem with cocaine or heroin, whatever he claims.'

'He hasn't claimed that,' I said.

'Good,' said the headmaster, clearly relieved. 'You see, once something like that gets into the public domain – however wrongly – it's difficult to persuade people that it's untrue. The Chinese parents here take a very dim view of that sort of thing. It wasn't an easy market to break into. Did I say we were planning a campus in Hong Kong?'

'Yes,' I said. 'You did.'

I looked beyond the headmaster at the pennant on the

wall. It was made of a shiny blue fabric with a gold fringe. Printed on it were the words: 'Presented to Mr Roger Thwaites BA MBA MEd by the Cordwainers Alumni of Hong Kong'. A colourful dragon hovered above the words, as if about to seize and devour them.

'It's so important to protect the brand,' he said. 'Since I became headmaster, enrolment of overseas students has increased by three hundred per cent.'

Like a lot of heads of organisations, he preferred to date all improvements to his own arrival. I nodded politely and took a sip of tea. Earl Grey. Perfectly made. There were no biscuits.

'You've introduced a lot of changes,' I said.

'Of course, Cordwainers is one of the very oldest schools in the country. King's Canterbury may claim to be older, but it's all a bit patchy – so-and-so was recorded as being a schoolmaster near the abbey in Edward the Confessor's time, then a cathedral charter refers in passing to a school in much the same place a couple of hundred years later. That sort of thing. I know the names of all of my predecessors going back to 1378. I have the original charter granting us this site in Holborn by King Henry in 1402. Eton wasn't even founded until 1440. We'd had three generations through the school by then – Henry V's assistant chaplain was one of our boys. By 1500, we'd had seven bishops who'd been taught here and two Lord Mayors of London. And we were always recognised as one of the major public schools.' He frowned and ticked them off on his fingers. 'It was us, Eton, Harrow, St Paul's, Charterhouse, Winchester, Rugby, Westminster – Shrewsbury just about in the same class. Of course, things slipped a bit under my immediate predecessors. When I arrived we weren't even in the Sunday Times league tables. Didn't care to submit the figures. Can you credit it? Frankly, we had a bit of a reputation for producing well-heeled thickos. There's a story about three public school boys at a party. They notice that an old lady is finding it difficult to stand. "Fetch a chair for the lady, one of you chaps," says the Etonian. The well-mannered Wykehamist goes off to fetch one and the Cordwainer promptly sits in it. That was us – rich and rude, and we didn't much care if that's what people thought. Now we're comfortably in the top twenty for A-level results – I wouldn't have settled for less. We'll be in the top ten by the year after next. The Chinese intake helps, of course. Bright kids. Keen to learn. Grade A at maths guaranteed in every case. I spend a lot of time out in the Far East, promoting the brand. You have to. We have a new marketing unit – we've put them in Lessergate where the Classics Department used to be. We're phasing out Latin. And Greek. The Chinese parents don't really see the point of it.'

We both looked at the pennant. The headmaster's name had, I noticed, been misspelt, but the dragon was well done. Its wings shone in purple, red and green silk threads.

'I visited Dr Slide,' I said.

Mr Thwaite raised an eyebrow. 'How is the old boy these days?'

'In good health,' I said.

'My predecessor used to make a point of going out to see him occasionally and inviting him back to events here – speech days and so on. I have to say we haven't issued an invitation lately. He doesn't quite fit the image we want to project.'

I recalled the leather patches and stained trousers and, now I thought of it, the slightly odd smell in his sitting room.

'No,' I said. 'I suppose he doesn't. You know he was Roger Vane's housemaster?'

'Yes, of course. Poor man.'

'You mean the character-naming business?'

'That and other things. I think he was rather fond of Vane to begin with – I'm not suggesting anything improper. We have a zero-tolerance attitude to that sort of thing – staff and students – abuse of a position of trust – our child protection policies make that very clear, as I explain in the prospectus. But earlier generations would not have frowned on romantic friendships between older boys and younger boys, or even between boys and masters . . .' For a moment there was an almost wistful look in his eye. Then his expression hardened again. 'Anyway, Vane later took against him. I'm not sure why. Finally there was the car business. At first they didn't know whose car it was . . .'

'Whose it was? I thought that it was the deputy head's car?'

'Of course. But the question was: in whose car had Vane learnt to drive? After he was reported, Vane's parents demanded to know how on earth he'd been able to do it. They'd never let him anywhere near the steering wheel of the family Daimler. The answer, of course, was that Slide had been giving Vane lessons in his own Ford Prefect – no driving licence, no insurance – certainly no risk assessment form. That's why it had to be hushed up. We couldn't really expel him under the circumstances.

Slide was pretty upset by it all – felt Vane had let the side down – refused to give him a reference for university, but Vane got in anyway – he was pretty bright. Nobody was too surprised when Vane's first book came out and there was a character called Slide in it.'

I nodded. 'Being a writer gives you a vast capacity for revenge – you use somebody's name or something very much like it – sometimes it's only the victim who knows what you've done. Or the victim and their friends.'

'In this case it was rather more than that,' said Mr Thwaite. 'The whole school knew. Everyone Slide really cared about. He held out for four books, then he had a nervous breakdown. He was off work for a year. The school took him back, of course, but the boys never really respected him afterwards. The insults in the books had made him a sort of celebrity, but his breakdown was just seen as weakness. They still liked him but they never forgave him. Made his life hell on earth. Wrote English essays with obnoxious characters called Mr Slither or Professor Slid in them. Got them published in the school magazine – even the one featuring Dr Jonathan Shite got past the censor. Quite amusing some of them. But completely heartless. That's boys for you. I've never yet met a headmaster who didn't believe in Original Sin.'

'Did Vane have anything in the magazine? It would be good to be able to quote from it.'

'I'm not sure. I'll look through the old copies and scan anything that looks interesting. I've got your email address.'

'Thank you. Do you know anything about an erotic poem that he wrote while he was here?'

Mr Thwaite flinched as if I had struck him. 'I've never read it myself,' he said.

'Do you know who helped him distribute it?'

He shook his head. 'I've no idea. I think we were talking about Dr Slide? As I say, the boys were not kind to him. He struggled on for a while but eventually he was sidelined into admin.'

'Careers advice,' I said.

'Was it?' asked Mr Thwaite with interest. 'I didn't know that. On the other hand – yes, I can see how that might have fitted in with other things . . .'

I waited for him to expand on this last point, but he didn't.

'Well, admin obviously suited him,' I said. 'I suppose these days you could put him into marketing,' I added mischievously.

'Not really. Our head of marketing gets almost as much as I do, including performance bonuses. The sad thing was that the school was Dr Slide's life. He'd been a pupil here, on a scholarship. As soon as he'd won his doctorate, he returned to teach. Then he was offered his own House. He'd have expected to go on and become headmaster somewhere. But it was not to be. After he retired the staff in his old department kept in touch – monthly visits to Putney – tea and crumpets, watching the rowers. Slide had been quite a good oarsman in his time. Just missed a Blue.'

'What subject did he teach?'

'Latin. That's why there's not much point in having him back. He wouldn't really fit in.'

'Quite a few people must remember him . . . and Roger Vane.'

'Oh yes, they remember Roger Vane all right. Badly though they treated Dr Slide themselves, a lot of them resent the way Vane treated him.'

'I can see that. There must be one or two old boys who would have preferred it if Roger Vane had remained dead.'

'There are some who would happily return him to that state today.'

'Are there many?'

'Six phoned me this morning alone. But hopefully most of them weren't serious. People say things they don't really mean. More tea?'

CHAPTER FOURTEEN

'Sex?'

'Not at the moment,' I said.

'When, then?' asked Roger Vane.

I realised that I had got myself into a difficult position.

'Mr Thwaite implied that there had been what he described as romantic friendships in the past – that relationships had existed between pupils and staff. But that there was nothing of the sort now. Or indeed in your day.'

'That's all he knows,' said Vane. 'I had more sex at school than at any other time in my life. Lost my virginity on a school trip to the seaside.'

'Can I quote you on that?'

'You bet. I'll give you names, if you like. And I'll let Thwaite know how his school works when he's not looking. That's the problem – you get in some snotty little grammar school boy like Thwaite, with his M-bloody-BA from some dump like . . .' (he named the most prestigious business school in the country) '. . . and they imagine they understand a great public school. Not in a million years. He'll get the A-level results, but he'll kill an ethos that has taken almost seven centuries to develop.'

I wondered if Vane knew that I was a snotty little grammar school boy. Probably.

'I'm sure you're right,' I said. 'But I imagined it would rather please you . . . the changes . . . making it more modern . . . I mean, you've rather distanced yourself from the place as it used to be. I thought somewhere you'd said that private education was outmoded and should be abolished.'

'Yes,' said Vane. 'I probably did. That's my right because I know what I'm talking about. I was there. Those who don't know should shut up about it. None of their bloody business. Now, what can I help you with today, Ethelred?'

I opened my notebook. On the page in front of me were the questions concocted by Elsie, Tim and Cynthia. I wasn't at all sure this was going to work. I drew a deep breath.

'Maybe we could begin with what happened in Thailand – if you feel up to it.'

For some reason I'd expected him to find some reason for not doing so, but Roger Vane nodded. Looking into the distance he began his recitation.

'It was like this,' he said. 'Tim and I had been arguing since we left Heathrow. One thing after another. Well, that afternoon we went for a walk. Tim challenged me over a perfectly innocent chat I'd had with the boy who cleaned the swimming pool. I told him not to be an idiot. Sounds simple, but we made that one last about half an hour before we'd exhausted all of its possibilities. We walked in silence for a bit, then he started on about something else – or maybe it was the same thing. It doesn't matter. He got pretty abusive, anyway. I told him I did as I chose – anyway the pool boy was well out of his league – at which point he actually lashed out at me with his walking stick or pole or whatever it was. It had a metal spike on it, anyway. It ripped my T-shirt and cut me quite badly. I tried to grab it off him and he hit me again. This time he knocked me down a bank by the side of the path. I rolled for a bit – quite painful rolling over some of that stuff – most jungle plants seem to have spikes or thorns. Anyway, eventually I came to rest by a tree and just lay there regaining my breath.

'He called down to me and told me that I wasn't hurt, which was only his opinion. I opened one eye and could see him watching me, so I decided that I didn't want to go back up there for him to take another swing at me. I pretended to be stunned or dead; I wasn't sure which, but it involved not moving. After a bit he called down again to say he was going back to the hotel and I could stay there if I wished.

'When I was sure he'd gone I sat up and leant against the tree and wondered what to do next. The gash on my shoulder was bleeding quite badly and I knew that it would be getting dark soon. I didn't fancy the climb back up the slope but then I noticed, just below me, another track, almost hidden by the foliage. In the days when they were logging in that area, the whole mountainside must have been criss-crossed with paths of all sorts – roads for the lorries, tracks used by the workers to get home at the end of the day. Most had become overgrown – takes just weeks out there for an unused path to vanish – but this one was clearly still used by somebody and, I reckoned, had to lead back eventually to the main path and the hotel. I inched down towards it and set off on what seemed to be the right bearing. But my sense of direction never was that good. As the track wound slowly downwards, I realised I was completely lost. Eventually I stumbled on a group of young men in a makeshift hut. I had no idea exactly what they were doing there, but I doubted somehow that it was legal. There was, in fact, a flurry of activity as I opened the door, but they didn't quite manage to clear up the crime scene as well as they might. There, on the table, sat a grubby, unlabelled bottle of the local hooch. Later, once I got to know them better, they conceded it was just one of a couple of hundred they happened to have with them. They were the proprietors of a small factory producing it in bulk, fifty yards down another path that led into the forest. They were waiting the necessary thirty-six hours or so that it needed to mature into something that didn't take the back of your throat off. Tomorrow, they said, they'd feed a bit of it to the dog. If the dog was still alive by the evening, the batch had passed quality control and could be shipped and sold.

'They proved to be very hospitable once they realised I had nothing to do with revenue enforcement. I stayed for a couple of days. The second afternoon we heard police helicopters overhead, which worried my new friends a bit, but they assured me they'd bribed all the right people and had avoided detection before. That evening they gave me a lift in their lorry – I sat at the back with a consignment of one-litre plastic containers of dog-endorsed alcohol, and they dropped me off in a village on the coast. It wasn't the sort of place tourists go to. I rather liked it. I stayed there for a few weeks, sold my watch, bought some new clothes in the market, then headed along the coast one night into Cambodia, courtesy of some nice smugglers – I think I've told you that bit before. Later I went upriver into Laos. Lived in various places. Eventually, I shacked up in Vientiane with a young man who looked rather like the pool boy from the hotel. Never really saw the point in going home. Not until I heard they were going to have me declared dead, in fact.'

He looked at me and raised an eyebrow.

'Can I quote all of that?' I asked.

'As far as I'm concerned you can,' he said. 'Don't you believe me?'

'Yes, of course,' I said.

Without taking his eyes off me, he started to unbutton his shirt, then yanked the collar downwards and to one side. Across his shoulder was an old scar. 'One wound, inflicted by my former partner,' he said. 'Is that OK with you?'

'Perfectly,' I said.

'You can touch it if you like.'

'I'm good,' I said.

'What next?' he asked, slowly rebuttoning his shirt.

'Maybe we can go back a bit,' I said. 'Your brother was quite a fan of your writing?'

I knew I was jumping about all over the place, but I was trying to do it subtly.

'I suppose so,' he said. 'If he thought it was shit, he'd have probably told me. Brothers don't spare each other's feelings.'

'You got on fairly well together?'

He looked at me oddly. 'Well enough.'

'Did you spend Christmases together?' I asked.

'Yes. Mainly. He was the closest family I had.'

'I suppose you had the usual family rows at Christmas?'

'Not many.'

'I mean, families often do.'

'Is that what yours did? Sorry to disappoint you but we didn't. Drunken family rows at Christmas are a bit common, don't you think?'

'Fair enough,' I said. I flicked to the next page in my notebook, cursing Elsie and seeking a more promising line of enquiry.

Then I heard Vane add: 'Of course, there was that Christmas when I told Cynthia that there was no Santa Claus.'

I looked up suddenly. 'Did you?'

Vane smiled benignly. 'Oh, there was a bit of a fuss over it and I didn't get any Christmas lunch, but it all blew over. Pobble forgave me.'

'Pobble?' I asked as innocently as I knew how.

He smiled. 'Cynthia used to call herself that,' he said. 'I doubt if she even still remembers. She actually gave me a little Boxing Day present to make things better – one or two of her Christmas chocolates in a small box that she had made and coloured, just for me. It had a smiling Santa Claus on it. I was deeply touched, I don't mind telling you. I kept it for years. That was the sort of kid she was . . . in those days.'

I scribbled a note or two.

'How did you get on with your sister-in-law?'

'Margery? All right. I noticed she wasn't at my memorial service. She should have been. Missed a good do.'

'To be fair,' I said, 'you shouldn't have been there, but you were.'

'Even so . . .' he said. 'Dead brother-in-law . . . I rather thought she liked me. Well, she did once.'

Falling out with people appeared to be one of Roger Vane's key competences. I waited to see if he would add to what he had said, but he didn't.

'What sort of car did you drive then?' I asked eventually.

'Car? I thought we were talking about my brother and his love of crime fiction. Or my absent sister-in-law.'

'Sorry – just running through the questions in the order that they occurred to me.'

'That's the order, is it? Christmas. Margery. Car. Well, I had all sorts of cars over the years – a Triumph, an old MG Midget, a Jaguar. How does that fit into anything you need for the book?'

'I'm just curious,' I said.

'Really?'

'Yes,' I said. 'Now about the MG—'

'Or is it that somebody else is just curious?' he asked.

'I don't know what you mean.'

Roger Vane shook his head. 'Do you remember that I told you that Cynthia had been quizzing me to see if I was the real deal? Well, her questions felt a lot like the ones you've just asked me. Do I remember this? What colour was that? What was your first car? All the standard tests except my mother's maiden name and my favourite author. She hasn't put you up to this, by any chance?'

The truthful answer was: 'No, it was Elsie'. I abbreviated that.

'No,' I said.

'Of course not. You wouldn't act as her dupe, would you? You're not that stupid. Or then again . . . So, have I given you enough information for you to report back to my niece?'

There was a long silence. I looked again through the questions. Sometimes, when you have been rumbled, the best thing is to press on regardless. You've got nothing at all to lose.

'That will all be very useful for the book,' I said. 'I wonder if you could also tell me a bit about—'

'No, Ethelred, I can't. That's it for today. You've used up all of your minutes on dear little Cynthia's questions. And your trick has been rumbled. Game over. And tomorrow I shall be out most of the day, unless you fancy a breakfast meeting. But, purely out of interest, did I pass? Do I get my diploma in Roger Vane Studies?'

It seemed churlish to deny him that.

'With distinction,' I said. 'Summa cum laude.'

'Idiot,' said Elsie. 'I ask you to do one thing . . .'

'They were your questions,' I reminded her. 'As you said, all I had to do was read them out. That's what I did. Now you have his answers. Anyway, I at least hope that it removes any remaining doubt from your mind that the man we have is the real Roger Vane. He was pretty well word-perfect.'

'Maybe, maybe not,' she said.

'But you told me that these were things only the real Roger Norton Vane could possibly know about. His description of the events in Thailand matched what Tim told you almost exactly. And he knew all about that Christmas argument. And Cynthia's nickname. And the car. How many hoops do you want him to jump through?'

'Just because he can jump through hoops doesn't mean he's not fishy. Dolphins do it all the time.'

'Dolphins are aquatic mammals,' I said. 'Not fish. If it helps, I don't much like him myself. He's an arrogant snob with little concern for anyone except himself. The only extenuating circumstance is that Cordwainers probably contributed a lot to developing him into what he is today. He is a victim of his upbringing. But he is who he says he is. Ask Cynthia about the box – that's something that only the two of them could possibly know about.'

'And Cynthia's mother,' said Elsie.

'Yes, I was forgetting that. Margery and Roger used to be quite close, apparently. But not now. She's had no contact with Roger since he got back.'

'You mean she's had no contact with the imposter.'

'Well, that's something on which we'll have to agree to differ.'

'Yes. Until I prove you wrong. Then you'll have to agree with me. I'll get some more questions for you to ask him.'

'No, you won't. Today cost me a perfectly good session with him – I did have some genuine questions for him. Or don't you want the book written by the ridiculous deadline that you agreed? You can ask him yourself, if you wish. I'm not wasting any more time.'

'So, you won't help me? Not even a little bit? After all I've done for you?'

'I pay you commission. That's what you get in return for what you do.'

'That's commission as in fifteen per cent of nothing?'

'Elsie, I'm happy to do anything that's in the contract. But there's nothing there saying I have to make myself look a complete idiot just in order to please you.'

'Are you sure there isn't?'

'Yes.'

'Fine. Then I'll have to sort it out myself, as usual. One of us, at least, has the ability to be a detective in real life.'

I tried to think of any occasion when Elsie had sorted things out. Her attempts to be a detective usually ended in her own arrest for breaking and entering, or various degrees of humiliation for her or me. Mainly the latter.

'Don't even think of going to his flat,' I said.

'But you told me: he's out after breakfast tomorrow – all day.'

'That won't make it legal.'

'Look, I won't have to break in. Tim still has a set of keys. Unless Roger has changed the locks. Then I admit it might have to be slightly less legal than I'd like.'

'Stealing somebody's keys doesn't make it more legal than if you break the door down.'

'I bet it does. Otherwise why is it called breaking and entering?'

I sighed. 'Have it your way. Legally it's not theft if you don't actually break the door down. What are you hoping to find?'

'Well, he'll have a passport, won't he?'

'He said it was in a false name.'

'Interesting to know what name though, eh? And he may have a driving licence or letters or credit cards or anything. You can't get through more than a day or two anywhere without using something with your name on it.'

'He said he'd lost his driving licence in the jungle.'

'He also says he's Roger Norton Vane. So let's not jump to too many conclusions about what we'll find.'

'You'll get caught,' I said.

'Don't worry, I'll have a good story prepared. If push comes to shove, I'll just claim I'm following up your visit. What have you and he talked about lately?'

I thought for a bit. 'Sex and drugs,' I said.

'OK,' said Elsie. 'That leaves just one other thing.'

CHAPTER FIFTEEN

Elsie

'Rock and roll?'

I looked up from the bottom of Roger Vane's wardrobe.

'Absolutely,' I said.

'You're sure of that?' asked Roger Vane.

Well no, not totally. I tried another tack.

'This isn't what it looks like,' I said.

'It looks like you're hiding at the bottom of my wardrobe,' he said.

'OK, then it is what it looks like, but I can explain,' I said.

'Fine,' he said. 'Explain how you got there. Because I haven't got a clue what's going on here. Not a clue.'

I was, frankly, still trying to work it all out myself. And it had all started so promisingly. That morning I had borrowed Tim's keys and set off for Canonbury – just a few stops on the North London Line from my own dear Hampstead. I'd waited in the square's gardens, sitting on a bench, plausibly immersed in The Guardian and watching for the soi-disant Roger Norton Vane to depart for whatever appointment was going to keep him out all day. Finally, round about nine-thirty, when I had only the sports and business sections left to read, I saw him leave and head in a fairly leisurely manner towards Highbury and Islington Station. I waited for five minutes, then binned my paper and sauntered in an equally casual way up to his front door. I selected the right key and found myself in the hallway and then, with the aid of two other keys (Yale and Chubb), inside the flat itself. It had taken about forty-five seconds, from bench to sitting room – all completely unobserved.

The flat was the ground floor and basement of a once stately residence – high ceilings and tall narrow Georgian windows on the ground floor and, though I hadn't seen it yet, probably slightly more cosy accommodation below. The layout of the sitting room was much as you would have expected: sofa, two armchairs, desk, television, books. Over in one corner was an untidy stack of what looked like the tools of Tim Macdonald's trade as an illustrator – now awaiting collection. I quickly scanned what I assumed must be their joint collection of CDs. Quite a few of those but no clues there. It was the desk to which I gave most of my attention. One drawer was full of pens and pencils, staplers, glue and the rest of it. One contained files – a couple of decades of utility bills addressed to Roger Norton Vane as the owner (albeit absent) of the flat. There were also folders with Tim's bank statements, plus bits of miscellaneous correspondence, including several letters on a disputed parking ticket. So, paint, CDs, bank statements . . . Plenty of stuff, then, that I could claim Tim had asked me to pop in and collect if I was interrupted. But nothing constituting evidence of the sort I was seeking.

At that point a phone rang in one of the other drawers. I jumped, as you do when you're breaking and entering and hear a sudden noise. I opened the drawer to find a newish mobile – Vane's presumably. So, that was OK.

Up to a point. Of course, the question was: if you leave your phone behind when you go off to an appointment, what do you do? Say, never mind, I don't need a phone today? Or do you run back and get it once you realise what you've done?

It was just then that I heard a key turn in a lock. It was the work of a moment to shove the phone back in the drawer and tiptoe into the next room, which proved to be Vane's bedroom. I figured he would collect the phone and be on his way fairly quickly. He would not go and take a quick nap first. Just to make absolutely sure, however, I opened the wardrobe door to see whether there was room for a small literary agent amongst his shirts and suits. There was. I hunkered down for a few minutes, regretting only that I had failed to bring any chocolate with me.

It took Vane a while to get into his flat from the hallway. I heard a key rattle repeatedly in the lock. Then I realised my first mistake. I had unlocked the Chubb lock but not locked it again. Vane, knowing he had locked it, was now trying to unlock it all over again and he couldn't work out why the key wouldn't turn. There was a pause as he put two and two together, then I heard the door open very, very slowly.

Vane's footsteps were quite loud on the old wooden boards, so I could track his movements well. He paused momentarily at the entrance, doubtless checking for intruders. Then he walked intrepidly and at a steady pace across the sitting room. Now I realised my second mistake. I should have left the phone on the desk where he would see it straight away and pick it up. Instead, clearly having forgotten where he put it, he recrossed the room several times, hunting for it, then swore loudly.

At that point he apparently decided he must have left it elsewhere, because his footsteps approached the bedroom, then I heard him descending the stairs towards the kitchen to check whether he'd left it on the table or by the cooker. I wondered for a moment whether to make a break for it, but I felt that if I could hear his footsteps so clearly then he would hear mine. Though I'm smaller and lighter than he is, of course. I quickly rehearsed the reasons why what I was doing was legal, but they didn't seem as good as they had been. I then quickly rehearsed the reasons why, though I knew nothing about the man impersonating Vane, he definitely wouldn't beat me to a pulp when he found me in his wardrobe. I could no longer remember them at all.

I'm losing track of the exact numbering, but at this point I made my fourth or possibly fifth mistake. I don't know if you watched *The Night Manager* when it was on television, but there's a scene in which Olivia Colman, having broken into a hotel room to obtain a vital clue, hears the bad guy returning. She hides in the bathroom (better, now I thought about it, than a wardrobe) and texts her colleague to ask him to phone the bad guy and get him to go down to the hotel lobby, allowing her to escape. I didn't have time to text the entire plot of *The Night Manager* to Ethelred but settled for: 'Stuck in wardrobe. Like Olivia Colman. Phone Vane and tell him something to get him out of flat.' That seemed clear enough to me. The problem was, of course, that it might be next week before Ethelred checked his messages.

Then a series of things happened. The first thing was this: I heard Vane start to climb the stairs again towards me. The third thing was that Ethelred texted back: 'Why are you in a wardrobe with Olivia Colman?' That was fine. It was the second thing that was the real problem. As the text came through it had made a sort of der-der-di-di-der noise at about the same volume as a pneumatic drill. Vane's footsteps paused. The bedroom door opened. Even from where I was, at the bottom of his wardrobe, I could sense his puzzlement. He was looking for a phone. He had heard a phone go off. But he couldn't remember leaving it in the bedroom. Or changing the ringtone. I heard him hunting on the bedside table. Then he came towards my hiding place. Of course, he was thinking, he must have left the phone in a jacket pocket . . .

'Hi,' I said. 'I'm Elsie Thirkettle. Tim's agent? I don't think we've met before.'

He didn't take my proffered hand. He looked at me with a sort of polite distaste, as if I'd pitched up on his doorstep and he didn't want to buy whatever it was I was planning to sell. Just for a split second I had an insight into what it is like to be a Jehovah's Witness with a bundle of Watchtowers in your bag.

'And you are in my wardrobe because . . .'

I quickly reviewed all of the stories I had prepared and chose this one: 'Tim asked me to pick up a few of his CDs if I was passing. I rang the bell and you weren't around so I used his keys . . .'

'Which CDs?' he asked.

'Buddy Holly?' I suggested. Everyone likes Buddy Holly, don't they?

'Rock and roll?' he asked.

'Absolutely,' I said.

'You're sure of that?'

Which is where I offered to explain – possibly my sixth mistake, but I no longer cared about keeping a precise tally.

'It was like this,' I said, stepping primly out of the wardrobe and brushing my skirt down. 'Tim asked me to pick up the CDs for him.'

'From the wardrobe?'

'Clearly not. Because that's not where you keep CDs. I was looking through the collection in the sitting room when I heard a key in the front door. I immediately thought that it must be an intruder . . .'

'Why?'

Good point.

'That just happened to be the first thing that occurred to me.'

'Wasn't it more logical to suppose that it was me returning? It's my flat.'

It was the word logical that gave me the key to it. Of course, he was a logical man and I was merely a scatty woman. On hearing a noise I would assume it was: 1) an

134

intruder 2) a unicorn 3) George Clooney. Obviously.

'Gosh,' I said, really admiringly. 'I should have thought of that, shouldn't I? Silly me. I'll bear that in mind if it happens again.'

He said nothing. He had no wish for it to happen again. I noticed he was tapping his foot, but not in time to any tune that I could hear.

'Anyway,' I continued, picking a bit of wardrobe-fluff off my sleeve, 'thinking that an intruder wouldn't look for me in the bedroom, I hid there. In your wardrobe. With your suits. That blue one looks very smart. Wool blend? With just a touch of cashmere?'

He said nothing.

'So, great chatting to you like this – getting to know you – hanging out – having a laugh together – but probably I'll just pick up the CDs and go, if that's OK?'

If this had been a John le Carré novel, he'd have drawn a gun at this point and told me to sit down and shut up. Actually what he said was: 'OK. Why don't you go and pick up all the Buddy Holly CDs, then. I can see why Tim wanted them.'

There was slightly more irony in his voice than was really called for, but so far no guns. I could almost hear Olivia Colman telling me to hang in there. We walked through to the sitting room together and he motioned me towards the CDs.

'All yours,' he said.

I checked the top row. Wolfgang Amadeus Mozart. I checked the second row. Wolfgang Amadeus Mozart. I checked the third row. Leopold Mozart and a few of Haydn's symphonies. Fourth row, the rest of Haydn's symphonies. Fifth row Boccherini and Vivaldi. Sixth row . . .

'Got to the Buddy Hollys yet?' he asked. (See previous note on irony.)

'I'm only guessing, so stop me if I'm way off target, but maybe there aren't any Buddy Holly CDs here at all?' I said.

'Got it in one.'

'Maybe Tim said Boccherini . . .'

'Easily confused. These names with B and H in them.'

I looked to see if there was a smile on his face. There wasn't.

Well, two can play at that game. Without saying another word, I scooped up Boccherini, Beethoven and, to be safe, both JC and CPE Bach. I dropped them in my bag.

'You wouldn't like to take the rest of his junk, I suppose?'

We looked at the drawing table and boxes of pencils and the desk lights all piled up in the corner. It would need a small van.

'Next time,' I said.

I made to depart, but Vane placed his hand against my shoulder. In an interesting turn of events, it seemed that he was going to gift me the CPE Bach CDs and then beat me to a pulp.

'So, Elsie,' said Vane, 'first time round, Cynthia sends Ethelred to check me out, then she sends you.'

There was an implication that this was going downhill. I resented that.

'It was Tim,' I said. 'He wanted his—'

'Buddy Holly CDs,' Vane interrupted. 'I can of course see that a number of you would benefit financially from establishing that I am not who I say I am. Your problem is that what you want isn't going to happen. I am and always have been Roger Norton Vane, man and boy. Never been anyone else. But would you like to search the whole flat? It would be doing me a service, if it would save my discovering you under the sink or in the recycling bin when I next come home.'

I was tempted to say 'yes', because it was the answer he deserved, but if he was offering, then the chances were that nothing was there to find. And he'd enjoy watching me fruitlessly sift through junk in cupboard after cupboard.

'I'm good,' I said. But I glanced round the room anyway. Now I could take it all in, it contained a lot of Roger Vane's life. There were a couple of certificates on the wall, an original drawing for one of his book covers and heaps of framed photographs. One appeared to be Vane himself on a film set. He was playing some part – I wasn't sure what. I might not have recognised him, because it was clearly taken some years before and his hair was done differently and he was wearing make-up. But, now I looked at the person in front of me and at the photo, I noticed one small detail on both that I might not have taken in if I'd been looking at just one or the other – a small scar at the corner of his mouth. There on the photo and there on the man in front of me. The scar. Neat, and not unattractive in a strange way. But distinctive. Better proof, in its own little way, than our carefully compiled questions.

'Nice photo – when was it taken?' I asked.

He started and for a moment seemed very confused – almost embarrassed.

'Oh, that thing . . .' he said.

'It's fine,' I said. 'Dexter does it all the time. And I can't quite say why it occurs to me now, but Le Carré did it in *The Night Manager*. Playing a minor role in one of your own TV episodes, I mean. So, you have a credit as an actor?'

'A credit?'

'That's you there – acting some part in *Gascoyne*.'

He stared almost uncomprehendingly at the photograph. Then the penny appeared to have dropped.

'Yes,' he said sheepishly. 'That's me. But it was uncredited. Just a walk-on part. First series. It just seemed . . . fun. You won't find it listed anywhere. I don't . . .'

Yes, he was really embarrassed. Most of the time he didn't seem to care what people thought and now he was almost blushing to be detected in this very minor vanity, if it qualified even as that. One point to me. Time to quit while I was fractionally ahead.

'Tim will be really pleased with the CDs,' I said.

Vane looked at me, still strangely concerned. 'Oh, yes, the CDs . . .' he said vaguely.

'Don't worry,' I said, playfully. 'Your little secret is safe with me.'

'That photo? It doesn't bother me one way or the other, Elsie,' he said.

But it did. Very much.

'I'm sure you did your best,' said Tim, fingering a CPE Bach sonata. 'You know this isn't mine, I suppose? CPE Bach was such a lightweight. Hardly a Bach at all.'

'Look,' I said to the assembled team. 'I realise it could

have gone better, in the sense that we might have actually discovered something that would help us prove the man is a fraud, but it could have been worse.'

'Could it?' asked Tim. 'You might have brought some of my drawing equipment.'

'You're writing a book. You don't have time to draw. I'll get you some crayons at the supermarket.'

Tim looked at me with almost as much contempt as Roger Vane.

'So was there nothing at all?' he asked.

I thought of the photo with the telltale scar. 'There was a picture of him from twenty years ago,' I said. 'It was on the wall. It really looked like him . . .'

I tailed off, aware that my audience was not impressed. This wasn't the sort of evidence they wanted.

'We know that,' said Tim. 'We're all agreed he looks like the person we knew – only older. And I know what pictures I have on the wall, thank you. Telling us that this person looks like Roger in one of the photos is not helpful.'

'His mouth—' I began.

'. . . is just like Roger's,' said Tim. 'Thank you, Elsie. Yes, we get it.'

He clearly still resented the fact that I had not brought him anything to colour in with.

'How did Ethelred get on?' asked Cynthia, tactfully changing the subject.

'I was coming to that,' I said. 'He reported that Vane answered all the questions correctly. Vane clearly knew roughly what had happened in Thailand – just as Tim told us. He knew about the Christmas argument. He even added a small detail of his own – that you'd made him a little box of chocolates on Boxing Day.' I smiled, awaiting an indignant refutation.

'With Father Christmas on it?' asked Cynthia.

'Yes . . .' I said.

'Good grief. I never even told my parents I'd done that,' said Cynthia.

We looked at each other. The accurate account of the Last Day in the Jungle, the telltale scar that I had spotted, the Father Christmas box – slowly the evidence was shifting in Vane's favour. You could almost hear the group's revised opinions clicking into place. I made one final attempt to dismiss them.

'It's still not conclusive,' I said. 'He could have found out somehow. You may not have told anyone about the box but your uncle might have done, and that person then told the man claiming to be Roger Vane . . .'

'That sounds very far-fetched to me,' said Tim with a sniff. Whatever I said this morning, he was going to disagree with as a matter of principle.

'No, that must be it,' said Cynthia, clutching at the straw I had offered. 'He has a source of information that we don't know about . . .'

'Precisely,' I said. 'There has to be an explanation in each case.'

I thought again of the scar by Vane's lip – it matched the photo perfectly. That had been conclusive for me. But he could have done that himself. Couldn't he? You'd just need a sharp knife and a steady hand – hell, Van Gogh chopped off an entire ear.

Or then again . . . Maybe, for reasons I understood only too well we were all simply hoping, as the evidence relentlessly built up, that it nevertheless wasn't true: he might have found an obscure source of information, he might have made a lucky guess, he might have taken a penknife to his face one morning.

'No, it's actually him,' said Tim. He sighed. 'I really haven't mentioned the Thailand business to anyone before. Scout's honour. That one thing on its own is conclusive as far as I'm concerned.'

So, Tim was now in the same camp as Ethelred. So, I realised, was I. Only Cynthia seemed determined to hold out, but she had a lot of cash to lose. She was staring ahead, not looking at any of us.

'It can't be him,' she said.

'Look,' I said to her, 'perhaps Tim's right. Perhaps we should at least consider the possibility that we were mistaken – that this man is who he says he is. Tim says the stuff on Thailand is conclusive. For me, it's that photo up on the wall – identical even down to the smallest detail. And in your case you said that the box—'

Cynthia stood up. She wasn't interested in conclusive anything. 'He isn't my uncle,' she said. 'He may be able to take you in, but he doesn't fool me. I'll find a way of proving who he is, then both of you, and he, will look pretty silly.'

She stood up. We watched her go. My front door slammed and then, a little later and further off, the street door did the same. That was all the doors I had, but we still sat there in silence for a long while afterwards.

'I really need my drawing table back,' said Tim eventually.

141

'I've got my graphics tablet, but I can't do everything on that. You'll have to ask Roger. I'm not going to. Not if it really is him.'

'I'll get it shipped back in a taxi,' I said. 'Now, go and write that bloody biography. And be careful not to libel him, because he can sue us.'

CHAPTER SIXTEEN

'And you can wipe that smug expression off your face,' said Elsie.

'I'm phoning you. You can't see my face. You've no idea what sort of expression I have.'

'On the contrary, Tressider, I know all your looks by now and when and where you use them. Your being at the far end of a telephone line is no impediment. You are currently employing look 72B – extreme pleasure at being proved right, in spite of having arrived at that conclusion entirely by luck.'

'If you could see me, you would also notice that my look concedes there is still a possibility that Vane could be a fake.'

'Really? The scar proves it for me,' she said. 'Precisely the same in the photo and in the flesh. I had them side by side. Just for a moment it occurred to me he might have faked it. But even if he would have cut his lip like that on purpose, it was clearly an old scar, not something he'd done yesterday or even last week.'

'You did well to spot it,' I said. 'I'd never noticed it myself and I've seen loads of pictures of him.'

'It was just seeing him and the photo side by side,' said Elsie, with a hint of pride.

'He also had a scar on his shoulder,' I reminded her, 'so he'd have been quite busy with his knife if he was faking it all.'

'There you are,' she said. 'I am conceding you were right all along. I am also upgrading your expression to 75G – smile so broad your head may drop off – with immediate effect.'

'Not quite,' I said. 'Let's not forget there's a lot of money involved in this – enough to endure a little pain for. No pain, no gain, as I believe the expression is – and, as for the age of the scar, who's to say he hasn't been planning it for some time? My guess is that a scar a couple of months old and one twenty years old won't look that dissimilar.'

'You're saying he could be a fake after all?'

'Cynthia clearly thinks so.'

'And the account of the last day in Thailand? How do you explain that? Tim says he's told nobody.'

'Again, you might care to cross-examine your witness a little more closely. I bet Tim's told somebody in strict confidence. When you have something like that on your conscience, you must feel you have to confess . . .'

'Possibly,' she said. 'But who?'

'There's a missing piece of the jigsaw,' I went on. 'Roger clearly had a number of partners in Laos – he's told us

144

that. But we're expected to believe Tim has been single for twenty years?'

'You have,' said Elsie.

'On the contrary,' I said. 'There have been several women in my life—'

'. . . who simply imposed on your good nature,' said Elsie. 'They weren't serious about you, Ethelred. You do know that now, don't you? You've been really lucky to have me around to get rid of them for you. Or at least, to get rid of the ones who didn't dump you.'

'Returning to Tim,' I said, 'my guess is that there have been various partners, one or other of which he may have decided to tell.'

There was silence as Elsie thought about this.

'And the Father Christmas thing?' she asked.

'Cynthia's parents knew.'

'She says not.'

'How would she know that for certain? Roger probably showed them the box. They probably told all sorts of people: guess what our cute little Cynthia did? Margery might still tell the story around the village.'

'So, do you still have genuine reservations? Or are you being irritatingly even-handed?'

'Neither,' I said. 'I'll come clean. I'd begun to feel that the most interesting thing about Roger Vane's reappearance was whether it really was him or not. It would have been good to publish the book with the public in genuine confusion. So, I wanted to examine the evidence again. But sadly I think Cynthia is the only genuine doubter left amongst us. Let's run through the facts. This person, if he wasn't Roger Vane, would have to have had the foresight to cut his lip some months ago at least – to imitate a scar that was too insignificant to show up anywhere but in a high-quality professional photo from the studio that nobody else knew existed – as I say, I'd certainly not noticed it on the snapshot I supplied for the memorial service. So that isn't something you'd easily get from the Internet: you'd have to know and see it first-hand. As for the scar on his shoulder – it was quite a large wound – a simple cut with a sharp knife wouldn't do it. Likewise we have to assume that this false Roger Vane then tracked down a former boyfriend of Tim's, who both knew and was willing to tell what had happened in Thailand. Moreover, he also ran into Margery or alternatively some friend of the family who happened to have been told about the Father Christmas Box and still remembered it and thought it a story worth telling to this total stranger. If this was a Golden Age crime novel and the author had a couple of chapters to spare at the end of the book, then maybe we could envisage a plot of that complexity. But real life's not like that. The simple explanation is that the man in the flat in Canonbury Square is Roger Norton Vane, who didn't need to fake anything or run into anyone.'

'As you say, that's what everyone seems to think except Cynthia,' said Elsie. 'Tim says even the bank has now accepted that Roger Vane is who he says he is and has given him access to his bank account.'

'Really?' I asked.

'Really. He apparently managed to gather together all of

the documentation they needed. Even found his old driving licence somewhere.'

'He said he'd lost it in the jungle.'

'Well, Ethelred, he's clearly found it again. I'm afraid that's about it. Roger Vane was never declared dead, so he doesn't need to get himself declared undead. He's back in residence in his flat and is in funds. As you say, it's only Cynthia who seems ready to hold out in the face of all of the evidence. And she arguably has good sound financial reasons for doing so.'

'In short, I don't even get to speculate in my biography that it might be somebody else.'

'Neither you nor Tim. The whole thing will have to be squeaky clean. How is the research going?'

'I'm off to the studios tomorrow morning. It seemed worth having a tour of the *Gascoyne* set and a chat to one or two people there.'

I heard Elsie yawn at the other end of the phone.

'Exactly,' I said. 'Well, at least we know the truth now. I rather think the excitement is over.'

CHAPTER SEVENTEEN

'I probably shouldn't say this, but the first series was rubbish,' said Gloria. 'I've been here all the way through – series one to series fifteen, and counting. Haven't missed any of them. First on the set every morning with my clipboard. Last to leave most evenings. It's why I never got a dog, I think. Or a cat. Or a boyfriend. One of these days I'll go on *Mastermind* with Roger Norton Vane as my specialist subject.'

'I'm sure you'd do very well,' I said.

She paused then said: 'You're not planning to do that yourself, are you, Ethelred?'

'Heaven forbid,' I said.

Gloria looked relieved. 'You could have it as your specialist subject if you really wanted to,' she offered. 'I mean, you're writing the book about him.'

Just for a moment her patent insincerity tempted me to claim it as my own.

'No, it's all yours,' I said after a wicked pause.

'Well, I probably do know more about it than you do,' she said. 'I probably know more about it than anyone in the world. Not that I'm boasting or anything. It's just that it's true. I'm the world's leading expert on *Gascoyne*.'

We were in an office at Oaklawn Studios, where the company that produced Vane's Gascoyne series was based. I was about to be shown round one of the sets by Gloria, whose precise role was still unknown to me, other than that it allowed her to use a clipboard and to have her good nature exploited by her employer. But, before I was permitted to go anywhere, it appeared that I had to submit to a period of instruction. Gloria had started talking when I walked into the office and had not yet paused properly for breath.

'We do most of the filming in villages around the M25,' Gloria continued. 'But we do some here – especially interiors. The police station, for example. I'll show you that. There's still a dent in the wall, if you look closely, from where Inspector Gascoyne threw a stapler at Sergeant Jacobs in series 4, episode 7. You'll remember that, of course. Everyone does. Then in series 4 episode 9, Gascoyne and Jones are having an argument and the camera pans in for a moment on the dented wall – so clever. "Show us the dent!" people say when I take them on a tour – the real fans, I mean. The ones who've watched every episode half a dozen times. "That dent should get an acting credit," somebody said to me recently. Laugh? We all fell about.'

I wondered whether to pretend that I found it funny. There was probably no need. I had already been made aware that I was not in the front rank of fans. I had no recollection at all of the scene in question.

'Often we'll use as many as four or five locations, maybe miles from each other, as the same village – it depends what we need – a watermill, a blacksmith, a cottage hospital. One of my jobs is to keep track of where we have filmed and where we haven't. Viewers can be quite harsh if you offer them the same farmhouse twice as different places in different episodes. They remember little details – a funny-shaped inglenook, say, or a stained-glass window. I use a card index with different coloured inks for each series. You'd think I'd have run out of colours by now, wouldn't you, but I found some beige ink the other day. You can't read it that easily but it's very distinctive. Somebody said to me: why not put them all on a spreadsheet? But it's not the same, is it? We're a very traditional show. I told the producer: "Spreadsheet! What would Gascoyne say to that?" He couldn't think of a reply! And we get crowds of people volunteering to be extras. But again, we can't use the same people too many times – not now. Fans stop the video recorder, wind back, then they say: "Didn't we see him as a drunk in series 7, episode 3? Why is he a vicar now?" It's a bit of a cult following, you see.'

I looked at her for a moment to see if she had intended 'vicar' and 'cult' as some sort of wordplay, but she hadn't.

'Roger Vane was an extra in series one,' I said. I expected some credit for knowing this obscure fact, or at least a look of recognition on Gloria's face, but there was none.

'Really?' she said rather resentfully.

'According to my agent. Roger told her that – he's got a photograph of it.'

'A photograph?' Gloria looked personally offended. 'It's not possible. I'd know about it. Something like that.'

'She's seen it,' I said.

'Well, nobody ever told me,' Gloria replied. I could see that tonight she would have the coloured inks out, scowling as she revised her records with savage swathes of Tipp-Ex.

'Elsie said he was a bit embarrassed about it. It was just series one.'

'Well, that might explain it,' said Gloria, slightly mollified. 'Series one wasn't a great success. Nobody wants to admit they had anything to do with series one. The scriptwriters tried to stick as much as possible to Roger's books – he was co-author of most of the scripts. But what works on the page doesn't always work on the screen. It was only once we got to the second series of *Gascoyne* and had some totally original scripts commissioned that we really started to get a following. Yes, it was when we began writing our own episodes with a proper television scriptwriter that it all took off. Sorry – you're a book writer yourself, of course – but you must have found the same thing with your own series?'

'My books? They've never been filmed,' I said. 'They've never even been optioned for filming.'

Gloria patted me on the arm. 'I'm sure they will be one day,' she said. 'Maybe in your own lifetime. It's surprising which books they choose to make into films. Sometimes you're watching television and you think – why did they choose this rubbish? So, you never know.'

'Thank you,' I said. 'That's kind. But Roy Johnston was just in the first series?'

'Yes, that's right. I think he was unfairly criticised – I shouldn't say this, but a lot of people blamed him for the standard of the first series. I mean, you can only work with the script you have. Though he never did much afterwards, either. So it could have been him and the scripts.'

'He and Roger were good friends?'

'Much of the time. They were very much alike in so many ways.'

'Equally argumentative?' I enquired.

'Oh, nobody was as argumentative as Roger. That's why he was eased out of his co-author role and became a consultant. Then he was eased out of the consultant role too . . .'

'Really?' I asked.

'Oh yes, that too. Of course, he kept his name in the credits – "based on the books by" – but nobody wanted to work with him. It didn't surprise anyone that he and Roy fell out. But once they had – well, I shouldn't tell you this, but Roy had to go. You couldn't have had both of them on set, and Roger was still a consultant then. It must have been terrible for Roy – he'd taken all the flack for the first series, got almost nothing in royalty payments, then had to sit by and watch the success of the second one. That's why he went to Australia. He got tired of watching all of the repeats over here. Even living in Australia was better than that. Then we sold it over there, of course – except series one; they didn't want that. They'd seen the UK ratings. Never showed it in Australia.'

'You don't ever hear from him now?'

'Roy? No, he's happy enough, I imagine. Sun. Sand. Booze. Whatever. Who wouldn't be?'

'No hard feelings on his part?'

'Oh no, I wouldn't say that. He hates Roger's guts. Wrote me a long letter from Brisbane one Christmas. In fact, if Roger were ever found murdered, I'd have Roy at the top of the list of suspects – though maybe I shouldn't say so, just in case he does it. Would you like to see the studio now? You must be dying to see the dent in the wall.'

As I'd said to Elsie – the excitement was well and truly over.

It was at a service station on the way home that my phone buzzed again.

'Ethelred? It's Roger Vane here. I need your help. Somebody has just tried to kill me.'

'Are you sure?' I asked. It seemed unlikely.

'Of course I'm sure. I think I'm in a better position to know than you are.'

I decided to ignore the contempt in his voice. 'But you're not actually hurt?' I asked.

'Thank you for getting round to asking that. No, I'm fine. I managed to get the better of them.'

'What happened?' I asked.

'No time for that. I'll tell you all about it when I see you and you can apologise then for doubting me. There are also some things I'll need you to do. I'll let you know what when we meet up.'

I wondered whether to explain that I was his biographer, not his PA.

'I'm not planning to come up to London for a few days,' I said.

'You don't need to. I'm travelling down to Sussex to stay with you.'

'Are you? When?'

'Tonight. I'll call you from the train once I know which one I'll be on, and you can come and pick me up at Chichester Station. I should be in well before twelve. If you could be there ten minutes or so beforehand, I won't have to hang around in the cold if the train is early.'

It was perhaps this final piece of presumption that sealed his fate.

'I'm out to dinner this evening,' I said. 'I've no idea what time I'll be back. If you come down in the morning there's a good bus service from Chichester to West Wittering. Ask the driver to tell you when you get to the Old House at Home. That's the closest stop.'

'Can't risk leaving it until then. I need to do something straight away. If you won't help I'll find a hotel for the night. There are hotels in Chichester, I assume?'

Well, if he wanted to waste his money hiding from imaginary assassins . . . I named a couple of perfectly good places to stay within walking distance of the station.

'I'll phone you in the morning,' he said and rang off abruptly.

But he didn't phone me. Because by the following morning he was already dead.

CHAPTER EIGHTEEN

The knock at my front door came early. I looked at my watch – seven-thirty. A little too soon for the post. Much too soon for any of my neighbours to be paying a social call. I placed my cup of coffee on the kitchen table, tightened the belt of my dressing gown, unlocked the door and opened it cautiously.

'Hello, Joe,' I said to the policeman. 'Anything wrong? Is this business or pleasure?'

'Hello, Ethelred,' he replied. 'Business, I'm afraid. Murder. Do you mind if we do this inside? It's starting to rain out here.'

I went back to the kitchen and poured him some coffee while he explained, apologetically, why he needed my help. I knew Joe well – we met from time to time so that he could keep me up to date with police procedure and so I could provide a little literary gossip in exchange. Strangely, it was literary gossip of a sort that he needed now.

'Yes,' I said eventually, in answer to his question. 'I did know Roger Norton Vane. I'm writing his biography – well, one of them anyway. I can't say I liked him much as a person, but I admired his work. I also probably ought to tell you now that if he was killed last night, then it's my fault in a way. He phoned and said that his life was in danger. I didn't believe him. I told him I couldn't see him until this morning.'

'But you changed your mind and phoned him at his hotel?'

'No,' I said. 'Definitely not. I was out to dinner. I got back around midnight. I'd recommended a couple of hotels where he could stay if he insisted on coming down to Chichester. But I didn't hear from him at all after that. I certainly didn't call him – I had no wish to find myself driving into Chichester to pick him up because he didn't like the hotel.'

'We think he was killed around eleven or eleven-thirty. A couple of blows to the head. The pathologist reckons that the second injury may have been when he fell to the ground – a lucky or unlucky blow, depending on how you look at it. When we were called to the crime scene we identified him straight away from the driving licence in his pocket – one of the old paper ones, but still in good nick. You don't see so many of those now and a lot of the ones you do see are held together with Sellotape. He also had his hotel key card with him, so we traced where he had been staying.

'It turned out he had arrived at his hotel around ten

o'clock, having walked there from the station. He checked in and went to his room but an hour later he left, having asked reception for directions to East Street. Earlier he'd told the receptionist a Mr Tressider would be picking him up the following day and so he needed a room just for the one night. She wondered if that was who he was going off to meet. Vane was found in an alleyway just off East Street, so the hotel seem to have remembered the conversation reasonably well. We checked Vane's phone – he'd received a call from an unidentified pay-as-you-go just before he went out. And interestingly, your mobile number was stored on it. I thought it odd, if you really had phoned him last night, that you hadn't used your own phone. But then being murdered just off East Street isn't routine either. So, I thought I'd better check.'

'You don't suspect me?' I asked.

'If we did, they'd have scarcely sent round a detective who knows you personally and might possibly be biased in your favour. You say somebody else had threatened to kill him, though?'

'He actually said somebody had already tried.'

'How?'

'He was going to tell me today. It must have been in London, because that was where he was until yesterday afternoon.'

'But he didn't say exactly where?'

'No.'

'Or who?'

'No.'

'That takes care of all my best questions, then.' Joe made

159

a couple of quick entries in a black notebook. 'Did he have any enemies?'

'The difficulty is knowing where to start. The number of people who wanted him dead was surprisingly large. But the number who would have actually killed him would be very much lower.'

'How many in the last group?'

'If it wasn't for the fact that he was dead, I'd have said none at all. His enemies were mainly highly respectable and had a lot to lose. They wouldn't have taken the risk.'

Joe looked at me with a sort of kindly sympathy. 'As you know, Ethelred, it's when you've got a lot to lose that you're prepared to take risks. So, who wouldn't have minded him dead if somebody else would do it for them? I'd be happy to start with the top dozen or so if there really are that many.'

I drew a deep breath. 'OK, what I have to begin by explaining is that Roger Vane had just re-emerged after a long absence—'

Joe held up his hand. 'It's OK, Ethelred. We googled him. It's all there. But the name was familiar, anyway. He's been on the news a bit lately.'

'Fine,' I said. 'Well, then you'll already know his enemies included his former partner, Tim Macdonald—'

'The artist?'

'Yes – well done for knowing that.'

'Not really. We got him off Google too. Illustrator of the Terry the Terrible Terrier series. I'll have to look them out for the grandchildren. Macdonald has an obvious motive.'

'Roger had evicted him from the flat,' I said.

'He was accused of murdering Vane before – in Thailand.'

'But never charged,' I said.

'Is that right?' He made another note. 'That will save me a lot of unnecessary checking. And, as his partner, he would inherit Vane's money?'

'No, it will go to his niece, Cynthia.'

'I see,' he said. 'One suspect down, eleven to go. Next?'

'Roger Vane and his agent were involved in some wrangle over fees. He'd accused the agent of fraud – not something agents ever do, according to my agent. But even if he did, I can't see that would be enough to kill for.'

'It might be enough if there genuinely was fraud and the agent didn't want anyone to find out. Who else?'

'There's a man named Slide – he was Roger Vane's housemaster. Roger ridiculed him in his books. Gave him a nervous breakdown. He had good cause, you might say. But he's pretty old and frail to have done it himself.'

'Could somebody have done it on his behalf?'

'Yes, anyone of that generation at Cordwainers.'

Joe looked up from his note-taking. 'The posh school in London?'

'That's the one,' I said. 'I understand that the school generally disliked Roger. They felt he had let the side down a bit. There was . . . I'm not sure . . . something the headmaster and Roger's contemporaries seemed keen to keep quiet. I talked to various people and always felt that something was being held back.'

'I bet. Anyone else?'

I hesitated. 'Maybe. But I don't really feel comfortable

speculating like this – I mean, I feel as if I'm grassing up people who've done me no harm.'

'That's how it works, Ethelred, though grassing up people who have done you some harm is more fun. Anyway, we'll need to talk to everyone who knew Roger Vane, so anything you say will merely speed up the process – get them cleared a bit faster, if they're innocent. If they're guilty we'll get them anyway. Hopefully. What about the niece who gets the money?'

'Cynthia. She stood to inherit a lot of money if Roger had been declared dead, but lost it all when he came back. And now he really is dead, the status quo is restored . . . But I really don't think—'

'How much money?'

'The accumulated royalties over twenty years must have run into hundreds of thousands – maybe millions.'

'Was she short of cash?'

'Apparently. So is her mother, Margery Vane. Cynthia wanted the money in part to help her mother – she's basically broke. Her mother was apparently once close to Roger Vane – later less so.'

'Close? Meaning what?'

'I'm not entirely sure,' I said. 'She implied a falling out.'

'Anyone else?' asked Joe.

I hesitated again. 'People may tell you that his former editor, Lucinda, disliked him. But she wouldn't—'

Joe held up his hand again. 'I'll be the judge of that. What did he do to her?'

'Got her sacked. Actually she wasn't the only sacking he was responsible for. There was Roy Johnston.'

'Oh yes, I remember – he was in the first series of *Gascoyne*.'

'Did you Google him too?'

'No, I've always been a bit of a fan of the series. I actually liked him better than the other one who replaced him. He was . . . how can I put it? . . . more like the Gascoyne in the books. What happened to him?'

'He went to Australia, apparently.'

'OK. I wouldn't mind a trip over there to interview him. Of course, if he's still there, it's unlikely he killed somebody in an alleyway off East Street last night. And if he isn't, I won't be able to interview him. But I might be able to swing it. You never know your luck. Next?'

'Lord Davies was at school with him – Vane knew something about his past that was not to his credit – but I wouldn't want to suggest that Davies might have killed him.'

'Very wise. Not with his legal team. But we can do that, of course. We'll have a word.'

'William Ogilvie, his lawyer, went to the same place. Also nervous about what Vane was going to say to me. You should probably talk to him too.'

Joe made further notes.

'So, what did happen to Roger Norton Vane in Thailand, then?' he asked. 'I probably owe it to my colleagues in London and Bangkok to clear that one up. Did he say where he'd been all this time?'

'He and Tim had an argument. Tim took a swing at him. Roger decided to clear off into the jungle to teach him a lesson. He rather liked it there so he stayed – first in

Thailand, then in Laos. He sold his watch to raise funds, then later he taught English. He heard he was about to be declared dead, and so he came back. There's not much more to it than that – or rather, Tim can fill you in on the detail if you need it.'

'Twenty years is a long time to stay away. It would have caused problems for all sorts of people.'

'Roger would have rather liked that,' I said. 'It was probably at least half of the reason why he stayed there.'

'And there'd be records of him living in Laos?'

'I assume so. But he lived there under a false name.'

'Which was . . . ?'

'I don't know. He never said.'

'Tricky, though it may not be impossible to find out if we need to. Where were you last night, by the way? You will notice the casual way I throw that in.'

'Out to dinner with some friends in Itchenor.'

'Names?'

I gave him their names and address. He wrote them in his notebook.

'Until when?' he asked.

'About midnight. I called a taxi company to get a cab home. They'll have records.'

Joe made a note of the company name and nodded. 'I'm sure they will. If we need to ask them.'

'Is there anything else?' I asked.

'Not for the moment. I'll let you know how it goes.'

'So, what do you think happened?'

'Well, based on the laws of probability, I'd have said he went for a stroll and was attacked by some druggie who needed twenty quid for his next fix. He was in a badly lit alleyway late at night – not wise, even round here. The guy coshes him, he falls awkwardly and hits his head against the wall or pavement. In the absence of other evidence, he died because he was in the wrong place at the wrong time. But the phone call to his mobile beforehand is interesting. Did somebody know Vane was down here and did they phone him and invite him to a rendezvous in an alleyway? If Vane was genuinely worried, it would have been an odd invitation to accept.'

'Vane implied that only I knew he was here – but it's quite possible that he told other people.'

'It might be convenient for you if he had told a few other people' said Joe. 'It's never good to be the only person with an opportunity to kill.'

'Why would I want to kill the subject of the biography I was writing? What's my motive?'

'Let's not worry too much about motive for the moment,' said Joe. 'You can kill somebody with no motive at all. But you can't kill them if there's no opportunity. It's always worth remembering that.'

'I was having dinner with friends—'

Joe gave me a friendly pat on the shoulder. 'Just winding you up, Ethelred. Unless we spot your face on the CCTV footage, of course. Then it will be another matter entirely. Why don't you focus on motive and I'll focus on opportunity? You never know – between us we might just get somewhere. Thanks for the coffee. I can find my own way out.'

* * *

'It's ironic,' I said to Elsie. 'Just as he proves who he is and gets hold of his money, somebody murders him.'

'Maybe that's why he was murdered,' said Elsie. 'So long as it wasn't clear who he was, he was in no danger. Once it was certain he was Roger Norton Vane, the killer decided it was time to act. The real Vane knew something that somebody was very keen to keep quiet.'

I thought about this. 'When I first saw him at the church, he said that the literary world should be trembling in its kitten heels.'

'There you are, then. Proving his identity sealed his fate. The whole time he was just digging his own grave. It's classic tragic irony, when you think about it. Of course, there's a silver lining. Now we can slag him off in the biography with no risk to anyone. You might earn out the advance, after all. First time for everything.'

'Profiting from his death? That would just make me feel even guiltier,' I said.

'Why should you feel guilty? Other than for the pitifully small amount of revenue you bring this agency? Of course, I'd never embarrass you by mentioning it.'

'If I'd just let him come and stay with me, he wouldn't have been at the hotel and wouldn't have been murdered. That's plenty to feel guilty about. To make it worse, I think the police see me as a suspect because I was the only person who knew he was down in Sussex. Or if they don't think that, they should. As Joe pointed out, it's all about opportunity. I was the only one who could have phoned him and lured him to the alleyway.'

'Cynthia knew,' said Elsie.

'Did she?'

'Roger told her in the strictest confidence.'

'And how do you know that?'

'Because she told me in the strictest confidence.'

'And who did you tell?'

'In the strictest confidence?'

'Yes.'

'Just Tim, I think.'

'And he told . . . ?'

'You mean yesterday afternoon or later?'

'Yesterday afternoon.'

'Four or five people, absolute tops. And Cynthia would have told her mum, of course. Roger's secret was absolutely safe with us. Which just leaves you, I'm afraid. Let me know if you're arrested. I'll come and see you on visiting days, if it's not too far away.'

I had no sooner ended the call than my phone rang again.

'Lord Davies' secretary here, you've been quite difficult to get hold of.'

'I was talking to the police, then I was on the phone to somebody,' I said.

'Lord Davies would like to speak to you,' said the secretary.

'Put him through, then,' I said.

'No, he wishes to speak to you here in London,' she said.

'Maybe tomorrow or the day after . . .' I suggested.

'He requests that you should be here by midday.'

'That might be tricky, even if I set off now . . .'

'If you look out of your window, you should see a limousine drawing up in front of your house. I'll put you in the diary for twelve-fifteen, just in case the traffic is heavy coming into London.'

CHAPTER NINETEEN

'I can get you some lunch, if you eat it. Never have time myself.'

'It's only just after twelve,' I said. 'Your driver put his foot down once we reached the motorway. We slowed only for the speed cameras.'

Lord Davies nodded approvingly. He was willing to spend money on a limousine to ensure that I was delivered when needed, but I could see he wasn't one to waste it on unnecessary speeding tickets.

'My secretary says that you've already spoken to the police?'

'Yes,' I said.

'So, what did they have to say for themselves?'

'I'm not sure how much I can tell you,' I said.

'Are you really uncertain? Perhaps I can clear that up for you, Ethelred. I have investments in several publishing houses, one of which publishes your books. I have dinner with the chairman on a regular basis. He won't, of course, have heard of you, but I can ensure he does. He won't have formed much of a view of your books, but I can advise him what to think – whether you are still worth publishing, and possibly even promoting, or whether you might be dropped back into the obscurity from which you came. It's quite a small company. I am quite a large shareholder. Their cash flow is not good at present. They'd like me to put some more money in. I'm thinking about it. Now, let me ask you again: what did the police have to say for themselves?'

'You overestimate my importance in this affair,' I said. 'I know very little that you won't have already heard on the news. Roger Vane was attacked in an alleyway in the centre of Chichester, late at night. You presumably don't need me to tell you that.'

'You are quite right in believing that I haven't had you ferried up here by limousine to confirm what I've just heard on the BBC, much though I suspect their left-wing bias and pleasant though it is to see you again. Do the police have any suspects lined up?'

'My source in Chichester says that they would have assumed it was a simple opportunist robbery that had gone wrong, had it not been for an earlier attempt on his life and a phone call that he had received just before he went out. He seems to have been lured to the alleyway and ambushed there.'

'So, he was killed by somebody who knew him?' asked Davies.

'Presumably.'

'Was my name mentioned?' he asked.

'What do you think?' I asked.

'And what did you say when it was mentioned?'

'I specifically said that I wasn't suggesting it was you,' I said.

'Thank you. That was kind. So, I can expect a visit from the Old Bill, then?'

'That is likely.'

'Then I am forewarned. I shall be ready for them. Was anything else said about me?'

'I don't think so.'

'Really? Don't you? Did I mention my meeting with your chairman?'

'Yes, I took your point. I may have to look for another publisher. These things happen.'

Davies looked at me. 'Was there any suggestion that I might have been in Chichester? I think you can tell me that.'

'No, there wasn't.'

'Did they speculate on what motive I might have for killing Roger Vane?'

'No. The police are more interested in who had the opportunity.'

He considered this for a moment. 'Perhaps we have less to discuss than I thought. I'm sorry to have brought you all this way for so little.'

'There's no need to apologise,' I said.

'That wasn't an apology,' he said.

He opened his diary to check his next appointment.

I stood. Then a thought occurred to me. 'So, where were you last night?' I asked.

I had expected him to damn my impertinence, but he simply looked up and said: 'Here. In my office. I had a conference call with some people in California – early evening their time. I needed to do some preparation for it, so I sat up until about three in the morning, took the call, then went to bed here – I have a bedroom in the building for when I need it. It's not that far to walk home, but it's often easier.'

'Do you have any proof of that?'

'Which bit? The bedroom? Or the distance home?'

'It's entirely your decision, Lord Davies,' I said, 'but when the police question you, I'd drop the flippant replies.'

'Would you? Well, you can tell the police they can begin by checking the CCTV footage of reception. They'll see me come in at about eight and they won't see me leave until I go home later today. And if you don't consider it unduly flippant, say I'd be happy to send them a copy if that would assist in any way.'

'I'll tell them,' I said.

'Good. I think that would be helpful for all concerned,' said Davies. He flicked through the diary, then looked up again as if surprised I was still there.

'Have you discussed Vane's murder with anyone else?' I asked.

'Other than talking to you, I haven't really had time to think about it. If I had discussed it with anyone else, it would be none of your business. You may like to imagine a great conspiracy taking place behind your back, but this isn't even my tenth most important meeting today. I'm sorry that Roger is dead, but he was never a friend of mine and not somebody I've thought about a great deal for the past twenty years. He means almost as little to me as you do.' He gave me a stiff, formal smile.

'So that's it, then? Shall I find the limousine again to take me home?'

'I'm sure my secretary could order you one, if you don't mind the expense. I needed you here, so I provided a car. I don't particularly need you anywhere else.'

'I'd better get the train, then,' I said.

'Entirely your choice,' said Lord Davies. 'My secretary will see you out of the building. Security is necessarily very strict. It is important to keep out undesirables. As you pass the CCTV camera you can wave at your policeman friend. He'll like that.'

I was heading for the Tube and Victoria Station when my phone rang again. This time I recognised the caller – it was a number I had entered in my contacts list.

'Good afternoon, Mr Ogilvie,' I said.

'Afternoon, Ethelred. Do you fancy a spot of lunch? I'll see you at my club at one o'clock. The Pagan Club in Pall Mall. My treat. I'll be waiting by the porter's lodge, just inside the entrance.'

'I was about to get the train back to Sussex,' I said.

'It's lucky I caught you, then. Don't be late.'

I put my plans for returning to Chichester on hold and checked the Tube map in my diary. I could just about get to the Pagan by one. I hadn't asked him how he knew I was in London. There probably wasn't much point. Davies had lied to me. I was fairly sure Ogilvie was planning to do the same.

CHAPTER TWENTY

'The beef Wellington is very good,' said Ogilvie over the top of his menu.

'Maybe something lighter . . .' I said.

'Nonsense. We'll both have the beef Wellington,' he said to the waiter, who had been hovering in the background. 'He needs building up. New potatoes. Peas. Buttered carrots. And a bottle of the 1998 Clos de Vougeot.'

'And some water,' I added.

'And some water,' said Ogilvie, as if the waiter had been unaware of my presence.

The waiter nodded and slipped the menus from our hands as if they had been made of silk.

Ogilvie leant back in his chair and stretched his legs out. We both briefly surveyed the room, taking in the high ceiling, the heavy plaster mouldings, the immensely thick royal-blue velvet curtains, the great gold tassels, the dark-blue leather of the chairs, the polished mahogany everywhere. 'Luncheon!' he exclaimed suddenly. 'Big mistake not to have it. Big mistake. Most important meal of the day. That and breakfast. And tea of course.' He paused, perhaps wondering if he could add dinner to the list. Or midnight feasts in the dorm. I thought of Elsie's comment about the Cordwainers' lifelong obsession with their stomachs. Roasting oxen on Big Side.

'I'm sure the beef Wellington will be very good,' I said.

'Roger always liked his food – we often lunched here – well, not so much in the last twenty years of course . . .' He lapsed into silence.

'Did you know he was planning to come down to Chichester?' I asked.

He looked at me for a moment. 'He mentioned it,' he said. 'Phoned me yesterday afternoon to update me on one or two things and mentioned it in passing. I was down in the constituency at the time.'

'Remind me – where's that?' I asked.

'Hampshire.'

'Yes, of course. I'm almost in Hampshire myself,' I said. 'Hayling Island's just across the water from us.'

'Yes, I suppose you are. You'd need to be a lot further west to vote for me, though.'

There was an assumption, if I were far enough west, I would not choose to vote for anyone else. The only impediment was geography.

'So did you come back last night?' I asked.

'Why do you ask that?'

'Because you're here now. You must have travelled back last night or early this morning.'

'Yes.' There was another pause. 'It was . . . last night, actually. Yes, last night. Ah, there's the wine waiter.'

We watched as the cork was carefully removed and a small libation was poured into Ogilvie's glass. Ogilvie sipped it thoughtfully and nodded. Our glasses were filled to the level that the waiter considered good for us and he departed.

'They decanted it in the old days. A decent wine like this one. Not any more. The wine committee decreed that because the French don't decant their wines, we shouldn't either. I always say, the French may know how to make wine, but we know how to drink it. Eh? What's your own wine committee say?'

'I don't possess one,' I said. 'I don't belong to any clubs.'

'Really?' he said. 'I'd propose you for this one but there's a very long waiting list, I'm told. And the committee's quite choosy. They won't accept everyone. Nothing gives them greater pleasure than turning down some jumped-up nobody. Pure snobbery, of course – I don't approve of it myself. You could always try one of the others along here – the Oxford and Cambridge, say. Or the Travellers. They'd probably take you.'

'I'm not up in London often enough,' I said.

Ogilvie nodded and took another sip of undecanted wine.

'So what do the police make of it all?' he asked casually.

I decided there could be no harm in telling him what I'd already told Davies. Anyway, I'd learnt something from Davies in the process. Perhaps I would learn something from Ogilvie too. 'They thought at first it was a mugging,' I said, 'but it is likely somebody deliberately lured him there to the alleyway.

That seemed odd in view of the fact that so few people knew he was in Sussex – but the more I speak to people, the more seemed to have been told. You said he phoned you. Did he mention that somebody had already tried to kill him?'

'Kill him? Ah . . . yes . . . I suppose he did. Well, he'd had some sort of threat, anyway. His account was difficult to follow – he'd spoken to somebody who said he deserved to die – then they admitted that they'd tried to push him under a Tube train earlier that day. Or was it that they'd instructed somebody to push him under a train? It all sounded a little confused and rather improbable. I mean, if somebody had attempted to kill him, would they then phone him up and tell him so? Hardly . . .'

'So you didn't take it seriously?'

'There might have been a small grain of veracity in it somewhere. Roger was in the habit of falling back on the truth when all else failed. And in the habit of expecting you to jump to it whenever he needed something doing. He wanted me to drop by and see him in Chichester on my way back to London – as if I had nothing better to do.'

'Did he say who had threatened to kill him?'

'No. He implied it was somebody I knew well. He was going to tell me when I saw him that evening.'

'And your journey back took you close to Chichester, enabling you to meet?'

'Did I say that? I suppose so . . . close enough . . . it depended which route I took. Not if I went along the M3, of course. But we didn't meet. I certainly wasn't in Chichester town centre when Roger was killed, if that's what you're implying.'

'I didn't imply anything. But what I say or what you tell me makes little difference. I'm sure that the police would pick up your car on CCTV if you had been there.'

He looked at me for a moment. 'Yes, good point – I suppose they would. Well, I'm always ready to assist the police with their enquiries,' he said. 'I'll write my registration down for you and you can give it to them. That should save them a bit of time.' He scribbled it on the back of one of his cards and passed it to me.

'I'm not sure when I'll talk to them next,' I said, placing the card in my wallet. 'I'm not helping them any more than any other witness.'

'But they've asked your advice?'

'Yes.'

'As Roger's biographer?'

'Yes.'

'So, they'll probably be asking who else knew him? Who might have held a grudge?'

'Yes.'

'And what have you said?'

'I've told them who knew him.'

'Including me?'

'I've said you are his lawyer. It's unlikely that that wouldn't have come to light.'

'I suppose not.' He looked at me for a moment, like a chess player trying to guess his opponent's next move. What would it be? A bold move with his queen? Or would he sacrifice a pawn? 'I suppose you know Jonathan Slide is on holiday in your part of the world?' he said.

'He told me he was planning to stay in Bognor . . . no,

Selsey. That was it. But he didn't say exactly when. Would he have known Roger Norton Vane was in Chichester?'

'I may have mentioned it to him. In passing. He phoned me. Asked whether I thought that it really was Roger. Said he wanted to talk to him – make it clear he bore him no ill will. That sort of thing. So, I probably did mention what I knew . . .'

'But last night Slide was in Selsey, some miles away.'

'Oh, I would think so. But he's in the habit of coming into Chichester quite often. There are various bars that he likes to visit – places he's been going to for years.'

'Well, if he was in Chichester last night, I'm sure the police will want to question him.'

'He did have a bit of a motive, of course. All those dubious characters in novels.'

'But he told you he wanted to make things up with Roger?' I asked.

'That's what he said. That's why I gave him Roger's number.'

'Well, I can't see Slide hitting somebody over the head,' I said.

'Is that what happened?'

'Yes, then Vane fell apparently, striking his head again.'

'It doesn't take a lot of strength to hit somebody hard enough to throw them off balance. Walking stick . . . something like that. And Roger wouldn't have been expecting it.'

'Sorry, are you saying Slide did it? He seems as harmless an old buffer as you could meet.'

'Now maybe. He wasn't always.'

'You mean he had a wild youth?'

'You'll have heard one of his roles was careers advice?'

'Yes. It sounds a bit of a sinecure. I'm surprised the school was so indulgent.'

'He was recruiting for MI6. That was how it was in those days. No application form. You simply got asked if you fancied that sort of thing. If you said yes, then you were given instructions to go and have an informal chat with a man near Waterloo Station. Slide spotted likely candidates and fed their names through. Old boys at MI6, and there were plenty, would have impressed on a succession of headmasters the need to keep Slide in place for the sake of national security.'

I thought back to my conversation with Thwaite. Something he had said – that Slide's role as career's master 'might have fitted in with other things'.

'So, did Dr Slide actually work for MI6? As a spy?'

'Some of us did a quick calculation and concluded that there were a couple of missing years in his CV – between the dates he was at university and the date of his joining the teaching staff at Cordwainers. Of course, he could have been in prison for gross indecency or something, but we reckoned he might have been spying. The masters at Cordwainers had collectively failed at an impressive range of things before settling on education as a vocation.'

I thought of my father, who had had many ambitions in his youth but ended up teaching Chaucer and Beowulf at our local grammar school. He never quite abandoned the idea that one day he might become prime minister. He eventually retired as acting deputy head of English.

'Well, Slide must be a suspect,' I said. 'So must Cynthia,

as the person who will now inherit Vane's estate.'

'Not really. She's not the heir. Hasn't been for some time. Roger asked me to change his will twenty years ago, just before he and Tim Macdonald went off to Thailand. He wanted Tim to inherit everything.'

'Does Cynthia know that?'

'She came to see me a week or so ago, when she was still trying to prove that it wasn't Roger. I felt obliged to tell her that even if she did prove he was an imposter – even if she proved conclusively that Roger Norton Vane had died – she still got nothing, poor kid. Not a penny.'

'Was she upset?'

'She did her best not to show it, but it was a lot of money – two or three million of accumulated royalties and other payments, I think. She could have used that. So could her mother.'

'You didn't think to tell her before?'

'Roger wasn't dead. I was under no obligation to tell anyone anything. Quite the reverse.'

'But you told her then?'

'It seemed helpful. I mean, the idea that she might inherit the money did appear to underlie her continuing campaign to prove he was a fraud . . . It was better for all concerned that she knew the truth. He'd cut her out of his will long ago – or to put it more positively, he'd cut Tim in. It wasn't unreasonable. Before Tim came on the scene, she was his next of kin – no other close family to leave it all to. After Tim became his partner, it was different. Had Roger got married, if he'd had children of his own, it would have been much the same for Cynthia. It's not uncommon. Many's the golden prize I've seen snatched from a devoted nephew or niece when their uncle decides, late in life, to shack up with some teenage floozy on the make.'

'So you thought it better to tell her and get her off your back? It didn't have quite that effect you expected, then. She was continuing to say that Vane was an imposter, right up to the last moment.'

'Was she? Fair play to her, then. It's just that her uncle's death would not have benefitted her, and she knew it. So, she had no motive of any sort. Tim's the one who will now collect. In spite of their being daggers drawn towards the end. When you think about it, Tim's lucky Roger died when he did – before he had a chance to change his will again. I'm sure he would have done in a week or two – possibly in Cynthia's favour. Did Tim know where Roger was, by any chance?'

'Yes,' I said. 'Elsie told him. In the strictest confidence.'

'Really? How interesting. Not that I'm suggesting anything, of course. Still, that's Slide and Macdonald with excellent motives and every opportunity. We're making progress at being detectives, aren't we? Eat up, Ethelred. You're having treacle tart and custard to follow.'

I left the Pagan Club feeling that I had eaten and drunk too much. Ogilvie had insisted that we should have cheese after the treacle tart and port with the cheese. In fact, I felt slightly nauseous as I descended into the Underground, but no worse by the time I had bought a single ticket to Chichester at Victoria Station. I'd had my phone switched off at the club but checked it quickly as the train slid away gently from the platform. There was a text from Joe, only a few minutes before.

'Drop by at the police station on your way home. There have been a couple of interesting developments. I just wish I understood them.'

CHAPTER TWENTY-ONE

'Biscuit?' asked Joe.

'Definitely not,' I said, taking a sip of coffee.

'Good of you to call round,' said Joe. 'But I thought it wouldn't be too much out of your way, us being so close to the railway station.'

'How did you know I'd been to London?' I asked.

'We phoned Mr Ogilvie to arrange to see him. He said he'd been lunching with you at his club. Nice place?'

'It was OK. I'm not planning to apply for membership. So whatever it is that you want to tell me is about Ogilvie? He gave me this to give to you, by the way.' I passed him Ogilvie's registration.

'Yes, he told us that too. I fear the Greeks, Ethelred, even when they bring gifts. If he's happy for us to have this, then it is almost certainly valueless.'

'You think he wasn't in Chichester?'

'Or he was in Chichester but in another car entirely.

That's the problem with police work. It makes you a bit cynical about generous offers of help. But it wasn't Ogilvie that I wanted to talk about. There are three things. The first is this . . . You remember you told me about a previous boyfriend – Roy Johnston?'

'Yes.'

'Well, my trip to Australia's off. Coincidentally he arrived in England last month. We checked immigration records. We haven't been able to find out where he's staying yet, but we were able to get information from his credit card company and his bank. There were a number of transactions in London – mainly around Oxford Street but one or two in Islington. So we reckon that he's based somewhere in the centre of town, but that he pops over to Islington from time to time. What do you make of that?'

'You think he's been checking on Roger Vane's movements?'

'That would seem likely. The transactions stop about four or five days ago. So maybe he's gone. Or is using some other card we haven't traced yet. No sign of him having paid a hotel bill, though. Of course, he could have paid it in cash, especially if he suspected we were on to him and might be checking card and phone records. But he may be staying with a friend. Any idea who might still be in touch with him?'

I shook my head. 'So you're looking for Johnston?'

'Yes, but we don't have a recent photograph of him. We've managed to get a copy of his passport photo – about nine years old. We've also come up with one or two on the Internet . . .' He passed me some blurred images. 'These would be twenty-four, maybe twenty-five years ago.'

'They're from the Gascoyne programmes,' I said. 'First series. The company that made the programmes might be able to let you have something that was slightly more high definition. But they'd still be pretty old. He was only ever—'

'. . . in the first series. Yes, we've got that. Anyway, our lack of a recent snapshot makes it a bit trickier trying to spot him on CCTV.' Joe turned the screen on his desk so that it was facing me. 'Here's footage from a camera quite close to the alleyway, facing west – there are no cameras in the alleyway itself and you can't quite see the entrance to the alleyway, but it's just behind us, as it were, from this viewpoint.'

He tapped his keyboard and the frozen view of Chichester's main shopping street started to move, cold and ghostly under the street lights. The windows of the closed shops still glowed, showing mannequins dressed in the latest fashions, stacks of chocolate bars, jumbles of DIY equipment. We watched various people pass by. Then Roger Vane came into view, striding towards us. He paused for a moment as if uncertain which way to go, looked around and then, as if having made a decision, confidently pressed on towards his death. Joe stopped the film.

'So, that's 11.32. He's coming from the direction of his hotel. You can see that he is about to turn right into the alleyway.'

Joe restarted the CCTV footage. A man walked his dog very slowly along the street. Shortly after, a man in a leather jacket glanced up at the camera and hurried on. A group of girls, on a night out, appeared, coming from the direction of the alleyway, one slightly behind the others. They lingered for a moment while one of the main group was sick on the pavement, then they passed unsteadily down the street. The girl who was on her own – maybe she'd had a row with the rest – also went on her way, a little behind the rest, her back turned to us. The man with the dog returned.

'That should now be shortly after the time of the murder, we think. The alleyway cuts through to another street. It's less well frequented than East Street. Here's the view from our camera there – this time facing east.'

A man and a woman walked down the road hand in hand. A couple of young men ran after them and overtook them. The couple seemed not to notice their intrusion. They paused, kissed, and drifted on. The street was empty for a while. Then the man in the leather jacket hurried past. Then a bit later the girls whom we had seen in the previous recording came into view, but as a single group. Joe stopped the recording.

'Both the girls and this guy obviously went through the alleyway at about the right time – the man first, then the girls maybe four or five minutes later. They're all picked up by both cameras. Do you recognise the man? Could it be Johnston?'

I shook my head. 'It's difficult to say, but he looks much too young. Too tall as well, I think. Johnston and Vane were of a similar build, apparently. On the footage there, the man in the leather jacket looks a lot taller than Vane.'

'Well, we thought he looked a bit young to be Johnston. Could it be any of the others you've spoken to? Ogilvie? Davies? Slide? Macdonald?'

'No,' I said. 'The picture's not good, but he's really too young for any of them. Too tall for Slide as well – much too tall. Slide's five six, maybe five seven. Possibly about right for Ogilvie or Davies. I can't see Davies in a leather jacket and jeans, though. Or Ogilvie.'

Joe started the recording again. The street was empty for some time, then a woman and dog appeared. Joe pointed to the screen.

'That's the woman who discovered the body,' he said. 'So Vane's already been killed by this point. His body was in a sort of dead end, a side passage leading off the main alleyway, so it might have been there half an hour or so – the man in the jacket and the girls could have walked straight past it in the dark. Of course, neither camera covers the actual entrance to or the exit from the alley – just our luck, eh?'

'So, somebody could have got in and out undetected?'

'By these cameras, yes – if the killer knew which way to enter and leave. But there are plenty of others in the centre of town. If we're ruling out the people we've seen so far, then it's a matter of going through lots and lots of CCTV in central Chichester. Routine stuff. We'll try to track down the man and the girls, anyway – they may have seen the killer. It's a shame about Leather Jacket; we thought we might be onto something.'

'I've never seen him before,' I said.

Joe made a brief pencilled note.

'Still,' I said, 'that's progress. We know Johnston is in the country and seems to have been stalking Vane. Maybe he'll show up on another camera, as you say. But it looks as if whoever killed Roger Vane knew the centre of Chichester well and knew where the cameras are.'

We turned back to the screen, where the occasional figure still flitted along the now eerily empty street. Somewhere, out of sight, Vane was dead and the police would already be inspecting the body.

'There was one other thing that we wondered if you could help us with,' said Joe. 'We have a report from the pathologist. He made a very odd discovery.'

'I'll help if I can,' I said.

'Vane appeared to have an old scar on his shoulder.'

'He did have one. I saw it.'

'Except he didn't. He only appeared to have one. It was theatrical make-up – five quid's worth of rubber. Very realistic for a Halloween party or a television programme. But not good enough to fool a pathologist, it would seem.'

'Why would he have done that?' I asked.

'That's what we wondered too. Any ideas?'

'Was the scar on his face faked too?' I asked. That had been what convinced Elsie that Vane was who he said he was. The scar that matched the photo on the wall.

Joe frowned and looked at the report again. 'Yes, it's mentioned briefly. Scar close to mouth. Is that the one?'

'He doesn't say that's also a prosthesis?'

'No. That must be real. Having spotted the one fake, I imagine he'd have been on the lookout for another. He just mentions the scar in passing. The real Vane had a scar there, then?'

'Yes,' I said. 'Just for a moment I wondered if we'd all got it wrong . . .'

'So did we. Fake scar, fake writer . . . But the real Vane had a scar by his mouth? Ah well. That's one theory we can cross off. But why would he fake the other scar? Especially if, as you say, he had a genuine one that proved who he was? What was this other scar supposed to be?'

'It was supposed to be the wound inflicted by Tim Macdonald when he'd hit Vane in Thailand years ago . . .'

'So Macdonald had hit Vane when they had their argument and Vane wanted to show that it had been worse than Macdonald had thought?' said Joe. 'What was the point of that? OK, so he scores off Macdonald in some way, but would he really have been that petty? After all that time?'

'Quite possibly,' I said. 'So you're saying the actual scar, underneath all the rubber, was insignificant?'

'The actual scar under the rubber was completely non-existent.'

We looked at each other.

'I had a case once,' said Joe, 'where the wife destroyed her husband's collection of vintage jazz records, having cancelled the insurance on them a couple of days before. She melted them using the kitchen blowtorch that he'd bought her for her birthday. She'd been hoping for diamond earrings, apparently. It's interesting what ideas people come up with once they set their mind to it.'

'True,' I said.

'In summary, then,' said Joe, 'the prime suspect has to be Roy Johnston. He hated Vane's guts and, by the most amazing coincidence, arrived back in England just before Vane was murdered. Motive and opportunity. Since his return he's done everything in his power to remain hidden. We've no evidence he ever travelled to Chichester and don't know what he looks like now well enough to pick him up on CCTV – or not so far. But I can't help feeling he has something to do with this. Well, at least we've cleared that up. Do you fancy another coffee before you go?'

CHAPTER TWENTY-TWO

'So, did you murder him?' asked Lucinda. 'I wouldn't blame you, of course, but we've already had to revise the jacket blurb three times. First we talked about Vane as having mysteriously disappeared. Then we had to talk about him as having unexpectedly reappeared. Now we're changing it again referring to him as the late and much-loved Roger Norton Vane. I don't want to have to come up with new wording to allow for your conviction as his killer. So, if you did it, please let me know now so I can finalise the cover design.'

'I was having dinner with friends,' I said. 'Somebody else killed him. I have no idea who.'

'No chance of finding out who did it before we go to print, I suppose?'

'You'll have to ask the police,' I said.

'But they are at least aware of your deadlines?'

'Totally,' I said.

'All right – just make sure they know that we can't make

any major changes after copy-editing. I'd like an arrest by then or not at all.'

'Just out of interest, where were you when Vane was killed?' I asked.

'Watching another rerun of *Gascoyne*,' she said. 'It's what I do when I can't sleep. It was the episode where the victim drowns in a vat of whisky and isn't found for a year. They get him out perfectly preserved and with a smile on his face.'

'Which book was that?' I asked.

'None of them. It was an original script. Vane's own plots were a bit more subtle – at least when I was editing the books.'

'Any witnesses?'

'Yes, it turns out that the foreman saw the victim entering the still room, followed by his disinherited half-brother. You don't suspect the half-brother because you don't know he's been disinherited at that point.'

'No, I mean witnesses to your being at home.'

'My husband and children,' said Lucinda. 'Good enough?'

'The police say it's all about opportunity,' I said.

'Which is why Vane survived this long,' said Lucinda. 'Laos is a long way to go and none of us knew he was there. Whereas Chichester would be much easier – plenty of cheap off-peak tickets. And a lot of people seem to live round there, anyway. If you do decide you killed him, Ethelred, could you let me know by tomorrow lunchtime, at the very latest?'

* * *

'You're almost becoming a Londoner,' said Elsie, depositing a small cappuccino on the table in front of me.

'Been there, done that,' I said. 'I used to be a Londoner, remember? Before my ex-wife took my flat and most of my money. I'm quite happy in Sussex. No plans to return to the Smoke.'

'Well, you're in London more than Sussex at the moment.'

'I needed to talk to Lucinda,' I said. 'There's the question of how we handle the biography now that Roger Vane is undoubtedly dead. Do we wait for the inquest and maybe even the murder trial? Or do we publish now?'

'And?' asked Elsie.

'Lucinda thought we should rush out an edition now – produce a revised version once the murderer is sentenced. She's happy I write it in prison if the murderer turns out to be me.'

'Two separate editions? We'll need a variation of contract,' said Elsie. 'I'll contact her. I hope you didn't say you'd do the revised version for nothing?'

'We didn't talk about money,' I said. 'Just my possible incarceration.'

'Good boy,' she said. 'Don't confess to the murder, though, without running it past me. It ought to increase the advance by two or three thousand.'

'I didn't do it,' I said.

'OK,' said Elsie. 'Well, if you claim you didn't, then I believe you. I'm just saying there's a couple of grand in it for you if you did.'

'I'd also hoped to talk to Cynthia,' I said, 'but I can't

get hold of her. I assume she's quite upset at her uncle's death . . . in spite of being cut out of the will. Actually, her uncle's death means she'll never get to see any of it.'

'I can't get her either,' said Elsie. 'She's not picking up or returning calls. I phoned her mother too, but she said she hadn't seen her – not worried or anything, just she hadn't been in touch. As for Cynthia being upset, I'm not sure she ever did accept that the murdered man was her uncle, in spite of all the evidence that he was. She held out to the bitter end, bless her.'

'You don't think that she could have been right?' I asked. 'That prosthetic scar was odd . . .'

'Well, you were the one who was always convinced it was him.'

'I'm just saying I don't understand it.'

'I hope you're not planning to tell me all the things you don't understand – I'm a busy woman.'

'It's just that one thing,' I said.

'Is it? Really? Are you sure? Nothing else puzzling your little brain? OK – I agree it is odd – but what was it supposed to prove? It was a weird thing for either a real or fake Vane to have done. It was the other scar – the one that he had before he vanished and that I so cleverly spotted – that proved who he was. He never needed to fake the shoulder injury. Not even Tim knew whether he'd really hurt Roger when he swung that walking stick at him. Clearly he hadn't hurt him at all, but Tim didn't know that. So why waste a fiver on joke-shop rubber?'

'Was it to make Tim feel guilty?' I asked. 'Joe thought it might be.'

'Always possible, because that's what people do. But to what end? They'd split up. Roger had thrown Tim out. It was all so over. So why does it matter if Tim feels a bit guilty? And he showed the scar to you, not to Tim.'

'So, the shoulder scar is irrelevant?' I asked.

'Far from it. I don't know if you ever read detective novels, Ethelred, so stop me if you've heard this before . . . but when something weird happens like somebody faking a shoulder wound, there's usually a reason for it. It's not something people do on impulse, like getting a tattoo with their girlfriend's name misspelt on it. So, whenever he did it, he probably thought he had a good reason for doing it at the time – like the tattoo, actually. If we knew what the reason was . . .'

'Well, we won't, because he's dead,' I pointed out. 'He didn't tell you or me or even Cynthia. In a way it's quite comforting to know that we can all take some of our weirder secrets to the grave.'

Elsie nodded. Perhaps she had a few weird secrets of her own. 'Anyway, Roger proved he was who he said he was in many other ways – also due to my cleverness in devising the questions – he knew all about that Christmas incident, for example. Only he and Cynthia – and Cynthia's mother, of course – could possibly have known about the box and stuff. I'm surprised that Cynthia still had doubts after that, but it convinced me.'

'Me too,' I said. 'You're right. Whatever doubts we had before, it is Vane who was killed in the alleyway – probably because he'd finally convinced somebody else that he was the genuine article. The police think Roy

Johnston is the most likely suspect. He had a long-term grudge against Vane for destroying his career. It would be an amazing coincidence that Johnston just happened to be in England when Vane was killed. So, let's say Johnston phoned him and arranged to meet him in the alleyway. God knows what excuse he gave for that being the meeting place, but Johnston killed him and made his getaway – all without appearing on CCTV, unless Johnston is a master of disguise. It's the perfect crime, except he has to leave the country at some point. He'll be stopped at the airport. Or, if he stays, he'll need to use a credit card and the police will at least know in which part of the country he's hiding out.'

Elsie considered this. 'Except,' she said, 'isn't Johnston in fact a master of disguise, in the sense that he is an actor, used to making himself look and act like somebody else? Wasn't there somebody who was caught on camera leaving the alleyway?'

'He looked much too young.'

'You could really tell that?'

I thought back to the blurred images. What had convinced me of his youth? The way he moved? The leather jacket? If anyone could disguise himself, then Johnston could.

'It didn't look like him to me,' I said.

'I wonder what Cynthia knew that she wasn't telling us?' said Elsie. 'Why was she the last one to disbelieve Vane? There has to be something. She wasn't stupid. She wasn't vindictive. She must have had a reason. I'm going to ask her again why she didn't think it was him. And this time she's going to tell me the truth.'

'I'll see if she's picking up now,' I said. 'It would be helpful to talk to her today, anyway.'

I rang her number. It switched immediately to answerphone. I left another brief message asking her to call as soon as she got it.

It was about fifteen minutes later that the phone rang to let me know it had received a text message. Only it wasn't Cynthia.

'It's Ogilvie,' I said. 'He wants to see me urgently.'

'I thought you saw him the other day?'

'I did. Must be something new. If I get the Tube now I can see him and still make my train to Chichester.'

I took a biscuit. Now I was doing the circuit for the second time, I was aware of the relative attractiveness of the bakery products on offer. I was as happy with these bright circles of hard icing as anything.

'The police seem fairly sure that it was Roy Johnston,' I said.

Ogilvie nodded. 'I'm aware that they have asked people to notify them if he is spotted. The artist's impression made him look like most people that the police are seeking.'

'They're still looking for an up-to-date picture. I think they've tried to age the passport photo a bit, which is all they have.'

'Well, I have no doubt they'll find him. That wasn't, however, what I wanted to talk to you about.'

'I'm happy to help in any way I can.'

'I never doubted it. You see, I'm Roger's executor.'

'Yes, I'd assumed you must be. You clearly drew up the will.'

'It doesn't follow automatically, but I am the only surviving executor – his brother would have been the other – and I'm now doing what all executors do: I'm gathering in information about what Roger owned and starting to pay any funds into our executors' account.'

'There'd be quite a bit there, I suppose.'

'Yes, there is. About a million pounds in his current account.'

'Not bad.'

'As you say. Not bad at all. But we'd expected closer to two million. We'd been in touch with Roger's agent and we know what he'd paid in. Roger had not had the opportunity to spend very much since regaining access to his account.'

'So, a million has gone missing?'

'Yes.'

'And you don't know where?'

Ogilvie pushed a bank statement across to me. 'There it is. That transfer there. One million pounds exactly.'

'Who is it to?'

'We had to check with the bank who owned the account it was transferred to.'

'Which was?'

'Cynthia Vane.'

I took a sip of tea and placed the cup back onto its bone china saucer.

'She was his niece, after all,' I said. 'Maybe he felt guilty about having cut her out of his will?'

'A million pounds worth of guilt? I would have thought

he could have just rewritten the will, leaving the estate to her again if he thought she had been unfairly disinherited. And maybe a small bunch of roses from Dansk Flowers in Upper Street. And let's not forget she was still stating very publicly that he was an imposter. She continued to accuse him of fraud to the very last. Actually, I'm not sure why he should have been in any way inclined to do anything for her under the circumstances. But he seems to have given her a million.'

We looked at each other for a moment. There was an obvious thought, at least if you're a crime writer.

'Blackmail?' I asked.

'Only if she could have proved he was a fake, which he clearly wasn't and she clearly couldn't.'

'No, I mean, what if the real Roger Vane had something to hide? Plenty of people involved in this business seem to have.'

'I hope you don't include me in that?' said Ogilvie.

I paused, then said: 'No, of course not. But it's possible, isn't it? She could have overheard something years before. Maybe she tries this piece of information on him as her final test and when he proves he knows all about it – whatever it is – she decides the best way to get the money to repair her mother's cottage is blackmail. She demands half his accumulated royalties, net of perfectly reasonable agency deductions, to keep quiet.'

I wondered if this was one speculation too far. Ogilvie certainly pulled a face.

'She was his niece,' he said. 'Blackmail would have been in very bad taste.'

'She wasn't a blood relation.'

'You know that?'

'Yes,' I said.

'OK – it's not something the family tended to talk about but it's true. Still, what could she possibly know that he'd want to keep quiet? Roger wasn't easy to embarrass.'

'I suppose it depends how many years you could spend in prison for it,' I said.

'That's true,' he said. 'She's not returning my calls, by the way.'

'Nor mine,' I said. 'Nor Elsie's.'

'Of course, you can go quite a long way on a million pounds,' he said.

The second text came as my train drew into Chichester.

IF YOU'VE GOT A FEW MINUTES TO SPARE AND YOU'RE NOT UP IN THE SMOKE, PLASE DROP IN TO THE STATION. I'VE GOT SOMETHING NEW TO SHOW YOU.

'Take a look at this,' said Joe.

The screen again showed East Street. There was police tape across the road and you could see a police car parked, lights still flashing, to one side. It looked cold. Somehow it always looks cold on CCTV, but this looked really bleak. It seemed to have started raining.

'This is about an hour after the footage you saw before,' said Joe. 'We looked at it up to the point where we knew Roger Vane had been killed, then a few minutes beyond. Then we looked at other cameras nearby. It was only after that that we thought to watch what happened here in the hour or two after the murder.'

We saw a few passers-by gawp at the police cars and then look in the direction of the alleyway, out of our view. They moved on. A man walked by with an umbrella, head down. We saw a policeman appear, go to the car, check something, then return the way he had come. He rubbed his hands briskly as he did so.

'I assume it gets a bit more interesting?' I asked.

'Maybe,' said Joe.

For a long time the street was empty. Then a figure emerged, indistinct at first, walking quickly towards us. The woman headed for the police tape, then stopped and looked around. A policeman appeared and she spoke to him briefly. She nodded at his reply. The policeman left. For a moment she remained where she was, staring towards the alleyway, then glanced up at the camera. She looked very worried indeed. After a while, she went back the way she had come, turning up the collar of her raincoat.

'Any idea who that was?' asked Joe.

'It was Cynthia Vane,' I said.

'We wondered about that,' said Joe. 'Thank you. That was very helpful.'

CHAPTER TWENTY-THREE

I was already on the bus heading for West Wittering when my phone rang yet again. I took it out. The number was not one I recognised. I accepted the call.

'Hello? Hello?' said a voice.

'Hello. Ethelred Tressider here. I can only just hear you.'

'Hello?' it repeated. 'Hello? Hello? Drat the thing. Hello?'

'I can hear you,' I said. 'But only just. Can you hear me?'

'Hello? Hello? Is there anybody there? Oh, maybe if I hold it the other way up . . . Hello?'

'Hello,' I said. 'That seems to be better. Ethelred Tressider here.'

'Is it? Well, why didn't you say so before?'

'I did.'

'Did you? It's the phone. It doesn't seem to work the other way up. Sorry, I don't use it much. But you gave me your number when you came to see me, so I thought I'd try to phone you. I'm not at home so I can't use a proper phone. But these things work anywhere, don't they?'

'They work in most places,' I said.

'Anyway, I thought we might meet up. You said you'd like to.'

'Is that Dr Slide?' I asked.

'Wasn't that what I said?'

'I don't think you did. I didn't recognise the number, but I recognise your voice.'

'The number? Can you do that? See who is phoning you?'

'On most phones. Maybe not on the older ones. I can't remember.'

'This one's quite new – not more than ten or fifteen years old. I bought it at a car boot fair. I was there to buy books but I ended up with a phone. A bit of a bargain, I think – not quite the latest model but it works perfectly well. You'll have to show me how to find out who is phoning you. I don't know how you'd do that. Anyway, this isn't sorting out when we're going to meet.'

'I'm not sure I'm free this week,' I said. 'Maybe . . .'

'This is important,' he said. 'I need you to explain to the police that I didn't kill Roger Vane.'

'Have they accused you of doing it?'

'Not to my knowledge. The point is that you need to prevent any such thing from happening.'

'I really have no influence with the police. Why don't you go and visit them yourself?'

'Because I don't want to do that. I want you to do it. I'll see you at ten tomorrow. Ten o'clock on the dot. Maison Blanc in South Street. You're not busy, are you?

There's only that book you're writing. I'm sure it will wait a day or two.'

'No,' I said. 'I'm not busy.'

I had just ordered my second cup of coffee when Dr Jonathan Slide came through the door. He was wearing what I took to be the holiday version of his schoolmaster's tweed jacket and flannels. He had on a white linen jacket and an old, shapeless panama hat with a blue and red band. He wore, over a crumpled white shirt, an orange and yellow tie. His trousers were khaki drill, surprisingly with very sharp creases down the front. His shoes were leather loafers. He carried a stick of a practical rather than decorative nature. There was in fact no element of his dress that you could not have bought in a menswear shop in Chichester fifty years before. I wondered if he possessed a pair of jeans. Probably not, though they too had been available in Chichester for over fifty years.

He looked around vaguely and had started, with some confidence, to approach an elderly balding gentleman sitting alone on the far side of the cafe, when he suddenly seemed to spot me and change direction.

'Ethelred Tressider!' he said, as if expecting to be congratulated on this feat of memory. 'You're early. We agreed ten-thirty.'

'You said ten,' I told him. 'And it's a little after ten-thirty now. But it's not a problem that you've been held up. I know the buses don't always arrive on time.'

'Ours do,' he said indignantly. 'I've no idea what the West Wittering buses are like, but ours are very punctual in Selsey. If yours aren't, you should do something about it, not sit there, drinking coffee all morning and complaining.'

'They're fine,' I said. 'The Witterings bus service is very good. Anyway, I came in by car today.'

'Is that why you arrived half an hour early? Don't expect me to pay for all the coffees that you've been drinking before I arrived.'

'The coffees are on me,' I said.

'Are they? All right. I'll have one of those frothy things with chocolate on them. A large one.'

The waitress placed my flat white on the table and I ordered a cappuccino for Dr Slide.

'So,' he said. 'What have the police told you?'

I looked at our neighbours on both sides, intent on their own conversations. It seemed unlikely that they would pay us much attention or that it would matter if they did.

'It's all in the papers, anyway,' I said, 'but they are looking for a man called Roy Johnston.'

'He plays Gascoyne in the television programmes, doesn't he?'

'Well done,' I said, genuinely impressed. 'He did, in the first series. But not many people seem to remember him. Another actor took over from him for series two.'

'Oh, so there was a second series, was there? I only watched the first one.'

I could understand that. I could see Slide anxiously watching the first series, waiting for his namesake to appear and humiliate him, only to discover that the production company's lawyers had advised very much against it. Then, relieved or disappointed, he would have lost interest.

'Yes, there was a second series,' I said. 'There have been about fifteen, I think.'

'Didn't know that. Fifteen? Why do they think it's him?'

'Roy Johnston was fired from the series. Roger dumped him as a boyfriend. His career was wrecked. Then, having stayed away for years as far as we know, he suddenly arrived in England shortly before Roger was killed. And before he was killed Roger received a call from an unidentified mobile. He seems to have been lured by the caller to the alleyway in which he was murdered. So the assumption is that he knew the person concerned. Finally, Johnston has now vanished – no trace of him.'

'It sounds as if it was Johnston, then,' said Slide dismissively. 'Can you get food here?' He was looking over at the serving counter, where the pastries were displayed.

'Would you like a croissant or something with the coffee?' I asked.

'That's kind of you. Yes, a chocolate one would be nice. Actually, you may as well ask her to bring me two while she's doing it. Just in case I'm still hungry after the first one.'

I caught the waitress's eye and ordered two pains au chocolat.

'But why do you think that the police would suspect you?' I asked. 'You were in Selsey, I assume, and have witnesses to prove it.'

Slide took a sip of coffee. 'Ah . . .' he said. 'No, not exactly. I was in Chichester that evening, as it happens. At a bar I know. I'm sure that you and Ogilvie wouldn't have mentioned anything to the police about my being here. Still, it might be awkward if either of you had.'

'But you have witnesses?' I repeated.

'For some of the time. Indeed, for a great deal of the time. But I may have gone to another club later on . . . Where I'm not known so well. The first place was a bit quiet. Not like it used to be. Ah, those must be my pains au chocolat!'

For a couple of minutes he sat, silently devouring the pastries.

'Not bad, these. You should have had one yourself,' he said.

'I had breakfast earlier,' I said.

'So did I. Now this phone thing – how can I tell who is phoning me?' He produced a phone of a type that I had not come across for ten years and handed it to me.

'Well, you'll see the number come up on the screen here,' I said.

'And their name?'

'Only if you've entered it in your contacts list.'

'Where would I find that?'

I brought up the contacts list. It was empty. 'Have you never put any contacts into the list? That makes it easier to phone them.'

'Didn't know you could. I thought you just dialled the number. So you can see the number of whoever is phoning you?'

'Yes. Haven't you noticed them come up?'

'I don't get many calls. Actually, I don't think I've ever had any calls. Not on this. I do on the other phone, of course. The proper one at home.'

I flicked through the menu. 'No,' I said. 'It doesn't look as if anyone has ever phoned you on this.'

'You can tell that?'

'Yes, there's a list of incoming calls. And outgoing ones.' I switched to the records of calls made. 'See, you made a call a couple of days ago. Actually a couple of calls to the same number.'

'Can you tell who it's to?'

'No, just the number.'

He sniffed. 'So, not so clever after all, then. As it happens, it was the cab company I sometimes use down here.' He picked up the last corner of his pastry, popped it in his mouth and chewed thoughtfully.

'Do you want me to put it in your contact list? That might be useful for you. What's the name of the company?'

'Thank you,' he said abruptly. 'But that won't be necessary. I'll have that back if you've finished playing with it.'

I passed the phone across the table.

'Where was Roger Vane killed?' he asked as he stuffed it in his pocket.

'In an alleyway, just off East Street. Why, were you close by?'

'East Street? Not close, exactly. Not very close, anyway.' He was thoughtful, then he said: 'Vane told me once he'd lost his virginity in an alleyway just off East Street.'

'Is that true?'

'How would I know? I wasn't there. It sounds unlikely. But it's perfectly possible. People lose their virginity in all sorts of places. He came down to Sussex with me more

211

than once, so he'd been to Chichester before. He knew it very well.'

'So, what you're saying is that the killer might be the person he lost his virginity to? Is that it?'

'Why would you think that?'

'Because the alleyway would have been a strange place to meet somebody at that or any other time. But if it had some meaning for the two of them . . .'

'Then it would probably have been one of the other boys who had travelled down with me. Or somebody he'd picked up. One or the other. Not me – I'd remember if it was.'

'Ogilvie was close by that evening,' I said. 'The night that Roger Vane was killed, he was driving back to London from his constituency.'

'Oh, I don't think it would have been him all those years ago. A very unlikely sexual partner for Vane, all things considered. Girls were his problem. No end of girls round him. His father had to pay one off – messy business.'

'But would he have heard the story?'

'Oh yes, Vane boasted of it all the time. I think most of the school knew. However, it does sound as if the killer was this actor fellow. So, if the police ask you, there's no need for you to mention I was in Chichester. Or even that I was in Selsey. What I told you was in complete confidence. One gentleman to another. Not for the biography. Not for the police. Ogilvie knows, but I can trust him totally.'

'I can't promise anything,' I said. 'Of course, not including it in my biography is within my power. But I can't withhold anything from the police, if they ask me, much though I'd like to help you.'

'So you'd like to help me?'

It was difficult under the circumstances to retract my casually given assurance.

'If I can,' I said cautiously.

He patted me on the arm. 'Thank you. Then I'm sure you'll find a way of keeping it quiet. I'm not asking you to do anything illegal, but nobody likes being a horrid little sneak, do they?'

'No,' I said.

'Excellent. I think I'll have just one more of those delicious pains au chocolat, then I'll leave you to pay the bill and I'll get back to Selsey if you'll excuse me. I don't want to miss lunch.'

CHAPTER TWENTY-FOUR

'I'm sorry,' I said. 'I don't think I've been much help.'

I had spent two hours at the police station, going through CCTV footage with Joe. We'd looked at the records of one camera after another – different streets, different passers-by, but all with the same lonely, cold midnight air to them.

'On the contrary,' said Joe. 'You've been able to rule one or two people out. Let's take another look at that one close to the Cross.'

He brought up the relevant camera and we watched again. A tallish man in an overcoat and hat went past, collar up, head down.

'It could be Davies,' I said. 'It's not easy to tell, especially when you can see so little of the face.'

'If so, he was about five minutes away from the alleyway at about the right time. He could have cut through one of the side streets . . . But we know that isn't Ogilvie, because this is . . .'

This time the screen showed a car park. There were only two or three cars visible, but somebody got out of one of them and took out his phone. For a while he seemed intent on his call. Then he got back in the car and drove slowly away.

'Yes,' I said. 'That's Ogilvie.'

'Dressed completely differently from our man seen at the Cross. And we've traced the car to a hire company. He normally drives a Jag apparently. Very clever him feeding you the registration details of a car he knew he wasn't using.'

'Yes,' I said.

'Here are the call records from Vane's phone,' said Joe. 'Quite a few calls that day. Any numbers you recognise?'

'That's my number,' I said. 'He phoned me during the morning to ask if he could stay with me.'

'The next one's his lawyer – Ogilvie. We googled the number. Vane phoned him at his office.'

'Yes, Ogilvie said.'

'And he told both of you there'd been an attempt on his life?' asked Joe.

'That's what he led me to believe. Ogilvie said it was more of a threat than an actual attempt. He didn't tell either of us exactly what had happened. He liked to hold things back for a dramatic reveal at the right moment – a crime writer to the bitter end.'

'OK – then there's another number here that we can't trace at all. Two calls received by Vane – one in the morning. One about 11.00 that evening – the last call, in fact, before he died.'

'So that's the one inviting him to a rendezvous in the alleyway?' I asked.

'By the look of it. Then there's this one – received around

midnight and corresponding to the time of the call made by Ogilvie from the car park.'

'Suggesting Ogilvie didn't know he was dead?'

'Or that's what he'd like us to believe,' said Joe. 'Don't forget that Ogilvie tried to lead us up the garden path with that number plate thing. So a call to a dead man that he knew would not be answered . . . That would be clever, wouldn't it? But a more likely sequence of events is this. Vane has asked to see him. Around midnight he passes by Chichester. He stops to make a call – perhaps to check which hotel Vane is staying in. He gets no reply. He is not best pleased, but he simply carries on to London. Later he hears Vane has been killed at about the time he was passing through. He knows we'll be looking at CCTV. He gives you the number of his car, which is safe in the garage in London, or wherever, and hopes we won't spot him in the car park.'

'Probably,' I said.

'So, the big question is this: is this mobile number that appears twice Johnston's?'

'I don't know. It could be.'

'In that case – and this has been worrying me for a while – how did he get Vane's number? When Johnston knew Vane twenty-odd years before, mobile phones scarcely existed. Even if Vane had a mobile then, it's unlikely he would have still had the same number now. So, it's improbable that Johnston simply had the number. In which case, who gave it to him? Nobody has admitted to ever seeing the man, let alone giving him Vane's phone number.'

I looked again at the digits on the paper. They were a bit familiar. I checked my own phone.

'You're right,' I said pointing to it. 'It's not Johnston. It's Dr Jonathan Slide. He's staying down here. And he had the number because Ogilvie gave it to him.'

The words 'horrid little sneak' crossed my mind, but if Dr Slide wished me to play fair with him, then he might have told me that he phoned the deceased shortly before he was coshed to death in an alleyway. It was not a completely irrelevant fact.

'Two calls from Slide, then. That's the old boy that Vane wrote about in his books?'

'Yes,' I said. 'Dr Slide was in fact in a bar in Chichester that evening. He also told me that Vane had lost his virginity in an alleyway in Chichester.'

'And that had some connection with the murder?'

'He implied it might.'

'But he had no evidence of that?'

'No,' I said.

'Odd thing to say, then.'

'He's an odd man.'

'So, Slide had Vane's number. He phoned him in the morning – is that the death threat? Then he arranged to meet Vane that evening . . .'

'If it was a death threat, why would Vane agree to meet him in a dark alleyway just before midnight?' I asked.

'Because Vane wasn't frightened of him?'

'He was concerned enough to leave London at short notice,' I said.

'And go to Sussex, where he knew Slide was? That does seem to be taking unnecessary risks.'

I tried to remember what Vane had told me. Somebody had tried to kill him, so he had to come down to Sussex.

But had he specifically said he was running scared? He said he needed to do something straight away. Something that wouldn't wait. Then the thought occurred to me: had Vane lured Slide to the alleyway rather than the other way round?

'It sounds as if we should speak to Dr Slide sooner rather than later,' said Joe.

'You've got his mobile number,' I said. 'If you can't hear him properly, just tell him to turn the phone the other way up and speak into the mouthpiece.'

'You haven't heard from Vane's niece, Cynthia, I suppose?' said Joe.

'No,' I said.

'Well, I'm sure we'll track her down too. She'd obviously followed him to Sussex. We think she may have been spying on him before that.'

'Really?'

'One of Vane's neighbours reported a small, plump woman acting suspiciously outside Vane's flat – she sat around in the square gardens for a long time, then, as soon as Vane left, she let herself into the building. Very unsubtle. She later left carrying what appeared to be a bag of CDs.'

'That was my agent,' I said. 'She has a key.'

'Well, I hope she doesn't plan further visits until we've finished searching the flat. It's pretty obvious to the meanest intelligence that that wouldn't be advisable, of course . . .'

'I'd better give her a call and tell her,' I said.

CHAPTER TWENTY-FIVE

Elsie

'So, what next?' Tim asked.

'You search the bedroom, I'll take the living room,' I said. 'This place has to be packed with clues.'

My phone rang. I checked it. It was Ethelred. I ignored it. There are some things that you know instinctively will wait an hour or two. I switched the phone to silent, because Ethelred can sometimes be quite irritating if you don't respond and will phone you every few minutes until you do.

'I'm not sure we should be here,' said Tim. 'The policeman said not to. And technically it isn't mine until probate has been obtained.'

'It's your home, Tim,' I assured him. 'You have every right to be here and, as your agent, I have fifteen per cent of the same right. Plus VAT where applicable.'

We looked round the room.

'Who put that hideous picture there?' asked Tim, pointing to Roger Vane in his uncredited TV role.

'I've no idea,' I said. 'I'd assumed you had.'

'Me? Put a picture of that dreadful man up on the wall? You must be joking.'

'OK, it wasn't you, then. So Roger must have done it. What was there before?'

'One of me, of course. Collecting an award. Best-illustrated children's book.'

Fair enough. Roger Vane had returned to the flat to discover a photo of his former lover and confessed assailant beaming down from the wall, tacky statuette in hand, and had substituted one of himself. I might have done the same.

'We'll bin it,' I said. 'The picture of you can't have gone far.'

'If he's thrown it away, I'll kill him,' said Tim.

'When the police question you . . .' I said.

'Yes, don't worry. I'll be careful what I say. I bore him no ill will. His death came as a complete shock.'

'Keep repeating that.' I said. 'You can write the book in prison. Loads of people do. But you'd be more comfortable writing it here. Now the flat is legally yours . . . or will be very shortly . . . it would be a shame to write anywhere else. You no longer get all the cash, of course, but the flat at least is left completely to you.'

'Why did he give Cynthia that money?' asked Tim. 'Just before he died. It's so unfair.'

'In the sense that you'd split up with Roger Vane and had done your best to kill him, but you still feel entitled to a hundred per cent of his stuff?'

'Put like that . . .'

'Of course, if the payment was in some way fraudulent, you'd have a case for getting it back.'

'Yes,' he said, brightening up. 'I would.'

Eventually we agreed that I'd take the bedroom while he took the sitting room and hunted for his awards picture. That was fine by me. I knew my way round the wardrobe quite well already.

Actually, the wardrobe was fairly empty. The section I'd hidden in before had a number of suits, which, now I had time to consider them properly, were mainly old ones, dating back to his pre-disappearance days. Men's suits have changed surprisingly little over the past twenty years – only the odd detail gave them away. There were one or two Savile Row ones – worth keeping. One or two from various chain stores. An old rowing blazer with green piping and a red dragon on the pocket. A sports jacket. Trousers to match. Jeans. A leather jacket. Some sweaters. There was also a new, blue overcoat. On the shelves were a variety of shirts, including about six new ones from M&S, four still in their wrappers. Pants and socks – all new as far as I could see, also M&S. In the other half of the wardrobe there were several bulging black plastic sacks. Otherwise it was empty. A work in progress, one might say.

I called Tim in.

'Yes,' he said. 'I never touched Roger's half of the wardrobe. I had this thing that, if I threw anything out, he might suddenly come back and ask where all his clothes were. So, I just made do with my half. Occasionally I'd get things out and brush them or shake them or refold them. I have to say that I think it's a bit much I looked after his things so nicely and he just dumps mine in plastic bags.'

'So Roger's half is much as it was?'

'I don't recognise those shirts. Oh, and he seems to have thrown out all his old socks and underwear. I can't quite see why. They were scarcely out of fashion.'

'So, there's the old stuff he had before you went to Thailand and new stuff he's bought since his return?'

'Yes,' said Tim. 'That seems to cover it. One or the other.'

'Don't you think that's odd?'

'No,' said Tim. 'Do you?'

'Let's go back to the living room,' I said.

Tim had assembled one or two of his own things on the floor, ready to take them back to my flat. The picture of Roger had, I noticed, been replaced by one of himself.

'So, any sign of a passport or driving licence?' I asked.

'Not here. He might have taken them to Chichester with him.'

'Yes, he might.'

I wandered round the room, checking bookshelves, opening drawers.

'I've done all that,' said Tim.

'So, in that case, you'll finally have to agree it's odd?'

'What is?'

'Think of his wardrobe – clothes from before he left, clothes from after he got back.'

'And?'

'He's been twenty years in Laos. Did he buy nothing there? I went to Vietnam for a couple of weeks. Came back with my suitcase stuffed with clothes – all well made, cheap, classy. Dresses. Jackets. Skirts. Trousers, made to measure.

Shoes made to measure. It's one of the things you do there – clothes shopping. Tailors touting for business all over. Fake designer stuff everywhere. Laos ought to be much the same. Even if it's a pale shadow of the shops in Hội An, you'd have at least expected a few shirts, wouldn't you?'

'I suppose so. Maybe he was just travelling light.'

'Why would he do that if he was coming back here to live?'

'I don't know.'

'And then no passport with any Lao visas, no Lao driving licence, no paperback with a price in Lao dollars or Baht or Dong or whatever they have. No airport taxi receipts in a strange script? No plastic bags with the name of some Lao department store on the side. No Lao loose change in his bedside table. I've checked. In short, nothing – absolutely nothing – to suggest Roger Vane ever went to Laos.'

'So, where was he all that time?'

'I don't know. But I wonder if Cynthia knows and whether what she knew was worth a million pounds.'

'To what do I owe this honour, Elsie?' asked George.

'I just thought I'd drop by. Chew the fat. Hang out. It's been a while.'

'No it hasn't. Always delighted to see you, of course, but this isn't a casual chat.'

'You are as astute as ever, George.'

'I detected no trace of sarcasm at all in that last remark. Now I'm really worried. What do you want?'

'It's about Roger Norton Vane,' I said. 'You represent him. You are his agent.'

'I now represent his estate,' said George. 'Much preferable in many ways to representing a living author.'

'Was he still giving you grief over missing royalties?'

'No. We seemed to have resolved that one. He came round, we went through the figures. He saw that it all added up. He was annoyed I'd paid some tax he thought we could have avoided, but you can't hold off the Revenue for twenty years, assuring them that you'll put in a tax return as soon as your client shows up again.'

'No,' I said.

'His only concern was that I should chase up some foreign royalties that were due. One or two publishers had taken liberties with our cash flow. He said he needed the money. I couldn't quite see it myself – he had a couple of million clear. Still, I said I'd get in anything that was owing – it probably amounted to ten or fifteen thousand – not peanuts but less than he thought. He didn't seem to realise – or maybe I should say didn't seem to remember – how the royalty system works. A publisher may account for sales for a period from March to October but that doesn't mean you get paid for that period on November the first. Far from it.'

'Tell me about it,' I said. 'Still, once an author has seen their first royalty statement they work it all out. They go back and read their contracts and are sadder but wiser.'

'True. But he'd apparently forgotten it all during his stay in the jungle. So I explained it all over again. All he wanted, he said when I'd finished, was as much as I could get as fast as I could get it. I could see he'd want everything he was owed, but I couldn't see why a week or two made that much difference to him. Unless there was some demand on his finances I knew nothing about.'

'Was he also pushing you to get an advance on his next book?'

'Not at all. If he needed money it would have been an obvious source of funds, but he never suggested that.'

'Had he written anything in his time in Laos?'

'Not that he ever mentioned.'

'Did he say that he had plans for future books?'

'Only in the most general way.'

'So, what's he been doing for the past twenty years, George?'

'Teaching English. Copy-writing. Living the dream.'

'He just chucked in writing books and went to eat lotus flowers in Laos?'

'That's the story.'

'For twenty years? Never a letter home?'

'Not even to check on his royalty statements.'

'It doesn't ring true.'

'It's what he told me. Look, he had a decent income from the television series and from the books he'd already written. He knew the money would be waiting for him when he wanted it. He had found fame. Maybe, in short, he felt he'd achieved what he set out to achieve. Maybe he decided he didn't want to write any more. Maybe he simply liked it out there. From where I'm sitting it looks pretty good.'

I looked at him. 'Where were you sitting, just out of interest, the night he was killed?'

'At home. We had a few friends round to dinner. They

left just before midnight. Roger was killed around 11.30, I think?'

'Apparently.'

'There you are, then. Whatever minor disagreements Roger and I might have had, we had resolved them. And, more to the point, I have a watertight alibi.'

'Good for you, George. You're probably one of the few people who does.'

CHAPTER TWENTY-SIX

'You are ignoring,' said Elsie, 'the immense value of what I have discovered.'

'There is,' I said, 'the small question of legality. The police said, stay out of Roger's flat. That meant don't go in it and, incidentally, don't remove stuff that you take a fancy to.'

'Yes, but there is also the large question of what I found out. I don't think Roger Vane went anywhere near Laos.'

'He went to Thailand. That's undisputed. And it's pretty close.'

'You know what I mean, Ethelred. I think, after Thailand, he went somewhere else entirely. Have the police found any trace of his stay in Vientiane?'

'He was there under a false name, which we don't yet know,' I said.

'In other words, they haven't.'

'No. But they may.'

'Or they may not.'

'You can't be certain,' I said.

'I can be more certain than you can.'

Conversations like this with Elsie could, I knew, go on for some time.

'What's your theory, then?' I asked.

'You said Slide was recruiting for MI6. What if he recruited Vane? What if Vane's disappearance twenty years ago was actually organised by MI6 – that they needed him to vanish?'

'Why would they need that?'

'All right – maybe that's not what happened. I do think that Cynthia knows what he's been doing, though.'

'Hence the giant and unexplained payout?'

'Hence the giant and unexplained payout. One million smackeroos. And Vane was desperately trying to get his hands on more cash, so maybe she was still squeezing him.'

'I suppose she hasn't returned your call?' I asked.

'No. I tried her mother again – she was insistent that she hadn't seen her. Do you think she could be in danger?' Elsie asked. 'I mean, if she knows this thing, whatever it is.'

'Roger Vane had received some sort of threat,' I said. 'Cynthia hadn't, as far as we know. The fact that she pitched up right at the murder scene is odd and so is the fact she's not returning calls. But there could be all sorts of reasons why she doesn't want to be contacted.'

'And the police are looking for her?'

'Yes. Also Roy Johnston. And the hen party. And the man in the leather jacket.'

'Have they found any of them?' she asked.

'Roy Johnston is still lying low somewhere. But the hen party was less concerned about not being noticed. It was simply a matter of asking round the various bars and clubs until somebody recognised them. To cut a long story short, none of the girls saw anything. But they were so off their faces that most didn't even remember going down that alleyway. A couple of them actually said they couldn't have gone that way because they'd never go down it after dark – there have been muggings there before.'

'Leather Jacket?'

'They're still working on him. They tried digitally enhancing the best shot of him, but it was nobody I recognised. Still, as a witness he was closer to the action than anyone and not obviously drunk. He may have seen something that the girls missed. But the prime suspect in my view remains Dr Jonathan Slide. He was at a bar in the centre of Chichester. The barman remembers him making a call at one point, but didn't overhear what he said. He doesn't recall what time Slide left. Maybe as early as eleven-thirty – he wasn't paying much attention.'

'Then Slide left in time to kill Roger?'

'Yes,' I said. 'Probably.'

'And we know that Jonathan Slide phoned Roger . . . ?' asked Elsie.

'Yes. Twice that day. Probably including at least one death threat.'

'So, in short, Slide could have lured him to the alleyway and killed him. But why? We know Roger treated him badly, but that was years before.'

'There's another possibility,' I said. 'It may be that Roger

Vane arranged the meeting in the alleyway so that he could kill Slide.'

'And it all went very wrong?'

'It's possible. It would at least explain why Roger Vane seems to have willingly gone to his death with a man who had already threatened to kill him.'

'So, if they had both been working for MI6 . . .'

I shook my head. 'I don't think so. But I admit, if we knew what he had been doing for the past twenty years, then it might be clearer why Roger Norton Vane left the mean streets of London, only to be murdered in an alleyway in the middle of the remarkably safe and law-abiding city of Chichester.'

'So, what next?' asked Elsie. 'It feels like a bit of a dead end.'

'On the contrary,' I said, 'while you've been blundering around in Vane's old flat, I have been going back through my notes.'

'And?'

'And I'm going to see Ogilvie and Davies again.'

'So that they can patronise you and pull the wool over your eyes?'

'No,' I said. 'Not this time. This time will be slightly different.'

CHAPTER TWENTY-SEVEN

There were no biscuits. No coffee was on offer. Ogilvie looked at his watch pointedly.

'I'm afraid I'm a little busy at present, Ethelred. I can spare you five minutes, then I really will have to ask you to leave. I have an important client coming here at eleven and I'll need you out of the office by then.'

'As you wish. I shall leave whenever you choose. You will only have to tell me when to go.'

Ogilvie looked at me suspiciously. 'So, what is it? Some missing detail from the biography?'

'Let me put my cards on the table,' I said. 'You've lied to me, Mr Ogilvie. You've also treated me as an idiot. I'm used to that, of course. My agent does it all the time. But lying to me was a mistake. I have relatively few skills that are of much use to anyone, but as a crime writer I do know how to spot inconsistencies – how to make connections. That's why it wasn't a good idea to assume that I wouldn't find out what was going on.'

'As I said, Ethelred, I don't have a lot of time. And since you have reminded me that you are a crime writer, let me remind you that I am a lawyer. If you have come here to slander me, or anyone else, then I would advise caution. I would advise you not to suggest anyone has been lying.'

'Thank you. That's kind of you. Let us begin with your most recent lie, then. You told me you hadn't been in Chichester the night that Vane was killed.'

'I told you that Roger Vane had asked me to go there. I don't think I said whether I had complied or not. It didn't seem especially relevant. If you chose to interpret my silence as meaning I didn't go, that is scarcely my fault. I was entirely truthful.'

'You have a strange idea of what constitutes the truth. An old friend is murdered and you think it's irrelevant that you were in the same town at the same time? I don't think so, do you? Nor do I think, when you gave me that registration number to pass to the police, that you had forgotten you were driving another car entirely. But, to cut to the chase, you were caught on CCTV in a car park in the centre of Chichester and you were making a phone call. The police have checked Roger Vane's phone records and I know that a call was made, at about that time, from your phone to his.'

'You're right, Ethelred,' said Ogilvie, with an unexpected display of contrition. 'It was very wrong of me to attempt to mislead you. I apologise unreservedly. Roger had told me he was going to Chichester and wanted to meet up. So, I stopped off in Chichester and phoned him to check which hotel he was in – that's the truth, I swear. I got no response, so I drove on to London. When I heard that Roger had been killed, I was naturally reluctant to say more than I had to. Now, perhaps, having cleared that up . . .'

'It wasn't wrong to mislead me,' I said. 'It was stupid. As you say, the CCTV just shows you stopping and making a call. But your lying made me go back and look at my notes again. All the way through our various discussions I felt you were covering something up – something from your past and Roger's – something that was not to your credit. Then I saw the CCTV of you . . . and the car. Nice motor, as they say. But apparently you usually drive a Jaguar. That was when it clicked. You've always liked driving, haven't you?'

I was watching his face very carefully. Ogilvie's mouth was hanging open slightly, but he had no idea he was doing it.

His phone rang. Without taking his eyes off me he picked it up. 'Yes?' he said.

'Mr Somerville is here,' I heard his secretary say.

'Tell him to wait,' said Ogilvie. 'No, I don't know how long I'll be.' He put the phone down.

'I'll go now if you wish,' I offered. 'You don't have to answer the question.'

'I've really no idea what you're talking about,' he replied.

'Yes, you do,' I said. 'You also lied, in a way, about that too. You told me not to believe the story that Roger Vane had stolen a car when he was at school. You went out of your way to assure me that it was probably untrue and that I'd get sued if I used it. But you know the story as well as any other living person, don't you? Because you were Roger

235

Vane's accomplice. You helped him steal the car. You were also arrested.'

'What if I did? It was a very long time ago.'

'It didn't bother Roger. It might not bother most people. But they are not standing for parliament. They are not trying to assure the voters of their commitment to law and order. Of course, you got away with it at the time, but only because the school pulled rank on your behalf and prevented it ever going to court. The story wouldn't have been about a youthful indiscretion, but about using rank and privilege to cover it all up. I would imagine your opponents at the next election would have great fun with that. As you say, the biggest majority can just evaporate if you're not careful.'

'How are you so certain?'

'I wasn't. I just said the words slowly and watched your reaction as I did it. If I can give you further advice, Mr Ogilvie, it's that you don't have a great future as a poker player.'

'It doesn't mean I killed Roger Vane,' said Ogilvie.

'It gives you a very strong motive. You couldn't be sure what Roger would tell me to put in the biography and you could scarcely sue any of us if we accused you of car theft, because it would have been true. So long as nobody was sure that it really was Roger Vane, you could hope that the person concerned had no personal knowledge of the crime. Once it was clear it really was Roger, you knew you had to act. Because you knew he was just the sort of person who would enjoy watching people squirm. To save your political career, he had to be put out of the way. So, knowing Vane was in Chichester you arranged to meet him. You chose a place that you knew had some associations for him, because he boasted of losing his virginity there – something only a few people would have known . . .'

'Oh, hold on!' said Ogilvie. 'I admit that it was me with Vane when he stole the car. But as for the rest of it – that's madness. Nothing remotely like that happened. Anyway, I was scarcely the only one who was worried what Vane might say about them.'

'Who else?' I asked. 'It might help if you told me.'

'Is that your price?' asked Ogilvie incredulously. 'I sneak on somebody else and you let me off?'

I shook my head. 'No, that's not my price. But if there was somebody with a better motive, then it can hardly hurt your cause to tell me. I notice that you were quite happy before to reveal that Dr Slide was in Selsey in the hope that that would take some of the pressure off you. So, tell me, who else had a better motive?'

Ogilvie's phone rang again. He ignored it.

'Very well.' Ogilvie licked his bottom lip. 'Davies has much more cause to worry than I do. You said Vane lost his virginity in an alleyway in Chichester?'

'That was with Davies?'

'You bet. Again, it might have amused Vane to tell the story but Davies might have felt otherwise . . . Now, there's a motive.'

I nodded. Davies' love of privacy was, as I have said, only too well known. No story about him was allowed out into the world until it had been meticulously groomed by his PR team. With the best will in the world, this would be a difficult one to groom.

'He has an alibi for that evening,' I said. 'He was in his office. He said that the CCTV cameras would show that he never left the building.'

'You mean the CCTV in reception?' asked Ogilvie. 'There's no CCTV for his private entrance. There's a lift straight down to his parking space.'

'Thank you,' I said, making a note in my book. 'That's very helpful. I think you should see Mr Somerville now. He's been waiting out there for some time.'

'Ethelred, you won't repeat anything I've told you? I mean it was in confidence . . .'

'I'd like to be able to do that for you,' I said. 'As to whether I can . . . the one thing I'm not going to do is to lie to you, Mr Ogilvie. It really doesn't pay.'

CHAPTER TWENTY-EIGHT

'I'm afraid,' said Lord Davies' secretary, 'that Lord Davies is very busy at the moment. It may be some time – some weeks, in fact – before he can see you. But if you email me and let me know what it is you wish to discuss, then I'll let you have his response as soon as I can.'

I adjusted the handset while I consulted the sheet of paper in front of me. 'You might like to quote this to him,' I said. I read the words in front of me.

'I can't possibly say that to him,' she said.

'Try it,' I said. 'Then ask whether he'll see me.'

There was a long, slow intake of breath. I heard her put the phone down and her footsteps as she walked to Davies' office. I didn't hear exactly what happened next but when she picked up the phone there was a puzzled tone in her voice.

'He can fit you in at four-thirty,' she said. 'It was difficult to find you a slot, but he says he'll be happy to discuss it then.'

'Tell him I'll be there at three,' I said. 'Three on the dot. If he has another meeting then, tell him to cancel it.'

'I don't think—' she began. I didn't hear the rest because I had hung up.

At three o'clock I was ushered, with equal measures of suspicion and respect, into Lord Davies' office. He waited until the door had closed before he spoke to me.

'Well, Mr Tressider, you have a nerve, I must say. After all the help I've given you with your damned book, you dare to come in here and try to blackmail me. Just what I'd expect from your sort. No manners, no decency.'

'Thank you for agreeing to see me, Lord Davies,' I replied. 'It's good of you. I know that you have a busy schedule and I'm grateful to you for fitting me in in this way. I'll try not to take up more of your time than I have to.'

Davies laughed. 'All right. We'll do it your way. It's an enormous pleasure to see you, Ethelred. To what do I owe this honour?'

'I was hoping I could get you to grass up your mates,' I said. 'They have already grassed you up, as I shall relate.'

The smile left his face. 'Go on,' he said.

'First, however, I need to caution you that anything you say may be taken down and used in Roger Norton Vane's forthcoming biography. Oh, and I'd prefer the truth. I've had enough lies to last me some time. In your case you wanted me to tell the police that they should examine the CCTV footage of reception to see when you came and went. Did you think I was stupid?'

'To be perfectly frank, yes, I did. Forgive me, Mr

Tressider. When you have made a lot of money yourself – and I have made a great deal of money – you tend to judge others according to how much money they've made. You have clearly made very little. I may have judged you harshly as a result.'

'That's fine,' I said. 'I've probably learnt more because you and your friends looked down on me than I would have done if you had treated me as an equal. I know, for example, that you had sex with Roger Norton Vane in an alleyway in Chichester – some years ago, admittedly, but it does seem to be the one he was killed in.'

'Badly lit alleyways are useful for all sorts of things. Are you suggesting that there is any connection between the two you mention?'

'That would be for the police to decide. You are aware, however, that I know of another connection between you and Vane.'

'Why are you so sure?'

'Because you agreed to see me. Had the lines meant nothing to you, you would have told your secretary to tell me to get lost. But I'd suspected for some time. The editor and salesman of Roger Vane's pornographic poem had to be a close friend. There were only a few to choose from. Your ability as a businessman, which as you imply is considerable, made you an obvious choice. I thought there were some nice lines in it, by the way, though the one I quoted definitely plagiarises the Earl of Rochester's satire on Charles the Second. In Charles's case the comparison was with his sceptre – impressive if true.'

'It wasn't illegal.'

'If you say so. In that case, you won't object to its inclusion in the biography. Copyright probably prevents my quoting actual lines – if, as I suspect, it was co-authored – but I can paraphrase. It sheds an interesting light on your early career.'

'Do you think I really care?'

'Yes, I do, bearing in mind how carefully you manage what gets into the press and what doesn't. It will probably amuse a lot of people.'

'Have you told anyone else about this?'

'Not yet.'

'How much do you want?'

'Sorry?'

'How much are you asking for to keep quiet? As long as the sum you mention is reasonable, then I shall ensure it is transferred into your bank account this afternoon. Or I can write a cheque now, if you prefer.'

'I knew your opinion of me was not high. Had I realised it was so low, I would have given some thought to how much I might ask for. A hundred thousand? Two hundred thousand? More? I think I saw that your wealth is measured in billions, so you'd hardly notice the odd quarter of a million. A missed opportunity for me but a small financial saving for you.'

'So what do you want then?'

'As I say, I want you to be my grass. I need information on Dr Jonathan Slide. Ogilvie was quite happy to sacrifice him. You won't be alone, by any means.'

Davies swallowed hard. 'All right. What do you want to know about him?'

'Is it true that he recruited for MI6?'

'So they said. I would have thought that your friends in the police could establish that.'

'Maybe. I don't know what MI6 can keep secret these days. It's all a lot more open than it was before. But maybe not the names of their contacts. Could he have recruited Vane?'

'He did recruit Vane. Or that's what some of us thought. It's not something you actually get told. If so, Vane was a strange choice – not good at keeping secrets – not subtle in any way. And it didn't stop him ridiculing Slide in his books. There was always a streak of cruelty in Roger Norton Vane. He was a nasty piece of work, when you think about it. But, yes, rumour was that he joined MI6.'

'So Vane was a secret agent?'

Davies laughed. 'Do you know the best bit about all this? If he was, it's pretty much the most interesting thing about the man. And you won't be able to use it. If you try, you'll be stopped in your tracks – and not by me or Ogilvie.'

CHAPTER TWENTY-NINE

'It's possible,' said Tim. 'I mean, I often thought that might be what he was doing. He travelled round a lot – book tours, he said. The British Council arranged them. China. Eastern Europe. One to Iran, when nobody went there. I mean absolutely nobody. A couple to Iraq, where the market for police procedurals isn't great. Sometimes he'd get a call and just dash off without telling me what it was. It was one of the reasons we argued, if you really want to know. I thought there might be somebody else . . . Of course, he could have been in MI6 and had somebody else on the side.'

We were in Elsie's flat, mugs of coffee in front of us. I had explained to Elsie and Tim what I had discovered from Ogilvie and Davies. Elsie made a pretence at not being impressed, but for the most part she listened in silence.

'So,' I asked, 'was he working for MI6 on that last trip to Thailand?'

'There was something odd about it. You know he rewrote

his will just before we left. It was almost as if he didn't think he was coming back. And then for a week or two before we left he was so nice. It was quite unlike him. Once we were in Thailand, though – actually on the plane going out – he suddenly started to get really difficult. It was as if he was deliberately starting arguments, building up to something . . .'

'Building up to a staged disappearance?' I asked.

'Yes,' said Tim. 'Staged is precisely the word I would have used. On that walk, when we stopped at the point he disappeared, he seemed to be trying to get me to hit him. Then, when I hardly touched him with my stick, he fell over and rolled down the slope. I'm not saying he was working to an exact script, but I think the plan was always that we would go out, have an argument and that he would storm off into the jungle. Afterwards people would say, yes, we'd seen them shouting at each other over breakfast – it's what we expected . . .'

'Then you said it took some time for a search to get started?'

'Precisely. Even at the time I wondered if that was because the authorities knew where he was. For years after, I expected Roger to suddenly pitch up and explain what he'd been doing – then, when he does return, he comes up with this extraordinary story that he's been an English teacher in Laos.'

'Except,' said Elsie, 'one of us has established that he never went to Laos.'

'Two of us,' said Tim. 'I helped check the sitting room.'

'So,' I said, 'our working hypothesis is that Roger was working for MI6, who needed him to vanish for reasons we don't entirely understand. He took a trip to Thailand where he was spirited away, possibly with the aid of the Thai authorities. When he returns he has a fake scar, perhaps because he still needed to maintain some pretence around the reasons for his disappearance. Having returned, he receives a threat and shortly after is found beaten to death.'

'A bit like Jim Thompson,' said Elsie. 'Except that Thompson was American. And vanished in the Malaysian jungle. And never came back at all. And there's no Roger Norton Vane Silk Shop at Bangkok Airport, though in all honesty they probably don't need another silk shop at Bangkok airport. Still, in many other respects the two cases are not dissimilar.'

'The problem is,' I said, 'that the whole MI6 thing is only a hypothesis. We don't even know that Roger was recruited to work for them. The same with his disappearance – it all looks planned but we can't be sure.'

'He definitely wasn't in Laos,' said Elsie. 'Fact.'

'Wherever he'd been, he'd changed,' said Tim. 'The person I saw wasn't the Roger that I knew.'

'It had been twenty years,' I said. 'We've all changed in that time. Anyway, how long did you actually see him for?'

'It was just the once,' said Tim. 'When he threw me out.'

'It's the small detail of the scar on his shoulder that strikes me as really odd,' I said. 'I mean, you might fake something like that for a few weeks or months – but not if you were coming back for good. And then he was harassing his agent to get in as much cash as he could as quickly as he could . . .'

'Nothing very unusual about that,' muttered Elsie.

'I mean,' I said, 'it's as if he wasn't planning to hang around longer than he needed to. The gift to Cynthia is much the same – he might have just included her in his will, but it had to be done straight away. On the one hand he's trying to gather together as much money as possible – on the other he simply hands over a very large sum in cash, almost as if he doesn't need it any more.'

'So are we back to Cynthia blackmailing him?' asked Elsie.

'But about what?' I said. 'I think we're close to resolving this puzzle – there's just a missing piece that I can't quite find. Maybe Dr Slide has it in his possession. He's back in Putney now, I think. I should just have time to get over there and back in time for the last train home.'

'If you'd given me more notice I would have provided you with dinner,' said Slide. 'You don't mind my eating mine while we talk?'

'No,' I said.

Slide had piled a tin of beans onto four slices of buttered toast. By carrying the plate with care to the table he was able to avoid spilling any onto the floor. The skill with which he tilted the plate whenever the sea of tomato sauce threatened to overflow the plate one side or the other suggested long and diligent practice.

The rain beat against the window, as a bitter wind swirled across the wide, empty expanse of the Tideway. Through the streaming glass, on the edge of the dark river, I could make out the gleaming low-tide mudflats, streaked with yellow from the street lights, and, further off, the grey silhouettes of the moored barges, far out in the stream.

'I love that view,' said Slide. 'The tidal Thames. Winter or summer. Never looks the same two days running. Always something going on. Something to look forward to. I never think about the past. Never. Some people might dwell over how they've been wronged. How they've been betrayed by those they trusted most. How they've never been properly rewarded while other people have made money they didn't deserve. Pots of money from television. Go on and on about it until they bore people rigid. Some people do that. Not me. Never think about it. Never talk about it.'

During this last speech he had been cutting into his toast with grim determination. He looked at the results of his work and then stuffed a mangled mess of bread and beans into his mouth.

'I won't keep you long,' I said. 'I just wanted to check about your work for MI6.'

Slide paused, his fork halfway to his lips. 'Who says I worked for MI6?'

'It seemed to be reasonably well known at the school.'

'Was it?' Slide seemed pleased rather than otherwise. 'It wasn't true, of course.'

'I was told you recruited for MI6?'

Slide looked down at his plate, as if trying to remember what he had been doing when he was interrupted.

'Oh that . . . I was careers master. I suggested all sorts of trades and professions to the boys. Finance. The Diplomatic Service. The Bar. Mainly those three, now I come to think of it. But a few seemed suitable for intelligence work and I knew where to direct them. I suspect a lot of careers masters did. At least, those at the better schools.'

'And you directed Vane?'

'If Vane joined MI6 it would have been from university. I'd have had nothing to do with that.'

'But it's possible?'

'Possible. But unlikely, I'd have said. Can't think of many people less suitable for the work. Complete liability.'

'There was something odd about Vane's disappearance, though . . . Do you remember Jim Thompson?'

'American businessman. Ex CIA, I think – something like that. Lived in Bangkok. Very successful in the silk trade. Vanished in the Thai jungle, didn't he? Body never found. Lots of conspiracy theories.'

'It was the Malaysian jungle, but otherwise that's right. Vane's disappearance seemed a bit like Thompson's . . .'

Slide shook his head. 'You're barking up the wrong tree there. Lots of people vanish in the jungle without any intervention from the security agencies. Look, Mr Tressider, I knew Roger Norton Vane. Knew him much better than you did. No agency in its right mind would have sent him on any sort of mission. Asking for trouble. But storming off in a fit of pique – yes, that's the Vane I knew. Nasty child. Badly brought up. Unpleasant parents too: complaining that we'd taught him a few useful motoring skills – casting aspersions on my relationship with my pupils – wanting to report me to the police, if you don't mind! Thank goodness we had a sensible headmaster in those days – not like the idiot who writes the school's business plan now. You know they've stopped teaching Latin, I suppose?'

'Yes,' I said.

'Well, if you'll excuse me a moment, I need to heat my spotted dick. I'd offer you some, but I've only got the one. I might have some biscuits somewhere if you're hungry.'

'Thanks, but I'd better be going,' I said.

'I hope you've got an umbrella,' said Slide. 'It's not very nice out there at the moment. Not very nice at all. You could catch your death if you're not careful.'

CHAPTER THIRTY

'This is completely unofficial,' said Joe. 'I'm not telling my bosses I've dropped round to see you. The idea of a policeman working side by side with an amateur detective is strictly for crime fiction.'

'Of course,' I said.

'Still, it's been helpful getting your perspective on things as Vane's biographer, so I thought I'd just bring you up to date. It seemed only fair. We've had some news from Australia.'

'Have you tracked down Johnston, then?'

'In a manner of speaking. My Australian colleagues have spoken to a few of his friends. It would seem that he told a couple of them that he was going to England and wasn't planning to return. He'd been renting a flat in Melbourne. He gave up the lease about a month ago. He'd been staying with a friend just before he left.'

'Did he say what he was going to do in England?'

'No, but he hinted that he was going to be very rich.'

'How was he going to achieve that?' I asked.

'Not by mugging Vane in an alleyway,' said Joe. 'Forty or fifty quid max. Hardly pays the taxi fare in from Heathrow these days.'

'Are you saying that some money was stolen?'

'There was loose change in Vane's pockets. No notes in the wallet, but there were two very new credit cards untouched – could have made a few thousand out of them. Odd they didn't take the cards, if it was just a mugging. Odd they took the cash if it wasn't.'

'Maybe he didn't have any on him,' I said. 'A lot of people don't carry much cash these days.'

'Possibly. Under these circumstances the best advice is always to take the simplest explanation.'

'Which is what?' I asked.

'I'm not sure yet. We've also had news of Cynthia, by the way.'

'You know where she is?'

'Again, no. But we had a sighting. She was seen talking to Vane at the hotel by one of the cleaning staff, shortly before Vane was killed. Vane was looking worried, Cynthia apparently said to him: "I wouldn't if I were you. What can he do, anyway?"'

'Who were they talking about?'

'Oddly enough, the cleaner didn't think to stop and ask them. You have to take that sort of thing with a pinch of salt. People rarely remember conversations as well as they think they do. Still, the guy was certain it was Vane and Cynthia – picked them straight away from the photos we showed him.'

'But you've no idea where she is now?'

'No. She's vanished every bit as much as Johnston has.'

'You mean they've gone off together?'

'I didn't say that. And why would they? Remember that thing about the simplest explanation? It doesn't have to be a plot. Anyway, how is the biography progressing?'

I told Joe about Ogilvie and Davies and their possible motives. He was distinctly sniffy that either might have murdered Vane, though not as sniffy as he was over Vane's possible MI6 links. It clearly wasn't, in his view, the simplest explanation.

'Secret mission in the jungle? All a bit complicated for a simple copper like me,' Joe said. 'So, the British and Thai authorities would have to be complicit in some way? And maybe the Lao government?'

'We think he was never in Laos,' I said. I decided not to explain exactly why we thought that. It was possible that Elsie had left few enough fingerprints to get away with it.

'Yes, we were coming to much the same conclusion,' said Joe. 'For all sorts of reasons. The police in Vientiane have still to come up with records of anyone like Vane. The British Council doesn't know of any English teacher matching his description – and the expat community there isn't that large. If he'd been in Laos for twenty years, somebody would have heard of him. Sounds like that was a straight lie.'

'Maybe MI6 might tell you if he had ever been one of their people?'

Joe laughed. 'They might tell you, if you knew somebody there and they owed you a very big favour. But I doubt they'd tell me. Not for something as routine as murder.'

I was heading for Oaklawn Studios, but I had time for a short detour. The clock in the village church was striking nine as I pulled up outside Margery Vane's cottage. Somebody else was there before me – a white van with the name and telephone number of a thatcher painted on it. Margery was in the garden talking to a man who I assumed must be the owner of the van. She excused herself and came down the path to meet me.

'Sorry, are you busy?' I asked.

'Yes, as you can see.'

'So, are you having the thatch repaired? I thought it was too expensive.'

'I decided that I could afford to have some of it done, after all,' she said. 'Did you have more questions about Roger? I'm not really free at the moment. You should have phoned before you came. You've had a wasted journey.'

'It's fine,' I said. 'I just dropped in on my way up to London. It wasn't out of my way. I'm still trying to get in touch with Cynthia – I wondered if she'd called you?'

'She's not here, if that's what you mean.'

'No. I didn't say she was. I just wondered if she'd contacted you since we spoke?'

'I said I would let you know when I had anything to report.'

'Yes, of course. Look, I don't want to worry you but—'

'You're not worrying me – just stopping me talking to my builder. I've told you and I've told the police – I simply can't tell you where she is. But I'm sure she's fine. She's been very busy at work lately – she'll probably give me a call at the weekend.'

'Maybe if you texted and said you were concerned . . .'

'I'm not remotely concerned. You and the police are concerned. I'm trying to get my roof fixed. You text her if you wish. Is that all, Mr Tressider? If you are on your way to London, I'm sure you don't have time for aimless chat with an old woman. So, I repeat, is that all?'

'Yes,' I said. 'That's all. And you're right. Time's getting on. I have a meeting to go to myself.'

'Can't keep you away, Ethelred, can we? Would you like me to sign you up for our newsletter – all the latest gen on the next series, exclusive interviews with the *Gascoyne* cast. We've got one with April Chambers this month – she plays DC Penny Forsyth – not a major character, but after all these years we've done most of the actors people are actually interested in two or three times. So we did her, even though she only gets a line or two per programme, poor cow. She gets written out of the series soon, so it's our last chance to do her . . . Oh, don't tell anyone I said that – it's not official yet – only heard myself a few days ago. Not sure even April knows yet. I asked her recently what she was doing after she leaves *Gascoyne* and she just looked completely blank as if she had no idea what I meant.'

'She may have worked it out now,' I said.

'Do you think so? She's quite thick. She'll probably need to see it in the newsletter before she believes it.'

'I assume I can go online and sign myself up for that?'

'Yes, of course,' said Gloria. 'It's very easy. It's just that I do it sometimes for our older fans who aren't so familiar with the Internet. They can get confused.'

'I can manage it,' I said.

'You sure? OK, then. You can always ring me if you get into difficulties.'

'Thank you,' I said. 'That's kind of you. But I really only

wanted to go through your picture library – I mentioned it in my email.'

'Yes, of course. We've looked some photos out for you. They're down in the archives. You know you can't take that coffee in with you? We've had so many accidents.'

'No, of course,' I said. I gulped what remained in the plastic cup and followed her down a spiral staircase into the very bowels of Oaklawn Studios.

There were two piles of photographs on the table. I flicked through each, as Gloria looked over my shoulder.

'That's series two,' she said. 'There's Sergeant Parthenope Williams. She was in just one episode – strangled at the very end of it by the serial killer. If you ever go to a *Gascoyne*-themed quiz night, it's worth remembering that. There's often a question on her.'

'It's not something I do a lot,' I said.

'Oh, you should. They're great fun.'

'Do you have any of Roy Johnston?' I asked. 'That was what I really needed.'

'That's him in costume as Gascoyne. But he didn't look like that in real life – not quite as good-looking as that. And they've touched it up a bit – taken out a few lines here and there. And an inch or two off the waist, I'd have said. You men can be very vain.'

'Any of him without make-up? Untouched?'

'None that we can find.'

'Can I keep this one at least?'

Gloria hesitated. 'Go on, then,' she said. 'You're obviously a big fan of series one.'

'Absolutely,' I said.

'You could start a Series One Facebook Group. Nobody's done that yet.'

'I wonder why not?' I said.

'I'd join it,' said Gloria. 'That picture there is George Mumbee.'

'The current Gascoyne?'

'Of course! I don't think they'll replace him in a hurry!'

'No, I suppose not. Was it intentional to make him look as much like Johnston as possible?'

'Yes. He was supposed to be the same person. Inspector Gascoyne.' She explained it slowly, no doubt making due allowance for my age.

I looked at the two photos side by side.

'You know Roger based Gascoyne on himself?' said Gloria. 'In the books.'

'Yes,' I said. 'I suppose I can see the resemblance, having met him. It's quite strong, actually.'

'Really? I never quite saw it myself. But some say they can. Roy Johnston was at least the right height and build. George is three inches taller. But not many people remember Roy now, so I suppose that didn't matter. No, when I said he based Gascoyne on himself, I meant more personality and so on; but I can't really see that either. Gascoyne is a cantankerous old bastard but nothing like as difficult as Roger could be – though I shouldn't speak ill of the dead. Frankly, Ethelred, there were days when I could have cheerfully murdered him myself. You're wrong, by the way, about him acting in one of the programmes. I've checked the records and there's nothing at all. It's not important, but just so as you know. I was right and you were wrong. I wouldn't want you to put things in your book that weren't true.' Having set things right, she smiled and offered me a sugar coating to my pill of disappointment. 'Now, I've got some really funny out-takes on DVD – if you've got an hour or two to spare, you should take a look at them, you really should.'

I phoned Elsie the following day.

'It's a different planet there,' I said. 'Gloria actually suggested that I should set up a Series One Facebook Group.'

'And will you?' she asked.

I decided to ignore the fatuous reply.

'Anyway, I've got some photographs that may be helpful,' I said. 'If you've got time I thought we might meet up at a coffee shop and I can show them to you. I could come to one near the office.'

'Maybe come to the office. I can't leave it at the moment.'

'Is the agency that busy?'

There was a long pause. 'It's just that I'm about to make an arrest.'

'At your office?'

'Yes.'

'How do you propose to do that?'

She told me.

'Elsie, that is the most ridiculous thing I have ever heard. And one of the most dangerous. And almost certainly illegal. Stay where you are. I'm coming over. And, for God's sake, don't try to arrest anyone until I get there.'

CHAPTER THIRTY-ONE

But that wasn't the only thing that happened that morning. No sooner had I ended the call to Elsie than my phone rang.

'Ethelred, it's Cynthia here. Ethelred, I've been so stupid – and now I don't know what to do.'

'Where are you?'

'London. I'm back at my flat.'

'Do you know where Elsie's office is?'

'Yes.'

'Then get the Tube down to Oxford Circus and meet me there. We're gathering all the stupid people together in one place, apparently.'

CHAPTER THIRTY-TWO

Elsie

'Whatever,' I said.

'It cannot possibly work,' said Ethelred. He wasn't actually frothing at the mouth but he was working up to it nicely. 'I forbid you to do it.'

'Where in your contract,' I asked, 'does it give you authority to forbid me to do anything? Nowhere. That's where. I, conversely, have you tied in more legal knots than you could count. So I hereby forbid you to forbid me. Legally I can do that. Check your contract.'

'Where does it say that?' asked Ethelred.

'Section seven, para twenty-three,' I informed him.

'I bet it doesn't.'

'Do you have a copy of your contract to hand?' I asked.

'It's in Sussex.'

'Well, mine's here and that's what it says.'

I checked his mouth. Mmm . . . yes, the first signs of froth.

'Look, Elsie, you can't gather all of the suspects together in your office. It doesn't work.'

'Obviously. I know that. After last time. So, I am gathering just one suspect together.'

'Who?'

'I can't say. Not until he or she arrives. I have, as I explained on the phone, written to all of the main suspects – plus one or two others just to be sure. I have told them that I know their dirty little secret and that they should meet me here at three o'clock. Failure to do so will result in my going to the police with the evidence I have. Most of the people receiving the letter will be innocent. They will assume that they have been included in the circulation list by accident. They will recycle the letter in a responsible manner and think nothing more of it. But the actual murderer will know they have to act swiftly. And at three o'clock precisely they will come through that door and I – or if you prefer we – shall arrest them . . . What?'

Ethelred was looking less impressed than I had hoped.

'Who have you sent it to?' he asked.

I ticked them off on my fingers. 'Lord Davies – don't pull a face like that; Ogilvie the lawyer – that face is no better than the last one; Dr Slide – the wind may change, Ethelred, and you'll be stuck with it. Then I thought I'd include Lucinda because you never know. Oh, and Cynthia's mother on the grounds that it's always the one you least expect. And she doesn't get out much, so she'll probably enjoy the trip up to London. I'd have sent an invitation to Roy Johnston but I don't know where he is. My theory is, however, that it's one of the other four.'

'What about George, Vane's agent?'

'He has witnesses he was elsewhere. Anyway, it goes completely against the Agents' Code to murder clients. It is specifically forbidden, in fact, however annoying the author in question happens to be. Whenever we're tempted, we remember the Code and regretfully desist. There are hundreds, perhaps thousands, of writers out there today who are alive only because of the precise wording of the Agents' Code.'

'And Cynthia?'

'I couldn't contact her, but you say she's coming anyway. When you think about it, she's a bit too obvious a suspect, but we shouldn't rule out a double bluff.'

Ethelred looked at me as if I was an idiot and checked his watch. 'We have twenty minutes to prevent a complete fiasco,' he said. 'I would suggest you email all four of your suspects and tell them that it was a stupid joke and that there is no need—'

There was a knock on the door.

'It looks as if he or she is early,' I said.

CHAPTER THIRTY-THREE

Elsie

The door opened. It was Tim.

'I thought I ought to come and give you support,' he said. 'Hello, Ethelred. I didn't know you were joining us.'

'I wasn't,' Ethelred replied. 'Could you please talk some sense into our agent?'

'It seemed a very good plan to me,' said Tim.

Ethelred made a strange gargling noise and said something about it being great we'd managed to get all of the idiots together in one room.

'Ethelred's just been over to Oaklawn Studios,' I said.

'That's nice,' said Tim.

'He's going to start a Series One Facebook Group,' I said.

Ethelred made another spluttering noise.

'Well, you can count me out of that. I have no wish to have anything to do with Roy Johnston. Is there any coffee?'

I summoned Tuesday, who had already anticipated my request. She placed the coffee pot and cups on the table in front of us.

'Ethelred's starting a Series One Facebook Group,' said Tim.

'That's nice,' said Tuesday.

'I am not starting any sort of Facebook Group,' said Ethelred. 'I don't do Facebook.'

'I could show you how,' said Tuesday. 'Older people often think it's difficult, but it's not really.'

'Thank you,' said Ethelred. 'I'll take your word for it. What I was doing at Oaklawn was in fact to get hold of a decent photograph of Roy Johnston.'

'Why?' asked Tim. 'You've got a perfectly good one already on the wall of the flat.'

I looked at Ethelred and he looked at Tim and Tim looked at both of us. 'What?' said Tim.

'Which picture?' I asked. But I knew the answer already.

'The one on the wall. The one that Roger put there in place of my award picture. The one I got him to take down years ago when I first moved in. I didn't want his former boyfriend looking down on me the whole time.'

'But that's Roger in the picture,' I said.

'Roger? It was clearly taken on set. In costume. Roger never acted in any of his programmes.'

'But Roger told me that it was him. That he'd had a walk-on part . . .' I said. Or had I told Roger that it was him and he'd gratefully accepted the suggestion? Yes, maybe that.

'Gloria always denied it,' said Ethelred. He seemed a bit smug for some reason.

'But he had the scar at the corner of his mouth,' I said. 'That's why I was so certain that Roger Vane was Roger Vane. The scar proved it. Small, almost unnoticeable scar but identical. I told you about it. Why didn't you tell me if I was wrong?'

'You said some old photo of Roger looked like the man claiming to be Roger. You seemed very pleased with yourself. You never mentioned a scar.'

'Didn't I?'

'Roger never had a scar at the corner of his mouth,' said Tim. 'Possibly Roy Johnston did. I wouldn't know. I've never kissed Roy Johnston. Actually I never met him at all – unless you're saying it was Roy Johnston who threw me out of the flat.'

There was a long silence.

'But you must have seen the scar on the man claiming to be Roger,' I said.

'Elsie, I was with him for ten minutes, most of which time I was chucking things into a suitcase. You said the scar was almost unnoticeable and you expect me to spot it instantly under circumstances that were, frankly, fraught.'

'Well,' I said, 'it would certainly have saved us a lot of time if you had bothered to check just one small thing.'

'So,' said Ethelred. 'The mystery of Roy Johnston's disappearance is explained. Shortly after arriving here, he became Roger Norton Vane. Gloria said that Roger and Roy Johnston were a similar build. She also commented to me how much alike they were generally. I've only ever seen photos of Johnston on the set, in make-up, but it's clear that they resembled each other facially – to some extent, at least. Johnston knew Roger well – as an actor he would have been able to reproduce Roger's accent and tone of voice. As an actor he would have experience in doing himself up to look like somebody else. As Roger's former partner he would have been able to study his character in some depth, would have known as much about him as almost anyone alive. We know that Johnston had left

Australia shortly before the memorial service – an event that was widely publicised – saying that he would soon be rich.

'So, he appeared dramatically at the church and then blustered his way back into his flat – behaving, oddly enough, exactly as Roger would have done. He took over Roger's life – his home, his royalties, his suits – though it would seem he went out and bought new shirts, pants and socks. I think I might have done that too. It's funny how so many small details – the new socks, for example – now suddenly make complete sense.'

'Hold on,' said Tim. 'I know Elsie was convinced by the scar, but that wasn't what swung it for me or Cynthia. Ethelred went and asked him a whole series of questions that he got right. How on earth was Roy Johnston supposed to know what had happened in Thailand twenty years ago. Or known that Cynthia's nickname was Pobble?'

'Unless,' I said, 'there was a spy in the camp.'

Ethelred looked at his watch. 'Important though this is, it could be that we now have only fifteen minutes until the murderer arrives,' he said. 'I really think you should phone the people that you wrote to . . .'

There was a knock on the door.

'Do any of you have a gun?' asked Tim. 'I think we need some way of protecting ourselves.'

'Clearly not,' said Ethelred. 'And I think I know who the spy in the camp was.'

The door opened and Cynthia came in. She looked around. 'I really do owe you all an apology,' she said.

CHAPTER THIRTY-FOUR

Elsie

Ethelred went out and found another chair for Cynthia. He's a bit of a gent. The office was, I had to admit, getting quite crowded now. I was in my chair behind my desk. Tim was in one of the two seats on the far side of the desk. Ethelred had been in the other one. The murderer, when he arrived, would have to stand – squeezed between the desk and the wall, probably – as we explained to him how we'd tracked him down and what we proposed to do next.

Tuesday brought more coffee and another cup. 'I thought there would just be two of you at this meeting,' she said. 'Is that all now?'

'Hopefully one more,' I said.

Tuesday looked doubtfully round my office. 'Shall I move you all to the meeting room? Robin's practising his book fair presentation in there, but I could get him out if you want.'

'No,' I said. 'One more, absolute tops.'

'Can I make a note of his name?' asked Tuesday.

'He'll introduce himself when he arrives.'

'So, you don't know who you've invited?' Tuesday gave a nervous laugh. 'Or are you just not telling me?' I was often, in her view, kind of weird, but not usually quite this weird.

'Exactly,' I said. 'One or other of those things. Now, if we could have a plate of biscuits, we'll continue.'

Ethelred returned with a chair from the meeting room and we all settled down again.

'So,' I said, in my most businesslike manner, 'I think everyone at this meeting already knows each other. Or perhaps we didn't know each other as well as we thought? OK. Let's do some introductions. On my right, Ethelred, the mid-list author and Facebook Group administrator. Then there's Tim, Roger's very unobservant former partner. And on my left, Cynthia, *the traitor in our midst*. Is that everyone? OK, introductions done. Thank you all for coming. And now it's over to you, Cynthia. How did you stitch us all up?'

Cynthia put down her coffee cup, not an easy task with three other cups and two coffee pots already vying for space with my paperwork and a couple of ironically cuddly toys.

'As you know,' she said, 'I was never convinced that the man claiming to be Uncle Roger actually was him.'

'We know it was Roy Johnston, if that helps at all,' said Ethelred.

'Thank you. It does,' said Cynthia. 'Though it took me a while to work it out who it was. At first all I could have said was that there was something wrong about him. He was brusque and unpleasant, but Uncle Roger was like that much of the time. He could be charming when he wanted to be, but usually he couldn't be bothered. Roy was somehow . . . less nuanced? The more I got to study Roy's performance, the more it was like somebody acting the part – the same phrases and gestures kept coming up, a bit like the villain in a melodrama having to twirl his moustache from time to time, so that people would understand he was still evil. And he got things wrong – Cousin Wilbert, for example. I knew there was no such person. And not knowing what sex his dog had been.'

Ethelred nodded sagely, though I seemed to remember that he had been the leading exponent of the school of thought that accepted the fake Vane as the real deal.

'I tried to convince you,' said Cynthia, 'but I could see you all drifting slowly and helplessly to the dark side – you were starting to believe that Uncle Roger really had come back. So, I went to see Mr Ogilvie. As Uncle Roger's schoolfriend and lawyer he'd known him for as long as anyone alive, pretty much, and kept in touch with him right up to the moment he disappeared. He was my last hope of finding another sane person.'

'And Ogilvie agreed with you?' I asked.

'No, he agreed with you lot. He had had doubts but on balance he was going to tell people that he thought the man was Uncle Roger and that he should be given access to his cash. But he also told me one other thing . . .'

'Which was?' asked Ethelred.

'That Uncle Roger had asked him to change his will just before going to Thailand. The money and the flat were

271

going to Tim. I was to get nothing at all. It seemed a bit rich that Tim, whom he'd clearly split up with, got the lot, while I, who was still very much his niece albeit adopted, got zilch. If I proved the man was a phoney, it just handed the cash to Tim. So I hatched a plan to rectify things.'

'Thanks a bunch,' said Tim.

'Always pleased to help,' said Cynthia.

'I'd have done as much for you,' said Tim.

'How sweet,' said Cynthia. 'Anyway, I went to my so-called "uncle" and told him I was onto his game. He'd clearly researched things quite well on the Internet – he'd checked me out on Facebook, for example, so he knew what I looked like and what I did. But he'd already made several mistakes, as I've said. So far, I told him, I was the only one who'd picked them up, but his luck couldn't possibly hold. There was a plan afoot to test him on his knowledge of Roger Norton Vane and he was going to fail it miserably. Gamma minus. Unless . . .' She looked round the room meaningfully.

'And he accepted your kind offer of cooperation?' I asked.

'"Cooperation"'s such a nasty word, isn't it? I prefer to think of it as blackmail. But I did indeed suggest that I fed him the information he needed in exchange for fifty per cent of the net takings. I also by chance had Uncle Roger's old driving licence, which he'd accidentally left behind on a visit to my parents shortly before he vanished – the old paper sort, no photo. Johnston – and he freely confessed that was who he was – could see that would be useful too, especially in proving his identity at the bank and elsewhere,

where an item of ID is either on their list or it isn't. The driving licence probably swung it, actually. It was a bit like being slipped the ace of spades in a slightly bent bridge tournament. We haggled, of course. He ended up with the Canonbury Square flat plus fifty per cent of the cash and as much of the outstanding royalties as he could call in. He pointed out he was taking most of the risk, if the fraud ever came to light, and was moreover having to be Roger Norton Vane full-time – not the most pleasant of experiences. I conversely had merely to act as a consultant. So, a million in my hand, payable as soon as he had access to the account, wasn't bad. We shook hands on it and opened a bottle of Sainsbury's own-brand Prosecco. Happy days.'

'And that's why he knew exactly what had happened in Thailand?'

'You've got it. I told him what Tim told us. We added a few interesting details of our own – Roy had actually once stumbled across an illicit distillery in the Thai jungle and did speak a bit of Lao, having gone there on holiday a couple of times. I made up a nickname for myself.'

'So you didn't really call yourself Pobble?' I asked.

'As if! I had some self-respect, even as a three-year-old. The hideous shoulder scar was entirely his idea, though. I said whatever damage Tim had inflicted would have healed by now, but he said that, as an actor, he was an old hand at prosthetic wounds and could make it look really convincing. Whoever saw it would be putty in his hands, if they didn't pass out first. Well, he was paying me a million, so I thought I wouldn't spoil his fun. In my defence I have to point out that all the good ideas were mine and all the crap ones were his – including taking a shortcut down the alleyway. I think somehow it was all a bit of a game to him.'

'Men!' I said sympathetically. 'They never grow up, do they?'

She nodded. 'Temperamentally he wasn't as well suited to deceit as I was. The male sex just lacks the nerve for it. No sooner had we got access to the bank account, than he started to worry that he couldn't keep up the deception much longer. I think he'd originally planned to be Uncle Roger indefinitely, but his agent kept asking when he'd deliver another book and festival organisers were inviting him to speak on The Golden Age of Crime Fiction, or whatever. Every newspaper or blog interview, if the interviewer had any knowledge of the genre, was fraught with the terrible risk that he'd say something inexplicably stupid. Then Oaklawn Studios wanted him to do some PR for them – Roy said there was a mad woman there who'd recognise him straight away – he couldn't possibly have anything to do with them. I said it would look suspicious if he didn't. To cut a long story short, he sort of freaked. He asked his agent to call in everything he could, with the intention of grabbing what was available, disappearing again and resuming life as Roy Johnston – much the same as before only richer and on a beach in the West Indies.'

'What stopped him?' asked Ethelred.

'Well, forgive me for stating the obvious, but what stopped him was being murdered in an alleyway in Chichester. He'd been jumpy for some days. Then somebody jostled him at Oxford Circus Station – the Central Line, I think – just as a train was coming in. He didn't think much of it. Until he received the phone call.'

'Phone call?' said Ethelred, on cue. They were developing into a bit of a double act, but not one you'd want to book for the O2 Arena.

'Yes, the phone call,' said Cynthia. 'A man called Slide phoned him.'

'Jonathan Slide,' said her straight man.

'That's right. Doctor Jonathan Slide. Uncle Roger's former driving instructor or something. It was a bit of a ramble, really. He said that, so long as it was uncertain that Uncle Roger was who he said he was, he'd held back. But now he – Slide – knew for certain he intended to give him – Uncle Roger, as he imagined – a piece of his mind. He said Uncle Roger had always been an unpleasant child and had grown into an unpleasant adult. Slide said Uncle Roger had wrecked his career as a driving instructor and he'd had to go and teach Latin at Cordwainers School. Something like that. Slide, taking his argument to its logical conclusion, stated that Uncle Roger therefore deserved to die. Johnston, though he was aware he was not actually Uncle Roger in real life, was quite worried about this and asked Slide whether the incident at Oxford Circus was in any way pertinent to their discussion. Slide said it most certainly was. He had, he implied, agents all over London and next time they'd do the job properly. He laughed in an evil manner and hung up.

'I tried to reassure Roy that Slide was just senile and vindictive, that the army of assassins was a figment of his imagination and that an evil laugh usually proved nothing one way or the other. Roy said that I hadn't heard the laugh. He wasn't planning to take any chances. He'd already got most of Uncle Roger's money together and, frankly, if there was another few thousand out there, it could go to Oxfam. It was time to cut and run. I pointed out that he had nowhere to go but he said that there was an idiot living down in Sussex who could be bullied into taking him for as long as he wished.'

'You knew who he meant at once?' I asked.

'Of course. But when he phoned Ethelred, he was told to get lost – well done for that, by the way, Ethelred – respect. Still, it did leave Roy in a bit of a mess. He thought Slide's friends were on his heels and that he'd better get down to Sussex ASAP. So, he packed a suitcase and took a train. But first he phoned his lawyer and one or two other people to tidy things up. He mentioned in passing he'd be in Sussex. Bad move if he really wanted it to stay a secret for long. He was so worked up, I felt sure he'd blow the whole thing, the police would become involved in a high-profile fraud case and the small matter of my acquiring a million by extortion might come up in court. So, I said I'd follow him down after work and we could meet up and talk it through properly.'

'Which you did,' said Ethelred.

'Which I did. I needed to get him onto a plane and back to Australia or wherever he wanted to go. I met him at the hotel. In my absence Slide had phoned him again. It turned out Slide had been in Sussex all the time – and only a few miles from Chichester. Slide had proposed they should have a drink or two and talk it through, man to man. I said there was no need at all to go. Roy said it was better to find out exactly what Slide knew – it might be that we'd need to pay him a few thousand to keep quiet. He sounded bribable. I offered to go with him, but he reckoned that that would wreck everything – Slide would be more cautious and would also know we were in it together. This last point convinced me. I had no wish for anyone to know that. We agreed he should go alone, see Slide, say as little as possible and report back. But he never returned. I didn't want to call him in case he was still in the middle of the meeting with Slide. Then I didn't want to call him because, if he had been killed by Slide, the police would be checking his mobile phone records and the less my name came up, from a fraud point of view, the better. Sometime after midnight I went looking for him. I found blue police tape sealing off East Street. I asked a couple of questions. I never doubted that it was Roy who'd been killed. I never doubted that Slide had killed him . . .'

Ethelred looked at his watch. 'Unless you phone people quickly, Elsie, they'll all be here in ten minutes,' he said.

'Plenty of time,' I said.

There was a knock at the door. Tuesday's head appeared round it.

'There's a Mrs Vane outside. She said she came as soon as she could. She had to see the builder about the roof.'

'You invited my mother?' asked Cynthia.

'Only as the person nobody suspected,' I said.

'Oh, good – she'll like being that,' said Cynthia.

CHAPTER THIRTY-FIVE

Elsie

'Anyway,' said Margery Vane, 'in the end I just got the two quotes and went for Mr Hepplewhite, partly because he had done the thatch on the Old Rectory, and partly because I liked the name. I suppose I'll have to tell him I can't afford it now – not if the blackmail money has to be paid back, as I assume it will. What a shame. But you now say you didn't really need me to come? I was of course very close to Chichester that evening, but only because I always am. I didn't kill anyone. Obviously I knew who had been killed because Cynthia explained it all to me. But sadly I was never a suspect – too old, I suppose. The police called round, though mainly to ask if I knew where Cynthia was – she's much younger. Cynthia was up in her room, but they could scarcely expect me to tell them that. It was rather fun concealing her – a bit like the games of hide-and-seek we used to play, but for slightly higher stakes. Anyway, I suppose she'll be able to go back to her flat now – or prison, depending on what we're all charged with.'

'Well, there's certainly no reason for charging you with murder, Mummy,' said Cynthia. 'You had nothing to do with it.'

'Might I remind you I was in on the blackmail from day one? I was the one who suggested that we should settle for a million if we could get it.'

'I wasn't planning to tell anyone that.'

'That's very sweet of you, but I'd hardly expect my own daughter to take the rap alone. Anyway, we're amongst friends here, aren't we?'

'Probably,' said Cynthia. 'But more to the point, you had no motive to kill anyone.'

'I might have done,' said Margery. 'I always rather fancied him. We might have had an affair for all you know.'

'You and Roy Johnston?'

'No, me and Uncle Roger. I never met Roy Johnston. Roger was really dishy. Much more so than your father. I knew he was gay, but I thought it was worth suggesting it to him. So I did. Anyway, it was Boxing Day and your father was drunk—'

'I'm quite happy if you stop there,' said Cynthia.

'I'd been meaning to tell you, but the right moment never really arose.'

'It was fine not knowing,' said Cynthia. 'If there's any more like that, it can wait.'

Margery nodded sympathetically. 'Yes, of course, darling.'

'And it couldn't have been a motive for killing Roy Johnston – whatever it was. I'm sorry, you're not a proper suspect and that's all there is to it.'

There was another knock at the door.

'There's a very odd-looking gentleman outside,' said Tuesday. 'I'm not sure if that's who you were expecting next.'

'Stains on his trousers? Slightly disconcerting smell?' I asked.

'Yes.'

'Excellent. A real suspect at last. You can show him in now,' I said. 'Oh, and another chair would be good.'

CHAPTER THIRTY-SIX

Elsie

'What a lot of people!' said Jonathan Slide. 'This looks very jolly. When you invited me, I'd assumed it would just be the two of us, Miss Thirkettle. But good to meet you all the same.'

'That's Miss Thirkettle,' said Cynthia, pointing in my direction. 'I'm Roger's niece, Cynthia.'

'Is that right?' he said, turning to me. 'I was expecting somebody younger. And not so fat. Anyway, Miss Thirkettle, you said you knew my guilty secret, so I thought I'd better come along.'

'To deny it?' I asked.

'No, to check which guilty secret you were talking about. You didn't say.'

'I mean the murder of Roy Johnston, posing as Roger Norton Vane.'

'Oh, so it was him, then. I did wonder. You see, right from the start there was something not quite right about him.

He looked like Vane, and he behaved like Vane, but there was – how can I put this without seeming like a snob? – a lack of class. However unpleasant a Cordwainers boy can be, and they can be very unpleasant indeed, there is always evidence of breeding in their unpleasantness. There is nothing accidental about it. An insult would be pitched perfectly to wound precisely as much as was intended. Never more than that. Never less. No wasted effort. A Cordwainers boy can be obnoxious with grace. It takes many generations to develop that sort of skill – you can't teach it. And Johnston, frankly, didn't have it at all. The real Vane didn't have much of it, of course, but you could still tell the difference. Anyway, that's what I thought. Fake. Then it was announced in the press that the man really was Roger Norton Vane. You could have knocked me over with a feather. But even Ogilvie, who is an Old Cordwainer himself, credited it. So, naturally, I phoned the man up straight away to tell him what a little shit he was.'

'Naturally?' said Ethelred.

'Well, I suppose it could have waited a week or two. But I'd had twenty years to think about what I would say to Roger Norton Vane if I ever saw him again. I wasn't doing much that morning, so I reasoned that now was as good a time as any. I rather enjoyed it in the end. No, I'm glad I took the opportunity to do it when I could, especially as he's dead now. Of course, I do realise that it was Roy Johnston that I was speaking to, so perhaps what I said was a little harsh, but if he insisted on impersonating Vane, then I don't know what else he expected.'

'Did you tell him you could have him killed?' asked Ethelred.

Slide thought for a moment. 'Yes,' he said. 'I did. He told me some story about having been pushed on the underground and asked if that had been one of my people. It seemed more amusing to tell him that it had been, and I asked if he'd caught sight of who it was so that I could write and thank them – we've always valued manners at Cordwainers. Then I added for good measure that there were simply dozens of Old Cordwainers who had volunteered to murder him on my behalf. That last bit was almost true, incidentally – two or three had said they would. They might have had second thoughts when it actually came to it, I suppose. I've been let down so often like that – promises that have come to nothing. When Vane – sorry Johnston – finally hung up on me, I could tell he was shitting himself. Real brown trousers job. As I say, great fun at the time . . . But then later . . .'

'You regretted showing your hand so early?' I asked.

'No, I just felt I'd been a little unkind. I remembered that I'd been quite fond of him once – Vane, not Johnston. I still thought it was Vane, you see. And I hadn't really given him a chance to put his side of the case. I hadn't taken into account the fact that the last twenty years had probably been a bit tough for him. He could be a changed character. I ruminated on that a lot during the afternoon. I didn't feel guilty, exactly – just that I could have handled it better. So I went into town to a place I know and had a few drinks – maybe a few more than I should. A dozen or so gin and tonics. I phoned Vane – sorry Johnston, I keep forgetting – and said I'd like to meet up with him. I said I knew all about him and what he'd been doing and wanted to meet up and talk things through. At first he said nothing, then, when he worked out what I was trying to say, he agreed to meet me.'

'So,' I said. 'You met and argued and you killed him.'

'Killed him? No, of course not. He never showed up. Waited in the bar for ages. I was quite cross after all the effort I'd gone to, phoning him twice in one day. Typical of Roger Vane, I thought. Nasty inconsiderate child. But I was wrong, because it wasn't Roger Vane at all. And the only reason he hadn't shown up was because he was dead. Perfectly reasonable, when you think about it.'

'You said two or three of the old boys had offered to kill Vane for you,' I said. 'So did that include Ogilvie or Davies?'

'I hate to point this out,' said Ethelred, 'but in five minutes both of them could be here.'

There was a knock at the door.

'Were you expecting another visitor?' asked Tuesday. 'Because there's somebody outside who says he's going to sue you – and I'm quoting him now – for every effing penny you've got.'

CHAPTER THIRTY-SEVEN

Elsie

I told Tim to sit on my desk and put Lord Davies in Tim's chair. I offered Davies coffee but he didn't seem to hear me, possibly because Tim was partially blocking his view of me. The room was getting quite warm, I noticed, and Tim's elbow was digging into my shoulder. Ethelred had nowhere to put his legs and was uncomfortably hunched up. Cynthia was regretting sitting next to Slide, who was giving off an odour of old and well-loved tweed. Margery was sitting bolt upright and enjoying every minute. Her expression suggested that she was wondering if there was still some way in which she might, even at this late hour, incriminate herself.

'Now, introductions,' I said briskly. 'Lord Davies, this is Ethelred—'

'I know,' he said.

'And this is Doctor Jonathan Slide.'

'I know,' he said. 'Good afternoon, Jonathan.'

'Nice to see you, Davies,' said Slide. 'It's been a while. You missed the thirtieth anniversary dinner for your year. Great fun. Your pal Rutherford was hospitalised. Almost died. Or maybe he did die. My memory's not what it was.'

'And this is Cynthia, Roger Vane's niece. And her mother. And this is Tim, Roger's former partner. And I'm Elsie Thirkettle, leading London literary agent. Well, I think that covers that.'

'And have you sent the same libellous letter to everyone here?' demanded Davies.

'No, you're all here for different reasons. I've accused only some of you of murder.'

'And why are you accusing me? I've already told Ethelred I had nothing to do with it. I was in London. I'm not sure how you propose to avoid legal action, Miss Thirkettle – what you say next had better be good.'

'Well,' I said. 'It's obviously up to you which of us you sue, but Ethelred told me quite clearly that you lied about the CCTV cameras. He also said it was perfectly possible for you to get out of your office undetected, drive down to Chichester, kill Vane – or Johnston as we now know him to be – and get back in time for your conference call. That was his view. And I'd probably go along with it, at least in part.'

'Which part?'

'The safe and legal part.'

'Would it help if I said that the police had already cleared me?' said Davies.

'Have they?' I asked.

'I have been subjected to DNA testing, fingerprinting, fibre analysis and an hour-long grilling on my movements.

The police have, however, confirmed that they cannot find me or my car on CCTV anywhere near the scene of the crime. They will shortly confirm that there is also no trace of my DNA anywhere near the site and no trace of the victim's DNA on my clothes. And I know that because I never stirred outside the office building all night. But you are presumably going to challenge all of this scientific evidence on the basis of a hunch that I might have had time to drive to Chichester and back?'

'Which you did have,' I said.

'Think carefully before you say that again.'

'It's more Ethelred saying it,' I said. 'You might like to note that for legal purposes. But I think you'll find it's true. Ethelred also says that you sold pornography to minors.'

Slide nodded. 'It was really a pastiche of the Earl of Rochester. I confiscated the copies that the third-formers bought, of course – slightly too sophisticated for them. The fourth-formers were doing the Stuarts, so in some ways it was quite educational.'

'I've had enough of this,' said Davies. 'I've already phoned my solicitor. You probably know him. Will Ogilvie. As soon as I can get to see him, I intend to start a libel action against you, Ms Thirkettle, and anyone else who has repeated these lies.'

'Three o'clock,' said Ethelred, as if he'd warned me before that that might happen.

There was a knock on the door.

'Mr William Ogilvie,' said Tuesday. 'Is he the last?'

'No, there will be one more,' growled Davies. 'I've already phoned him.'

'Shall I fetch more chairs?' asked Tuesday.

'No, I'll stand,' said Ogilvie, glancing round the room. 'No introductions needed. I think I know everybody. Good to see you all. I've got a bit of a bombshell for one of you, I'm afraid, but I'll wait my turn to speak. If there's any chance of coffee in the meantime, I'd love some. And . . . is it me or is it really hot and . . . er . . . slightly stuffy in here?'

CHAPTER THIRTY-EIGHT

Elsie

'So, have I missed anything exciting?' asked Ogilvie, as I wrenched open the window.

'Vane wasn't Vane; he was Roy Johnston,' I said. 'Johnston was trying to nick Vane's money by impersonating Vane. Cynthia helped him and blackmailed him into giving her a sizeable cut.'

'So did I,' said Margery. 'We were both in on the blackmail. Let's be clear about that.'

'Noted,' I said. 'For the record, she also had an affair with Roger Vane.'

'No, she didn't,' said Cynthia.

'Just a small one, perhaps,' Margery said. 'Would you all like me to tell you about it?'

'No,' said Cynthia. 'They wouldn't.'

'Anyway,' I said, 'Dr Slide told Johnston he'd like to kill him but, to be fair, actually meant the threat for Vane. Later he told him he knew everything, meaning the past twenty years had been tough, but which Johnston interpreted as meaning something else. This enticed Johnston out of his hotel to his death. Those are the headlines. Now for the news where you are. A certain lawyer was seen in a Chichester car park at the right time and had a motive in that Vane knew he had done a bit of car theft in his youth and he didn't want that to get back to the constituency. So, you're a prime suspect, Mr Ogilvie. The weather is expected to remain cold with rainy intervals. Over to you.'

'Thank you,' said Ogilvie. 'I've heard worse summings up in court. But I must challenge you on one point. The Sussex police have been more efficient than you imply. I too have been interviewed, swabbed, fingerprinted and my clothes brushed for evidence. I won't say I enjoyed it, but it has given me greater empathy with some of my clients than I had previously. I was indeed in Chichester car park; but like Lord Davies – and we have already had the opportunity to compare notes – I am not expecting to be told that I have been caught on CCTV in the centre of town or that there is any evidence to connect me with an alleyway just off East Street. I never had strong views on DNA in the past, but now I think it's rather useful. So, I agree I was closer to the action than Lord Davies, but not close enough to do any damage.'

'Same here,' said Slide. 'Fingerprints. Swabs. The lot. Nothing to connect me with anything, apparently. Thank God for technology, I say.'

'So, it couldn't have been any of you . . .' I said.

'I haven't been fingerprinted,' said Margery, holding up her hand. 'Or any of the other things.'

292

'Precisely,' said Davies, looking at me. 'It was none of us. And since my solicitor is now here, I can begin legal action against you, on my behalf and Dr Slide's and indeed Mr Ogilvie's, if he wishes. I intend to instruct the best barrister we can find – don't worry about paying, Jonathan, this will be my treat. And we will take you, Ms Thirkettle, for every penny you have. As for Miss Cynthia Vane, who you say was complicit in Johnston's chicanery, she has fraudulently obtained money from Roger Vane's bank account. I think the police may have something to say about that.'

'Thanks for mentioning that, Elsie,' said Cynthia.

'And thank you so much, Cynthia, for snitching on us to Roy Johnston,' I said.

'Right,' said Davies. 'Where do we begin, Will? How long will it take to issue writs?'

Ogilvie frowned. 'Speaking as your lawyer, I would not advise you to do anything,' he said.

'Why not?' asked Davies.

'Let us consider,' said Ogilvie. 'Nobody here has committed a crime.'

'Cynthia has,' said Davies. 'Theft and blackmail. And her mother seems to have aided and abetted her.'

'So I did,' said Margery. 'Both of those things.'

'No, you didn't,' said Ogilvie. 'I'll come to all of that in a moment. But first we should each consider how much of this we wish to come out. Your involvement in the publication of the poem, for example. Or your previous relationship with Roger Vane, coincidentally linked to the place in which he was killed. The gutter press would enjoy reporting every detail. And Jonathan has a great deal in his past . . .'

293

'Gosh, yes,' said Slide. 'An enormous amount. My, I did have fun.'

'As to my own role in borrowing the deputy head's car . . . well, I'm not sure how much I want to be an MP anyway. If that comes out, then it comes out. It's not as though I was ever charged with anything, though explaining the cover up may be awkward. I'll talk it through with my constituency chairman and stand down if he wants me to stand down. But you can count me out of any legal action and my advice would be to let it go.'

'And the charges against Cynthia Vane?' asked Davies. 'Surely they can't be ignored?'

I noticed Tim nod at this point. A little harsh but Cynthia had no reason to expect our loyalty and, hell, it was his million she'd stolen.

'Ah yes . . . that was my bombshell, I'm afraid. I have an apology to make – to Cynthia and to all of you really.'

He paused and flashed a glance at Tim.

'Go on,' said Tim.

'Well, it's like this. Cynthia came to see me and I told her that Roger had made a new will. She was cut out and Tim got everything. And that was how I remembered it – indeed that was the will I drafted for Roger before he went to Thailand. I recalled every detail. Or almost every detail.'

'But?' said Tim.

'But he never signed it. When I got it out of store, I noticed the signature was missing. Then I remembered. He'd said he'd sign it when he got back. It was only a delay of a fortnight. Neither of us imagined that he wouldn't be coming back. So, the only valid will is his earlier one. Now he's dead again, the money's Cynthia's. I'll have to check what the legal position is if you attempt to steal your own money. I don't think it happens that often.'

'Excellent,' said Margery. 'I won't need to cancel Mr Hepplewhite. And Cynthia doesn't need to go to prison of course.'

'But Roger intended me to have the money . . .' said Tim. 'The drafting of the new will makes that clear.'

'He did intend you to have the money. Briefly. Less so perhaps after the events in Thailand. We'll never know. Maybe if you got a good lawyer he could make something of it. I'd refer them to Waghorn vs Waghorn in the first instance.'

'Will that help my case?' asked Tim.

'No,' said Ogilvie. 'Sadly not.'

'So,' said Cynthia, 'there was no need for me to do any deal with Johnston, because the money was always mine?'

'Yes.'

'No need to help him prove he was Roger Vane?'

'Not from your point of view.'

'So, he should have ended up going back to Australia with nothing – as he would if left to his own devices – rather than being murdered in an alleyway?'

'That too is true. I think it's called tragic irony when that happens.'

'And we have all consequently wasted a great deal of time and effort having to prove our innocence?' demanded Davies.

'I'm not saying everyone hasn't been inconvenienced to some extent,' said Ogilvie.

'All because of your incompetence?' asked Cynthia. 'We should be suing you.'

Ogilvie pursed his lips. 'I would be careful with your precise wording. I told you Roger had changed his will, as indeed he had. I also said that I wasn't sure how you could be prosecuted for stealing your own money. But the good thing about the law is that there are always two ways of looking at everything. It was still your intention to defraud the estate of Roger Norton Vane. Morally it was your money but legally it was yours only once the will was proved – another will, a signed one this time, might theoretically have come to light. A moderately clever prosecution lawyer might still make a case against you. But – and this is the good news – only if there is some evidence that you were planning to perpetrate a fraud. At the moment the police will obviously be aware that Johnston transferred money to you. But, unless anyone here cares to tell the police what we now know, there is no proof that Johnston even consulted you before doing so. It could have been simply because he felt guilty at his own deception . . . that he wanted to make some sort of reparation to the family. So, let us all think very, very carefully. Almost everyone of us has a certain amount to lose if the police are given more evidence than they actually deserve . . . and, Margery, you will be delighted to learn that I include you in this warning. So, my advice to everyone is that we should allow the authorities to conclude their investigations and not interfere any further in any way. Unless one of us knows otherwise, none of us killed Roger Vane.'

'That's good advice, as ever,' said Davies. 'There has been more than enough interference already. And that is why I have made a formal complaint to the West Sussex Police about your conduct, Miss Thirkettle. I am not without influence. I have spoken to their commissioner. I must warn you that he is sending one of their top men to sort this out.' He checked his watch. 'I think you'll find he should be here any minute.'

There was a knock at the door.

'I have no idea how you can fit anyone else into this room,' said Tuesday, 'but since he's a policeman I can't very well keep him out.'

'Hello,' said Joe. 'I am indeed one of their top men – thank you for saying so, Lord Davies. And I think I can finally sort this out for you. No, don't get up, Ethelred, I'll just perch on the other corner of the desk. Are you sitting comfortably? No, I didn't think you were. Well, I'll begin anyway, and I'll start by telling you the name of the murderer. I think you'll all find it pretty obvious, when you consider the evidence.'

CHAPTER THIRTY-NINE

Elsie

'The murderer,' said Joe, 'was Wayne Flood.'

'Who?' said Tim.

'Who?' said Ogilvie.

'Who?' said Davies.

'What?' said Ethelred, by way of elegant variation, I suppose.

'Well, I'm glad I'm not the only one who has no idea what's going on,' said Margery.

'Not an Old Cordwainer, I think,' said Slide. 'You don't mean Tristram Flood-Jones, the banker, I suppose? No, he's in prison already. Rate fixing. Can't be him.'

'Wayne Flood?' asked Cynthia. 'You said we would find it obvious but clearly none of us has even heard of Wayne Flood. It's hardly fair to expect us to have guessed it was him when we don't have a clue who he is.'

'On the contrary,' said Joe. 'It is entirely fair, as I shall demonstrate. Indeed, it could have been nobody else, and you should all be ashamed of yourselves for not spotting it.'

'But you've never mentioned his name before,' said Ethelred.

'That's right,' said Joe. 'I haven't. But before I explain why it had to be him, I'd like to say a few words on the subject of murder in real life.'

'That sounds like a chapter in its own right,' said Ethelred.

'Could be,' said Joe. 'You never know.'

CHAPTER FORTY

Elsie

'The problem with crime fiction,' said Joe, 'not that I read a lot of it, is that the murder victim is very often a mere cypher – a largely anonymous character whose only function is to act as the central point of the investigation, which is the real subject of the book.'

'I thought you didn't read much crime fiction?' said Cynthia.

'Well, maybe a bit,' said Joe. 'The point is that in real life, the victim is nothing of the sort and the pain and hurt don't end with the catching of the murderer. Real murder devastates lives – not just the victim but the victim's family, the victim's friends, the victim's community. And the hurt lasts as long as they last. They try to dull the pain with logic and meaning. One of the things that people who are caught up in a murder say to me all the time is that they hope that the death of their loved one will mean that no other child, no other young woman, no other human being ever has to suffer again in the same way. And they don't just say it to me. They say it to the papers, they say it on television. They set up funds and foundations. They want to know the reason why their loved one died. They want to take that information and apply logic to it. They want to come up with a formula that proves nobody will die that way again. They want to be able to learn from it. They want us to learn from it.

'The problem is that most real-life murders are messy and illogical. There isn't a reason for them. There's nothing to learn except that it's easier to kill another human being than you ever imagined. A kid says something to another kid in a nightclub that is misheard and the next thing you know the second kid has got ten of his mates together and they beat the shit out of the first kid and leave him dying by the side of the road, right by the CCTV, which has picked up the whole thing. That's murder. No motive. No plan. Just a minute and a half of opportunity and an arrest the following morning. We've got a farmer's wife over by Bognor – let her husband have it with both barrels from his shotgun. She said she regretted it as soon as she fired the first barrel, but she'd started so she thought she might as well finish. Most murders are pretty much unplanned. Most murders are regretted almost at once.

'But readers of crime novels expect a suitably convoluted motive, a carefully planned and executed crime. That's where you all went wrong.'

'Is that it?' asked Ethelred. 'Is that what you wanted to say about murder in general?'

'There's a lot more if you'd like it,' said Joe.

'We get the picture,' said Margery. 'Now tell us who the hell Wayne Flood is.'

CHAPTER FORTY-ONE

Elsie

'I understand your puzzlement,' said Joe, 'but the problem is that you have all been behaving like characters in a crime novel. You've allowed yourselves to be seduced by the ingenious rather than the probable. You've wanted to believe, for example, that because Roger Vane purportedly lost his virginity in an alleyway near here, somebody who knew him well would wish to lure him back to the same place and kill him there. Why on earth would they do that, other than to draw attention to their connection with him? And because the idea of revenge long deferred is so attractive, you were willing to believe that Dr Slide might be capable of ambushing and coshing Roy Johnston, believing him to be Roger Vane. But is that really likely? Dr Slide walks slowly, with a stick. You know that. Isn't it more likely that it was somebody younger and stronger? You, Ethelred, liked the idea that Roger Vane might have vanished because of some conspiracy involving MI6 – you invoked the interesting case of Jim Thompson. But again, how often do you think that happens? There was no conclusive proof that Vane had ever had any contact with MI6. Dr Slide said that he was most unsuitable – garrulous, petulant. Are these the qualities of an MI6 officer? Of course not and you know it. But you chose nevertheless to ignore this very accurate assessment and to believe that Dr Slide might have recruited him.

'And there was plenty of other much more mundane evidence that you also chose to ignore. I said right at the beginning that the most likely thing was that Vane – or rather Johnston – went for a stroll and was attacked by some druggie who needed twenty quid for his next fix. If we could have found evidence that any of your suspects had been near the alleyway at the right time it would have been a different matter. But we watched the CCTV and none of them appeared. It is true that I said there was a way you could get in and out of the alleyway without being caught on film, but I also said that you would be picked up by one of the other cameras nearby. Nobody was. On the other hand, and at exactly the right time, we saw a hen party pass through the alleyway and just before there was a man in a leather jacket – tall, relatively young. The girls saw nothing but gave us some useful evidence – they said they wouldn't normally have gone that way after dark – too dangerous. The alleyway is the kind of place where muggings happen. Then there was Johnston's wallet. I told Ethelred that there were no banknotes in it. He commented that some people didn't like carrying cash, which is true. But there was small change in Johnston's pocket. Wasn't it more likely that the absent notes had been stolen – and the cards ignored – by somebody who didn't fancy the risk of being caught with a dead man's credit cards on him? Somebody who needed cash urgently but was well enough known to the police to be at risk of being stopped and searched? I think you also fell into the trap of believing that because Johnston was found dead in the alleyway there was some good reason for his being there – that he had been lured there and killed. Isn't it more likely that it was just on his way between the hotel and wherever he was going? When we looked at the CCTV footage, he pauses as if unsure which way to go – might we not assume he was trying to work out whether the alleyway was the quickest route? Inadvisable, perhaps – and Vane, you might say, should have known better – he'd been visiting Chichester since he was in his teens. But it was of course Johnston who was killed, somebody who had never been to Chichester before and certainly wouldn't have known what the alleyway was like.

'Nor can you claim you shouldn't have realised that it was an imposter we were watching. Ethelred says that Gloria at Oaklawn Studios denied vehemently that Roger Vane had ever been an extra in the series – and she should have known. She was the world expert. And yet you preferred to believe that the picture of Johnston on the wall had to be Vane in costume and that the small scar by his mouth was the clinching evidence he was who he said he was. But take away that misapprehension – trust Gloria's evidence – and his identification becomes much shakier. The picture couldn't have been Vane because he was never an extra. So the man with a scar at the corner of his mouth had to be somebody else. So, Johnston's insistence that the picture was him should have made you doubly suspicious of everything else he said. And let me return briefly to my earlier point – the real Vane knew Chichester well. But the man who was murdered had to ask the hotel receptionist the way to East Street. That alone should have told you it wasn't Vane.

'But let's not ignore fiction completely. I think a great fictional detective once said: "When you have eliminated the impossible, whatever remains, however improbable, must be the truth". It was impossible that any of the suspects had committed the murder. You could eliminate them. In this particular case, the truth isn't even that improbable – it's routine. Hundreds of people are mugged in alleyways for every one who is spirited away mysteriously by the CIA. The only thing you could not reasonably be expected to know is that Leather Jacket's name was Wayne Flood, for that is what he is called in our records. One of our junior officers recognised him. He had form, as they say. Drug dealing. Theft. Assault. We knew where he lived. We picked him up this afternoon. He'd unwisely kept the jacket, because he nicked it from a high-class store and rather liked it. In the pocket was Johnston's passport. Wayne obviously thought it was worth nicking along with the cash. Case closed, I think.'

CHAPTER FORTY-TWO

'So,' Elsie said. 'I think that was one of our more successful investigations.'

'Really?' I asked.

'All things are relative,' she said. 'Neither of us was assaulted or arrested. That's always a plus. Nobody was made to look an idiot – or at least I wasn't. And the murderer has been caught, though admittedly not because of anything we actually did. Job done.'

The crowds had dispersed. Joe had gone as soon as he had cleared up for us the small matter of who had killed whom. Davies had been the next to go, with one parting reminder that he had the resources to sue us all, collectively or individually, if we breathed a word of his involvement. Ogilvie excused himself on the grounds of having to earn a living, offering his services at reasonable rates should any of us have residual legal problems arising from the case. Slide had been more difficult to remove, having a larger window in his diary than the others, but had eventually accepted that the best was over and that there were no more biscuits. Cynthia and her mother, their finances on safer grounds, had headed for nearby Oxford Street. Tim, Elsie and I remained.

'True,' I said. 'Job done.'

'Except,' said Elsie, 'I have a horrible feeling there's a suspect I missed. There was somebody else I was sure could have done it.'

Tuesday put her head round the door. 'Lucinda's just phoned. She says she got your email but she's running late. If you breathe a word of her guilty secret, she'll murder you. And she says she means it.'

'Now there is somebody who could have killed Roger Norton Vane,' said Elsie.

'Except she didn't,' I said. 'Because we know who did. What are you going to do when she arrives? It could be a tricky interview to handle.'

'I shall be elsewhere drinking hot chocolate with marshmallows,' said Elsie. 'Come on, you lot, I'm buying. Hot chocolate for four with plenty of cream.'

'I'll get my coat,' said Tuesday.

'Joe was right,' said Elsie as she picked up her handbag. 'We all got a bit carried away. In real life, most murders are dull and routine. It's only in crime fiction that they offer much entertainment. Of course, there's one big advantage of real life.'

'What's that?' I asked.

'When it's over, you can draw a line under it and get

on with whatever you had to do – dumping the diet, for example. There's no need for a long epilogue, explaining what happened next.'

'Now that is very true,' I said.

EPILOGUE

It was at his second memorial service that I finally accepted I would never meet Roger Norton Vane face-to-face.

I had got to know London quite well in the preceding months. As Elsie said, I had almost become a Londoner again. The Smoke felt like a second home. I had completed the manuscript of the Vane biography on time and the book had been rushed through editing, copy-editing and proofreading. It had appeared to good reviews, but modest sales. By then people had already started to forget Roger Norton Vane and his strange murder by proxy. It's the actors in series who are remembered – not the writers.

The wheels had been set in motion again to have him declared dead. Cynthia had quietly repaid the money to the estate – nobody had chosen to dispute her claim that she had had no idea why Johnston had made the transfer to her account – and was now waiting to receive it again slightly more legally. She had already completed a deed of variation leaving a legacy to Tim. I have no idea whether she actually believed it when she said that she was sure he would have done the same for her.

The church was perhaps a little less full than before. It was early autumn and a few people were still away in Tuscany or Provence or Corfu or Ho Chi Minh City. Others vaguely cited pressure of work as their reason for absence, perhaps feeling that one memorial service for a given writer was plenty. Nobody was naive enough to hope for a repeat of the fun and games of the first Vane commemoration.

And yet, we had no better idea now of what had happened to Roger Norton Vane – the real Roger Norton Vane – than we had at the beginning. It was not likely that he had been whisked off by MI6 or the CIA, but it was not impossible. The mundane explanation was that he had gone off in a fit of pique and got lost – that his bones were still lying somewhere close to the path, hidden in the dense undergrowth. That, I'm sure, would be what Joe would have told us was the simple, straightforward resolution of the puzzle. But real life is sometimes more colourful, more capricious than fiction. It certainly couldn't be quite that simple. Vane's watch had somehow made the journey from the jungle down to the coast, and it was unlikely that it had done so on its own.

Sitting in the front row of the church, I scanned the sheet of paper in my hand. This time I was due to speak at the service. I thought I had struck the right note in what I planned to say – that Roger could be difficult, but would not have been the well-loved author he was if he had been any other way. He had attracted many strange stories, of which his brief reappearance was the strangest. But we must now sadly accept that we had seen the last of Roger Norton Vane. It was his work that would live on.

The organ had started playing and there was a general shuffling as the congregation rose. As I too got to my feet, I took a brief glance behind me to check whether there was a late arrival at the door of the church. A man in a new green anorak, perhaps, and mended plastic sandals. A man with a scar on his shoulder and fluent in Malay or Cantonese or Tagalog. A man with a story to tell.

But only the low autumn sunlight streamed through.

AUTHOR'S NOTE

My apologies to the people of Selsey for implying that their morals are laxer than those of West Wittering, and possibly even on a par with the inhabitants of Brighton. They are Dr Jonathan Slide's views rather than my own. My apologies also to anyone who tries to discover the exact location of the places I describe – I have played around here and there with the geography of Chichester. Though it would be good to think that an alleyway so perfect for murder did exist, I have invented the scene of that particular crime. Other alleyways are however available. I must also stress that the information I provide on CCTV cameras is not to be relied on for real life crimes and readers will need to carry out their own survey before committing whatever murder they have in mind.

ACKNOWLEDGEMENTS

My thanks as ever to Susie Dunlop and everyone at Allison & Busby who helped me with this latest book in the Ethelred and Elsie series: in particular Kelly Smith, Christina Griffiths, Lesley Crooks, Daniel Scott, Ailsa Floyd, and Simon and Fliss Bage. Thanks too to my hard-working agent, David Headley, and to everyone at the DHH Agency. Congratulations and admiration to David Wardle for producing another cover that exactly matched the spirit of the book. And finally my thanks to my wife Ann for her love and support, to our daughter Catrin who read an early draft of the book, to Tom and Rachel, and to our first granddaughter Ella, who is currently more into chewing books than reading them. Hopefully this one will taste OK.

L. C. TYLER was born in Southend-on-Sea and then educated at Oxford and City Universities. His day jobs have included being a systems analyst, a cultural attaché and (for a few weeks one summer) working for Bomb Disposal. He has won awards for his writing, including the Last Laugh Award for the best comic crime novel of the year. He is Chair of the Crime Writers' Association and has been a CWA Daggers judge. L. C. Tyler has lived all over the world, but most recently in London and Sussex.

lctyler.com
@lenctyler